Next In Line

by

Donna Marie West

The Wild Rose Press, Inc.
PO Box 708
Adams Basin, NY 14410-0708
Visit us at www.thewildrosepress.com

Publishing History
First Edition, 2024
Trade Paperback ISBN 978-1-5092-5707-2
Digital ISBN 978-1-5092-5708-9

Published in the United States of America

Dedication

My deepest and most heartfelt gratitude to my partner, Serge, who has never once complained about the thousands of hours I've spent, month after month and year after year, with pen to paper or fingers to keyboard.

My most sincere thanks as well to my first editor, Edd Sowder, and dear fellow writers and valued friends, Charles H.K. West (no relation as far as we know) and John Irvine, without whose input and encouragement this story might never have made it out of my computer.

Special thanks to my editor at The Wild Rose Press, Kaycee John, who helped me with the finer points of getting my manuscript ready for publishing.

And finally, but not least, a humble thanks to you, the people who have taken the time to read my stories. I hope you enjoy reading them as much as I enjoy writing them. If you would like to follow me or leave a review, please do so on Amazon or Goodreads, or on my public Facebook page.

Chapter 1

Hit and Run
Alison

He came out of nowhere from between two parked cars.

I hit the brakes on reflex only, no time to think or even to scream. I felt the thud rather than heard it, and he was rolling on the tarmac in the ghostly glare of my headlights.

"Oh my God! Oh my—!" I fumbled frantically with my seatbelt. Wrenching the door open, I stumbled from the car. "I'm so sorry! I didn't see you. I—" I dropped to the street beside him, ignoring the fact that my knees were in a puddle of cold water.

He groaned and pushed slowly to his hands and knees.

"Are you okay?" I asked stupidly in panic. "I mean, of course you're not! Don't move. I'll call 911!"

"No!" He reached out to grab my arm with his grazed and bleeding right hand. He grimaced in pain and immediately let go. "No. Please do not call anyone. I… I'm all right."

There was a distinct accent to his words. Spanish, maybe, or French. No time to wonder about it now.

Grasping the arm I offered for support, he got to his feet, only to stagger and sway and sit heavily down again on the curb. "Give me a minute. Please."

In that minute, I saw that he wasn't much older than me. Early twenties, no more. His longish hair was disheveled and so were his clothes. He was soaking wet and scuffed from the accident; a thin trickle of blood ran from a scrape on his right cheek. He swiped at it with the palm of his uninjured left hand and contemplated the blood there before wiping it clean on the thigh of his jeans.

I realized I was trembling, but whether from cold or shock—or both—I had no idea. This afternoon's shower that had stopped a while ago was beginning again, and my car had stalled right there in the middle of the road. I wondered vaguely if it would start again.

A couple cars honked and rolled slowly past us. The drivers gawked but were either afraid to become involved or too concerned with getting wherever they were going to stop. A handful of passers-by gathered, pressing in closer until suddenly the guy looked up at them, his eyes startled and wide like the eyes of a hunted animal. Even under the dim light of the streetlamps, I noticed that they were a rich chocolate brown and framed by thick, dark lashes.

"I must get away from 'ere," he whispered, making a second and more successful attempt to stand.

"But what about… um… Shouldn't we wait for the police?" A siren wailed shrilly in the distance. I assumed someone had called 911.

"No police!" he hissed, limping away from the side of the road, his arms wrapped protectively around his ribs. He leaned back as if to hide in the substantial cedar hedge lining the sidewalk, still breathing in audible gasps.

"Okay then, whatever you say," I agreed hastily. I had no idea why, but I would have said anything to prevent his taking flight the way I suspected he was preparing to do. "Get in my car. I'll take you wherever you want to go."

He nodded and hobbled obediently around my car while I dove in and stretched across the front seat to unlock the passenger side door.

He collapsed in the seat and pulled the door closed with a heavy click. "Let's go."

"Where do you want to go?" I asked as the police siren grew louder.

"Anywhere but 'ere!" he yelled sharply, his accent becoming more pronounced. French, I decided. "Go!"

My hand shook as I turned the key in the ignition. My car promptly sprang to life in spite of whatever damage the collision with a human body might have caused, and I gingerly pressed the accelerator. We rolled down the street, passing the police car and ambulance with their lights flashing and sirens screaming as if all the commotion was no concern of ours.

"You need to go to the hospital." I glanced over at the guy in genuine concern for his well-being. "You might be really hurt. I mean, God, I hit you with my car!"

"No," he said through his teeth with a shake of his head. "No 'ospital."

"Then where?" I asked again, flustered but determined nonetheless to help him. The words spilled from my mouth almost before they'd formed in my mind. "I'm taking you home." I jerked the steering wheel and made a sharp right turn onto Waite Street. "My dad's a doctor. At least he can check you out and make sure you're not going to die." I expected him to object or

3

argue or maybe bail at the next stop sign, but he didn't.

He didn't say or do anything, just sat with his head bent slightly down, his hands clasped in his lap. I wondered if he might be praying.

I took a left onto tree-lined Ridge Road and pulled into the asphalt driveway beside my dad's navy SUV. I parked my car, turned the overhead light on, and looked hard at my curious passenger.

Blood was still trickling down the side of his face from the scrape on his cheek. A drop fell onto the front of his gray nylon windbreaker and glistened in the pale light.

"Can you walk?" I asked doubtfully.

"Yes, of course I can walk," he replied, but he stumbled getting out of the car and grabbed the wooden railing to prevent himself falling flat on the front stairs.

"Alison! Good heavens, what's... Who is this?" asked my dad as I helped the guy into the house. Dad was used to my arriving with all sorts of stray cats and dogs—our current pets were all rescues—but I had to admit I'd never before brought a bedraggled human home.

"I-I hit him with m-my car," I stammered. "But he's okay. I mean, I guess he isn't, really, but he won't go to the hospital." I stopped for a gulp of air. "I didn't know what else to do, Dad. Will you help him?"

"What's your name, son?" My dad went immediately into Dr. Mitchell mode, asking the simple question that hadn't even entered my mind.

That hunted animal look crossed his face again and it was a moment before he replied, "You may call me John."

"John," Dad repeated doubtfully. "Well, John... I'm Fred Mitchell, Alison's father. I'm a doctor. I don't have a clinic here at home, but if you come into the bathroom, I'll take a look at you and see if you shouldn't go to the hospital after all." He helped John hobble toward the bathroom with one long, exasperated look back over his shoulder at me.

I kicked off my wet sneakers and hung up my raincoat in the hall closet. I was shaking again as I sank down on the living room sofa. A dozen questions ran through my mind as I absently patted the head of Bax, our beagle, but two in particular returned over and over: *What—or who—was John running from that he nearly got himself killed in the street? And why did I invite him into my car without a second thought? That's totally wild, even for me.*

Fifteen minutes later, Dad came alone from the bathroom carrying John's clothes under one arm. "You're just like your mother," he said with a sigh and a shake of his head, and I saw what I recognized as a spark of admiration along with sadness in his blue eyes. "You can't resist an adventure, nor the chance to help someone."

The mention of my mom tugged at my heart. Barely more than a year had gone by since she'd passed away from cancer. My dad and I'd helped each other through the worst times, but now we almost never talked about Mom. In fact, we hardly ever talked about anything anymore. Dad had seemingly managed to move on, but I was stuck somewhere between an intense feeling of loss that still had me crying myself to sleep some nights and the need to strike out in anger and frustration at the injustice of a world that would let a loved and loving mother die so pointlessly.

I pushed thoughts of my mom away to a distant

corner of my mind. "What else could I do," I asked as I heard the faint drumming of the shower, "after I'd practically run him over?"

"You could've waited for the police, Alison. You don't know who this young man is, but he's obviously running from something. He may have committed a crime. Heaven knows what. Drugs? Rape? Terrorism? He was extremely evasive about answering my questions. He's certainly not from around here. All I could get out of him was that he's in good health." He looked down at John's clothes as if suddenly remembering them. He turned the pockets inside out and came up with nothing. No wallet. No cell phone. Not even any loose change. "Get these washed for him, will you?" he asked, handing me the bundle of wet clothes.

Despite the vague concern that we might be destroying evidence of some crime, I jogged downstairs and threw John's socks and underwear, black designer jeans, navy Yale golf shirt, and stained windbreaker into the washing machine with some detergent. I noted as I did so that they looked and smelled as though he'd worn them for days on end. Joining my dad in the living room, I asked, "He's not hurt too badly, is he?"

Dad shrugged. "He has a number of cuts and scrapes, and his entire upper left leg is banged up quite badly—"

"I hit him on the left side," I explained. "He ran out in front of the car; I couldn't stop in time."

"Yes, well… That's not what worries me most." Dad paused and his expression of confusion melted into a frown of deep concern. "He has quite a bump on the back of his head, some nasty bruising on his torso and as far as I can tell, a couple cracked ribs or torn rib cartilage.

But I don't think they're from the accident tonight. He's been involved in more than one incident recently."

I caught my breath. "Oh my—really? Did you ask him about it?"

"Of course I asked him!" He let out a long, frustrated sigh. "He said he got hurt playing soccer, but I don't be—" He stopped abruptly as the sound of the bathroom door opening.

I heard uneven footsteps in the hallway, and John appeared in the living room doorway wearing my dad's gray terry bathrobe, which he'd modestly snugged tight with the belt. His hair was still wet but combed back from his narrow, handsome face. He was badly in need of a shave—unless week-old stubble was his usual thing—and the scrape on his cheek, although no longer bleeding, looked painful. His muddy black high-end running shoes dangled by the laces from his left hand.

"May I 'ave my clothes?" he asked in a voice that left no doubt as to his intentions. He was planning to leave.

"They're in the wash. You couldn't put them back on the way they were," I said with a quick look at my dad. "Dad'll lend you something for the night. I mean, you can't just go back out tonight like nothing happened."

John smiled wistfully and shook his head. "I cannot stay 'ere."

"You need to rest," I insisted, getting ready for an argument from my dad.

"Alison's right," said Dad, sounding every bit like John's doctor now, although I could see the doubt in his face. "I want to examine you again, more thoroughly. I'll take you wherever you want to go in the morning."

John opened his mouth to object, then shut it again. Slowly, he admitted, "Per'aps you're right. A night of sleep would be nice."

The way he said it, I was pretty sure he hadn't had a good night's sleep in a while. I showed him to the spare bedroom, waiting for him at the top of the stairs while he limped up them one by one, leaning on the handrail for support. I pulled fresh white sheets, pillowcases, and a blanket from the closet, realizing as I did that no one had stayed over since before Mom died. I shook them to air them out and made up the bed.

John dropped his shoes on the floor in front of the closet and looked around the cozy, pastel pink room as though he'd never seen anything like it. "Thank you," he said solemnly when I was done.

"You're welcome," I replied as my dad joined us with his black bag and clean T-shirt and gray sweatpants which he offered to John. My mind was still reeling with questions, but before I could open my mouth, Dad was bustling me out of the room. I looked past him to John and called out, "See you in the morning," just as Dad closed the door in my face.

Suddenly remembering I'd left my book bag in my car, I hurried out to grab it before washing up and retiring to my bedroom.

"I'll put the load in the dryer," my dad said to me when he came into my room across the hall to say goodnight about twenty minutes later. "I want you to lock your door tonight, Alison. I'll be locking mine."

"What—why, Dad? Do you still think he's a dangerous criminal?"

"No, not really," he admitted. "I think he's probably a good guy going through some bad times, but I want to make sure we're safe. Just in case."

I lay in bed staring wide awake at the ceiling, thinking about the strange turn my day had taken. After this morning's class at the University of New Haven and a quick lunch in the cafeteria, I'd spent the afternoon in the university library looking for source material for my behavioral studies homework. I'd stayed later than planned, grabbed a burger that I'd subsequently forgotten and was probably now going soggy wherever it had landed inside my car, and headed home in a hurry. Then I'd committed something close to a hit-and-run—only the hapless victim had run along with me—and invited a total but admittedly intriguing stranger to stay the night.

I didn't feel like I was in danger. I felt insanely lucky to have turned onto Whitney Avenue at the exact moment I had. Thirty seconds sooner or later, and I would have missed John.

Who is he? I wondered as I finally drifted off to sleep. *Why doesn't he have a cell phone or wallet on him? And why do I feel like I absolutely have to get to know him?*

****

I awakened with a start from a dream I didn't remember to the sound of footsteps in the hallway. Early morning sunshine bathed my room in a gentle yellow light; a glance at the red digital numbers on the clock radio on my bedside table told me it was five past seven.

Of course. Dad's getting ready for another weekend shift at the hospital. But isn't there something—Oh! John spent the night right across the hall!

I stumbled out of bed, peeled off my pajamas, and threw on jeans and my blue U of New Haven sweatshirt.

I figured it would be a good conversation-starter, if John actually went to Yale. I hurriedly brushed my hair, pulled it up into a ponytail, and stroked some brown mascara on my lashes. I didn't dare take time for more. Dad had to be at the hospital by eight o'clock, and I was pretty damn sure he wasn't going to let John stay alone in the house with me.

I jogged downstairs barefoot, drawn by the aroma of peanut butter and fresh coffee.

"Hi, guys," I said cheerily, and two heads turned to look at me. Trying for nonchalance, although my heart raced at the mere sight of our guest, I poured myself a cup of coffee and sat at my usual place at the table to add milk and sugar.

John was sitting in my mom's chair, dressed in his own clothes with Molly, our five-year-old calico cat, in his lap. That surprised me; Molly was usually very wary of strangers. "Good morning," he said to me with a brilliant smile that went all the way to the corners of his soft brown eyes.

"Morning," I said back.

I couldn't take my eyes off him. He ate his peanut butter laden bagel slowly, chewing and swallowing deliberately, like he was relishing every bite. He looked much better than he had the night before. The scrape on his cheek had closed nicely, and my dad had bandaged his banged up right hand. His hair—dark brown with hints of auburn where the sun touched it through the window—was pushed back behind his ears, and I had to admit that the unshaven, swarthy look suited him. There was definitely something of the Old World aristocrat about him, from his precise, rather formal English to the way his slender, manicured fingers held his coffee cup, to how he endured my unabashed stares without so much as flinching as if he were used to drawing attention.

John drank his orange juice all at once, drained the last of his coffee, gently placed Molly on the floor, and rose with a low groan. "Thank you for breakfast," he said, looking first at Dad and then at me. "For everything."

I couldn't hold back a dry laugh. "I hit you with my car."

"You stopped for me," he pointed out, not laughing at all.

Dad also stood. "I'm going to take John to the bus station on my way to the hospital."

"You—what?" I pushed to my feet, turning on John as he reached for his jacket on the back of his chair. "Don't you live in town? You go to Yale, don't you?"

"Yes, but it's"—he pronounced it "*eetz*"—"a long story."

"But you told my dad?"

"He did not," Dad replied, coming to stand between John and me. "He made a call on my cell phone, which he subsequently deleted, and asked me to drive him to the bus station. I gave him enough cash for a ticket to… well, wherever he wants to go in the northeast, I guess." He leveled his no-nonsense physician's expression at John, adding, "I'll be ready to leave in a couple minutes." He took his dishes to the sink and headed for the bathroom.

John winced slightly as he shrugged on his jacket, which in addition to being far inferior in quality to the rest of his clothes was, I noticed now, at least two sizes too large for him. He started toward the living room and the front door, but he wasn't going to get rid of me that easily.

"So that's it?" I asked, nowhere near ready to let the most interesting guy I'd ever met walk out of my life so quickly. We reached the front foyer, John walking slowly, still limping slightly, and me nearly stepping on his heels. "Where are you going? Home?"

John turned abruptly to face me. He was a good six inches taller than me, but he tilted his head down and I lifted my chin, and we found ourselves pretty much eye-to-eye. His breath smelled of peanut butter and coffee. "I'm sorry, Alison. You 'ave been very kind to me, but it's better I do not tell you more than I 'ave already."

"You haven't told me anything!" I retorted, frustration making me snappy.

"I'm sorry," he said again, sounding like he meant it. He looked past me as Dad joined us.

And that was it. John left with my dad and I felt as though a chapter in my life had ended before it began.

Chapter 2

Family Secret
Joseph

Dr. Mitchell made one last attempt at convincing me to go to the hospital. When I declined, he dropped me off at the New Haven bus station and wished me luck. I could not help thinking that had he paid any attention to the news this week, he would have driven me directly to the police station.

I planned to take a bus to New York City, where my family had connections. They could quickly and quietly get me out of the mess I was in. Upon entering the bus station behind a woman overloaded with luggage and three children in tow, I glanced around the main room.

I saw him immediately. He was hiding beneath a baseball cap and sunglasses, his jacket zipped up to his chin, but there was no mistaking one of the four men who pursued me.

I spun on my heel, narrowly avoiding crashing into two giggling teenage girls behind me and walked across the parking lot as fast as my bruised hip and ribs would allow. There was a taxi stand to the right of me; I turned toward it without looking back to see if he followed me.

"Where to?" asked the cabby over his shoulder as I slipped into the back seat of his car.

"*Pardon? Ah oui, bien sûr*," I replied, rolling my Rs,

putting on my accent as strongly as possible and hoping that if anyone asked him, he would remember a French tourist with limited English. Dr. Mitchell had been more than generous, but I certainly did not have enough money for a taxi all the way to New York City. *Sans* wallet, cell phone, or passport, there was only one other place I could think to go. "Ridge Road, *s'il vous plaît*."

The cabby turned and grinned at me, showing the stained teeth of a smoker. "Address?"

I dared to peek out my window as we pulled away from the bus station but did not see anyone in pursuit. *Yet.* "Ridge Road," I repeated. "I do not know zee number."

The cabby snorted. "It's a long road, son."

I asked him to let me out as soon as he turned onto Ridge Road. I paid him the fare plus a modest tip and headed out on foot down the quiet road lined with oak trees.

Having taken pains to notice its appearance when I left this morning, I recognized the Mitchells' two-story brick house as soon as I saw it. Alison's white car was in the driveway. The front bumper was dented where I assumed it and I had made contact last night.

Now what? I just ring the doorbell? After a moment's hesitation, I decided that this was the best thing to do. I could not risk standing outside for long.

Alison opened the door. She gaped at me wide-eyed for about two seconds, then let out a strangled shriek and slammed the door in my face.

Merde! She has seen the news for sure…

I glanced to the right and saw a gray van coming down the road. It went past without slowing. The windows were tinted, and I could not say if it was the van and the men from Monday.

Hearing her fumble with the key in the lock, I grabbed the doorknob, turned it, and pushed my way into the house. I closed and locked the door behind me and turned to Alison.

"Wh-what are you do-doing here?" she stammered, taking a step backward. "Didn't my dad take you—?"

"He did," I said, "but I could not go." *How can I even begin to explain?*

"I saw your photo when I opened Facebook," Alison said, taking another step backward. Her eyes, blue as the sky, never left my face. She was clearly terrified. Of me. "The police are looking for you. It is you, isn't it?"

"You do not understand," I said, taking a step toward her.

"I understand that you killed some—"

"No! I did not." Another step. "Please. Listen to me."

"No way!" Her voice rose with each word. "For some crazy reason last night, I thought you were a good person. When I saw Molly on your lap this morning, I figured I was right. But I was wrong. You're a fugitive! I called the cops as soon as I read the news report on you. They're on their way. If you don't want to get caught, I suggest you get out of here. Right now!" She turned and fled, hitting the stairs to the second floor about five strides ahead of me.

I lunged after her. I almost caught up, but my injured leg gave out, sending me sprawling on the hardwood stairs. I landed on my previously battered ribs, making me lose my breath and bringing tears to my eyes. By the time I recovered and staggered to my feet, Alison had locked herself in her bedroom.

"Alison! Listen to me!" I shouted, pounding on the door with my uninjured fist. "*S'il vous plaît*! You have it all wrong!"

To my great surprise, the door opened, and I stumbled into the champagne-colored room.

"You have until the police arrive to explain things to me," Alison said, taking care to remain out of my reach. She held a riding whip defensively in one hand.

I limped past her and sat down heavily on the foot of her unmade bed. My hip and ribs were killing me.

"They said on the news... They said you're suspected of killing your roommate and setting your house on fire to cover it up."

"Philippe," I said, swallowing the lump that rose in my throat at the thought of him. I took a deep, steadying breath through my nose. "I did not kill him."

"But he was your roommate?"

"Yes. Philippe was my best friend and for the last few years, he was my... uh—"

"What? Your lover?" She rolled her eyes. "Come on, John. It's the twenty-first century. You can say it."

This almost made me smile. "My bodyguard."

Alison's mouth dropped open. "Your—you have—had—a bodyguard?"

I nodded. "Yes."

"Why do you need a bodyguard? Who the hell are you?"

"It's a long story," I said. "But I assure you, I neither killed Philippe, nor did I start the fire. I'm not a violent person, Alison. Please. You must believe me."

She shook her head, her eyes narrowing to blue slits. "It's not enough. You—" She stopped at the sound of the doorbell. "You wouldn't be afraid of the police if you were innocent."

It's not the police I'm afraid of.

The doorbell rang again, and Alison appeared to come to a decision. "Stay here," she said, heading for the door. "Hide in the closet. Don't make a sound. If they find you, I'll tell them you threatened me and made me let you hide. I won't go to jail for you."

I nodded. "I understand."

I crept to the closet and slipped in behind Alison's clothing. Had the situation been different, I might have found it amusing or even arousing to hide amid this nice American girl's clothing. As it was, all I could think about was my immediate dire situation.

I had not had time to remove my jacket, and I was soon sweltering in the stuffy space. I tried counting seconds to keep my mind off my discomfort and avoid its wandering to dark places. When this did not work, I turned to prayer for safety and guidance. Eventually, I heard the click of the bedroom door and footsteps in the room. I held my breath, afraid to move, until Alison called for me to come out.

Should I trust her? Or are the policemen out there with her?

Alison pulled open the louvered doors of the closet. "It's okay. I got rid of them." She no longer held the whip. I supposed she had put it down on her way to meet the police.

"How?" I asked. My throat was dry, my voice hoarse. I coughed, pulling off my jacket as I crossed the room. I peered cautiously out the window. Unfortunately, this room overlooked the back yard. I could not see if the police car was gone.

"I said on the phone that I'd seen you," she

explained. "When the cops got here, I told them about hitting you with my car. I said you got in my car and made me bring you home. Patch you up. This morning my dad drove you to the bus station. I haven't seen you since. I didn't know who you were until I saw the news this morning. Well, that part's true, at least."

"*Oui*? I could not believe it last night, that you did not recognize me."

She shrugged. "We don't watch the TV news much. Too depressing."

I could not help smiling. "Yes, I must agree with—"

"Now what I want to know," Alison interrupted, "is did I do the right thing? You said you didn't kill your roommate. So, tell me what happened. I want to know everything."

I looked past her at the dresser and the framed photographs standing on it: Alison riding a horse over a jump, which I supposed explained the whip. Others of her with her father and a woman who had to be her mother. "It's a long story," I said again.

"Well then, come downstairs. I… um… I'll make some more coffee and you can tell me. Then I'll decide if I call the police to come back."

****

"I do not know where to start," I admitted. We were sitting in the Mitchells' cheerful yellow kitchen with cups of coffee and a plate of chocolate chip cookies from a tin. This morning's wee cat had crawled back onto my lap. Molly. She appeared to like me.

"The beginning would be good," Alison suggested and sipped her coffee.

I nodded in resignation. "Yes. I suppose it would

be." I sipped my own coffee—strong and black, just the way I liked it—stroked the purring cat, and ate a cookie. I chewed slowly, thinking over what to say. Speaking of this went against everything I had been taught since I was a wee boy, but the urge to tell her was inexplicably overwhelming. "All right. But you must promise me you will not repeat it to anyone. Not even your father. My future—my life—and perhaps the future of millions of people depends on it."

She rolled her eyes as if she thought I was exaggerating. Then she shrugged one shoulder and nodded. "Okay. Whatever. I promise."

"*Bien alors...* I suppose you've heard of the *Da Vinci Code*?"

Alison's eyes widened in surprise. Clearly, she had not been expecting this. "The book and movie? Sure, hasn't everyone?"

"Yes, perhaps. Of course, the story is complete fabrication, but the basic premise is quite true. Yeshua bar Joseph—the man you know as Jesus Christ—did not die on the cross. He was revived, he recovered, and he traveled with his wife, Mariamne—uh... Mary of Magdala—and others close to him to the south of France. There are several historical texts now discovered that mention that Jesus was married, yes?

"Mary and Jesus had three children, and their bloodline continued through the ages. This secret and the knowledge of Jesus' true teachings were guarded by the *Templiers*—the Knights Templar—and a very old secret society called the *Prieuré de Sion*. The bloodline families wished to remain anonymous. They were afraid of persecution—or worse—and they were right to do so."

I peered across the table at Alison, who sat entranced, her eyes wide and jaw slack, coffee and cookies forgotten. "The Catholic Church suppressed this because… uh, the existence of the Jesus bloodline would prove that Jesus did not die on the cross, yes? This would destroy the Church and upset the balance of power around the world. Do you see?" From the blank expression on her face, I was not certain that she saw it at all, but I continued. Now that I had started, I could not stop. "The secret was almost revealed late in the nineteenth century, when a priest in—"

Alison suddenly came out of her stunned silence to exclaim, "What the hell are you talking about? That's no big family secret! It's one of those crazy conspiracy theories people are always kicking around, like the first moon landing was faked, or Oswald didn't kill President Kennedy. What does this even have to do with anything? With your friend getting killed, the fire, or you being wanted by the police?"

I rubbed at my temples with my middle fingers. I could feel a headache coming on, one of many since Monday night. "Of course, it's hard to understand. I'm trying to tell you—"

"Your name's not even really John, is it? The news report called you Joseph. So did the police." Alison shot to her feet, slamming her shaking hands down flat on the table. "Tell me right now! Who are you?"

Allowing the cat to slide to the floor, I rose as well. I ran the fingers of my bandaged hand through my hair, pushing it off my forehead. "I did not wish you to know who I am. Perhaps it was foolish of me, but you know, I was a wee bit out of my head last night." I took a deep breath through my nose and slowly let it out. "My name is Jean René Joseph de Lorraine." I pronounced it the French way. "I am the legitimate heir in the royal bloodline of Jesus Christ, and probable future Grand Master of the *Prieuré de Sion*."

Alison collapsed in her chair again, one hand on her cheek, her eyes narrow and full of doubt. Tiny freckles stood out in her full cheeks, which had gone white as I spoke. "You're a total nut job, that's what you are. I wouldn't be surprised if you did everything the police suspect—"

"No! I did nothing wrong!" I strode around the kitchen, needing to move, trying to put my thoughts in order. I knew I was breaking every rule by telling this girl my secret and yet, it felt incredibly liberating. When I was calm enough to speak again, I stood at her elbow, looking down at her. "There are several families with a claim to the *sang real*—the royal bloodline—of Jesus. One part of my family wishes the world to know the truth. They do not care what will come of such a revelation. They desire recognition and the power they believe will come with it. Since I reached the age of twenty-one, they wish me to declare myself to the world. But my side of the family—and I—do not wish to do so at this time. I'm not ready, and I do not believe the world is yet ready for this knowledge."

Alison snorted. "You think?"

I took a step back and gave her a long look. "*Bien alors*... to answer your questions. Last Monday night, a man from this opposing side of the family—a cousin in whose home I lived when I was a child—came to my house with three... uh... how do you say? Thugs? They asked me to agree to declare myself. I refused. Somehow, things went horribly wrong. Philippe overreacted and the men crossed a line they should not have crossed. One of them stabbed Philippe. I went a bit mad after this. We fought, but they were too many for me. Someone hit me over the head. They dragged me out and threw me in a van where I lost consciousness. I awoke on a bed in a house somewhere, locked in and under guard. They had taken all my personal things, even my neck chain and my watch. Gregory—my cousin—was there. He made me watch the news. That was how I learned that Philippe was dead. That I am suspected of terrible crimes."

I realized I was sweating. I wiped my hands on the thighs of my jeans and continued, "Gregory told me that if I refused to declare myself and claim my rightful place in the world"—I spit out the words as if they were dirty—"he would see me disgraced. Perhaps arrested by the American police. This would cause a scandal that would discredit me and my family. I would be out of the way, and he would be free to present Peter—his own son—upon his twenty-first birthday in the spring."

Alison opened her mouth to speak, closed it again with a click of her teeth. "You—you're telling me you were kidnapped by the same people who killed Philippe and set your place on fire?"

"*Oui.*" I wondered if by some miracle, she was starting to believe me.

"How did you get away?"

"I was compliant. The guards grew lazy. One of them neglected to lock the door of the room where I was held. I took advantage of this and found a way to escape through the garage. I had only the clothes I wore and the jacket I grabbed on my way out. I did not even know I was still in New Haven until I met you and your father. I just ran."

"You were running from them when I hit you last night."

"*Oui.*"

Alison propped her elbows on the table, cupping her chin in her hands. "Oh. My. God. That…" She shook her head. "That has to be the most unbelievable story I've ever heard. Totally nuts."

I sighed heavily. "You do not believe me."

Turning her head sideways, she looked up at me. Her eyes burned bright. "No. I mean, I don't know. But I believe that you believe it, and I guess that'll have to do for now."

Chapter 3

Fugitives
Alison

"You prefer Joseph, then?" I asked once my mind had wrapped itself around the implications of his tale. "Not John?"

"Yes, this is the way I'm called since I'm a wee boy." He'd sat down and we'd finished our now cold coffees in silence.

"So... are you like, a prince or a duke, or something?"

One corner of his mouth turned up in a half-smile. He shook his head. "No. I 'ave no title."

I studied him for a moment, wondering if he hadn't been the victim of an elaborate hoax himself. "How do you even know if what you've told me is true? That you're the hundred times-great-grandson of Jesus Christ?"

Joseph's shoulders rose and fell slightly in a non-committal shrug. "I know. But please do not ask me to explain to you 'ow I know this, Alison. I cannot."

I could see that it had taken a lot for him just to tell me what he had so far, so I temporarily dropped this line of questioning. "But you really are from France?"

The smile grew a little bit wider. "But of course. You cannot tell?"

I nodded. His accent was unmistakable. "So what are you doing at Yale? Don't you have any good universities in France?"

"*Oui*, we 'ave. I was educated in some of the best schools in Europe." It didn't sound like he was boasting; it was a simple statement of fact. "I 'ave a *Licenciate*—uh, like a bachelor's degree, yes?—in sociology from the Université de Paris." He pronounced it "*Paree*." "I read, write, and speak French—"

I giggled, a silly sound born of tension and excitement.

Joseph's eyes twinkled with a genuine smile, and I was struck by how the brown irises were speckled with tiny flecks of amber. "But of course! I read Latin and speak some 'ebrew. I learned my English in Scotland, but it's not yet what it needs to be. A few years of school in America seemed a good way to perfect it."

Scotland? Well, I guess that explains why you say "wee." I asked, "Why?"

His broad forehead creased in confusion. "*Pardon?*" He said this in French.

"Why learn Latin and Hebrew? And why does your English have to be perfect? What are you planning to do with your life?" *Other than being the supposed legitimate heir to none other than Jesus Christ, that is.*

"Ah! *Bien...* I do not yet know exactly, but I'm presently in my second year of studies in international law at Yale. As well as being the 'ead of my family, I will strive to one day 'old a position of power, per'aps in my own country, NATO, the United Nations, or some international human rights organization. Whatcvcr I do, I wish to make the world a better place."

"So, you're a humanitarian at heart?" I was aiming to tease, but the smile faded from Joseph's face.

"Yes. Do you now understand why my life is

important?"

Everyone's life is important, I thought, but instead, I said, "Yeah. I get it."

At that moment, Bax raced into the kitchen in hot pursuit of the cats. Molly leaped up onto Joseph's lap. Her brother, Mister, shot between my feet and back toward the living room.

Bax crashed into my legs, shook himself, and looked up at me expectantly.

"I'm sorry, boy," I said, coming back to the realities of everyday life. "We missed your morning walkie, didn't we?" I gave the beagle a brisk pat on the shoulder. "I'll put you out, but we can't—"

"Go for your walk," Joseph told me. "I could use some time alone to think about what I must do next. I will not touch anything."

"You can touch whatever you want. We've got nothing to hide," I said and immediately regretted it. "Oh! I didn't mean—"

"I understand, Alison," Joseph interrupted gently. "I 'ave turned your world upside down this morning. I'm sorry."

"Don't be. Just stay here, stay away from the windows. I'll be back in twenty minutes." *I could use some time to think too.*

I dressed for outdoors, snapped Bax's leash on his collar, and took him on our usual route around the block. My mind soon became lost in musings about what it might mean to the millions of devout Christians around the world if what Joseph had told me was true. What it would mean to me. I didn't notice the dark green two-door parked across the road from my house, nor the two men in nondescript black clothes who were inspecting my car until it was too late.

"Miss? A word with you. Please," said the larger of the two, striding toward me as I stopped in my tracks on the sidewalk. With his black skullcap pulled down to his ears, he looked totally disreputable and the kind of man who would have no trouble kidnapping someone. Usually a friendly dog, Bax lowered his head and emitted a deep growl aimed at the man's knees. "Is that your car?" asked the man, one eye cautiously on Bax.

I swallowed and managed to blurt, "Who's asking?"

Ignoring my question, he asked another of his own. "You hit someone with your car last night, didn't you? Name of Joseph Lorraine?" He pronounced the name the American way. In fact, he sounded as American as I did.

"Are you with the police?" I took a couple small steps backward, out of arm's reach. "I already told them everything I know."

The man gave me a sinister smile. "I'm not with the police, and I would appreciate your telling me everything too. Let's say I'm an interested party."

Seriously? What does that even mean?

Careful not to tip the man off that I was hiding something by glancing toward the house, I said, "Look… I hit the guy with my car and brought him home to get him patched up. Dad took him to the bus station this morning. That's all I know."

At that point, the second man joined us. He was sporting the fading remnants of a black eye, and I couldn't help chalking up a point for Joseph and Philippe. The two men conversed in low voices, and I was only able to make out a couple words: "bus" and "another way" stood out. A moment later, the first man thanked me coolly and the two strolled away to their car.

I watched the green car disappear around the corner before hurrying to the front door. It was locked, just the way I'd left it. I opened it, went inside, and locked it again behind me. "Joseph?" My voice shook. I took a deep breath and tried again. "Joseph! Did you see those men outside?"

Joseph crept cautiously down the stairs. "Yes, but they did not come to the door," he assured me when he reached me. "Are you all right? They did not touch you?" He looked and sounded genuinely concerned.

"No, they just… they scared me, that's all. I was afraid they'd do something to you. Or me." My hands were trembling so badly I couldn't unclip Bax's leash. Joseph reached down to do it for me, and Bax bounded away toward the kitchen. "I heard them talking," I added. "I don't think they believe you got on a bus this morning."

Joseph frowned. Shook his head.

I was beginning to calm down and think again. "What're you going to do?"

"I 'ave a plan," he said, "but I think I will need your 'elp."

"Okay. How about I make some lunch?" This sounded rather idiotic, but I realized dimly that I was trying for a few moments of normalcy in what had become a totally abnormal situation. "We can talk while we eat."

Joseph surprised me by agreeing. He helpfully slapped together a couple ham and cheese sandwiches while I heated up some canned tomato soup and set the table. A few minutes later, we sat down for lunch.

"I called my aunt Marguerite in New York City this morning," Joseph offered, elaborating on his plan. "I told 'er what 'appened to me since Monday. She knew already some of it. She saw the news. She said I must go to 'er. She will arrange for me to 'ave everything I need and 'elp me get things sorted out with the rest of the family. And the American police as well," he added as an afterthought.

"Good. That sounds good," I said. "Do you need some money for the bus or train or something?"

Joseph pressed his lips together and seemed to think about this for a moment. He ran his fingers through his lovely, thick hair and shook his head. "No. The bus and train stations are certainly watched. I need a car. Even if mine is not with the police, I do not 'ave the key. I know it's a lot to ask—"

"I'll drive you," I offered, my heartbeat picking up at the very prospect of this. "New York's only a couple hours from here taking I-95. I'll be back long before my dad gets home from his shift at the hospital."

"Yes?" Joseph's face brightened. "You will do this for me?"

"I will."

His eyes narrowed. "Why? I'm still a fugitive. If we're caught, the police will learn that you lied to them this morning. You said before that you will not go to jail for me. Why are you 'elping me now?"

Why? Now there's a question, Joseph. Because I hit you with my car. Because you're handsome and charming and mysterious. Because I haven't cared about anything or anyone but myself in years—until you showed up last night and I felt my world shift.

"Because you need help," I said after a moment. "Isn't that enough?"

****

- 29 -

An hour later, we were on our way out the door. We'd done the dishes and erased all evidence of Joseph's having returned. I'd texted my dad to say I was going shopping in New York City with my best friend, Roxie, all the while thinking that it was the first time I'd outright lied to him in some time. I'd texted Roxie to cover for me. I could count on her to do it; I'd covered for her often enough when she was seeing a guy her parents hated. I'd left fresh water and food for Bax and the cats. I'd changed from my jeans and hoodie into black leggings and a long-sleeved green sweater that showed off my curves and earned a discreet but approving look from Joseph. I'd lent him my I LOVE NY baseball cap and one of my dad's scarves to help avoid his being recognized by anyone glancing casually our way.

"I will drive, Alison. Please," Joseph said as we reached the car. "Just in case."

"In case? Seriously? Did you take a course in evasive driving or something?"

"Yes." Joseph held out his bandaged right hand for the keys.

I looked down at it. "Your hand's hurt."

"It's all right." He wiggled the thumb and fingers of the hand in question to prove it. They seemed functional enough.

I dropped the keys into his palm and sank into the passenger seat. My car smelled of burger; the fast-food bag still sat where it had fallen last night. I gave Joseph directions to the interstate but once we were on it, he assured me he knew the way to his aunt's home.

"Tell me something about you," Joseph said once we were cruising comfortably on the highway. "I know almost nothing."

"Huh. There's not much to tell," I said, reluctant to bore him with the details of my ordinary life.

"Please. I want to 'ear it."

"O—kay. Well, I'm an only child. I've lived in New Haven all my life. I was kind of wild as a teenager, always looking for a thrill. Until my mom got sick. Brain cancer. Inoperable," I added in answer to Joseph's questioning sideways glance. "She died a year ago April. I managed to graduate high school because I knew that was what she would've wanted. I quit my job at the New Haven Animal Shelter and took a year off to basically let myself go. Gained weight. Stopped caring." I paused, rubbing the top of my left thigh absently. "Finally, I registered in the University of New Haven's psychology program. Just started last month." I shrugged. "That's me."

"You were close to your mother, yes?" Joseph asked, looking over at me again.

"What?" I was startled. Most of my friends—even Roxie—wanted to avoid the uncomfortable subject, but Joseph seemed to honestly care. "Yes. She was… she was perfect. She worked as a family counselor and volunteered at the animal shelter. She put up with all my teenage rebellion crap without ever getting mad the way my dad did. When she got sick, she went downhill gradually over two years until finally… she was gone." I took a deep breath and blinked back sudden tears.

No way, Alison. You're not going to weep in front of Joseph. You're just not!

I gulped and finished with, "I still miss her every day."

"I'm sorry you lost your mother," Joseph said after a moment. He was looking straight ahead now and seemed to be searching for his words. Finally, he asked, "Are you a Christian?"

"What? Why? What does that have to do with anything?" *If you tell me Mom's in heaven with God, I just might scream.*

"I think"—he cleared his throat—"I should not 'ave told you about the Jesus bloodline. It must 'ave been a terrible shock, yes? Per'aps I upset you more than you let me see?"

"Well, it was a shock, for sure," I admitted. "And yes, we're Christians—Presbyterian—but I wouldn't say we're devout. We haven't been to church since… since my mom got too sick to go. I'm not sure I even believe in God anymore."

Joseph was quiet, focused on the road.

In hopes of breaking the awkward silence, I asked, "What about you? Do you believe there's a God?"

"*Oui.* I do."

"But I guess you can't be Christian, can you? I mean, if you believe—think—that Jesus didn't die on the cross? Are you Jewish?"

"No," he said, drawing the word out after some more silence. "My family left the Jewish faith in the early centuries of the Christian church. We pass for Catholic to avoid problems, but to be honest we're more correctly Gnostics." He smiled at the look of surprise and confusion that must have shown on my face. "We believe in the power of prayer, the importance of personal knowledge of God, and the true teachings of Jesus and 'is brother, Jacques—you would call 'im James, yes? We believe that every person possesses the spirit of Christ within. But you're right, we do not believe in the resurrection."

No, of course you don't.

All of a sudden I was hot. It seemed there was no air in the car. The back of my neck prickled with perspiration, and I was sure my cheeks were crimson. I rolled my window down halfway and let the cool wind blow across my face and ears. "Tell me about you," I said when eventually I felt normal again. I turned away from the window to look at Joseph.

"I already told you—"

"You told me about the bloodline. I want to know about you. About Joseph."

He didn't look at me, but I could see the corner of his mouth turn up in a smile. "*Bien alors*... I'm the eldest of three children. My sister, Élisabeth, is nineteen. She studies to become a doctor. The baby, Florence, is twelve. My mother runs an antique shop that's in our family since four generations in the city of Carcassonne, in the south of France. My father was the French ambassador to Israel for six years. Besides France, I 'ave lived in Scotland, Switzerland, Israel, and America. Every summer since I'm sixteen, I volunteer at some refugee camp, disaster area, or 'omeless shelter. I believe it's important for me to know this side of life. As I told you, I prepare for—"

"A position of power," I interrupted again, rudely. "Yeah. You told me."

He looked at me then, long enough and hard enough that I told him to put his eyes back on the road before we had an accident.

"Yes, it's true," he admitted—wearily, I thought. "I lead a life of wealth and privilege. It 'as many advantages. But it 'as disadvantages too." He glanced sideways at me. "I 'ave great responsibility. And it can be quite lonely, you know? I must choose carefully my friends. And then I must lie to them. Some people would put me on a *piédestal* because of the blood in my veins. Others would…" He shrugged and shook his head. "My cousin betrayed me. My best friend died trying to protect me. My family in France is mad with worry about me. I 'ave never spoken of the bloodline to anyone outside of it. I could be in big trouble for this. You must keep my secret, Alison."

"I told you I would," I said, even as I began to feel the enormity of that promise. *What if it really is true? Could I keep a thing like that from Roxie? From Dad? From the world?* I sank back in my seat feeling slightly sick to my stomach, staring out the window as urban sprawl gave way to the countryside of southern Connecticut and my eye lids slowly drifted closed.

I awoke with a jolt and the feeling of my stomach turning over. "W—are we there yet?" I asked, blinking, as I came around enough to remember where I was—and who I was with.

"We're followed," Joseph said, his voice low and intense. He jerked the steering wheel, and we crossed two lanes of the interstate at once.

"Huh? What?" Shooting up straight in my seat, I peered into the rear-view mirror. "Is it the men from before?"

"I think yes. The dark green car, three back."

I craned my neck to look back over my shoulder and spotted the car in question as it veered into our lane. "How did they find us?"

"I do not know," Joseph muttered, and stepped on the accelerator.

Chapter 4

Change of Plans
Joseph

*Merde! How can they follow us? Did they watch us
leave and we did not see them?*

I gripped the steering wheel so tightly my knuckles
turned white. My right hand gave a warning stab of pain,
and I eased off with it a wee bit. I made another drastic
lane change and looked in the mirror to see if the green
car followed.

It did.

My heart pounded in my throat and the headache
that had gone away during lunch was coming back. *Pas
de panique, Joseph,* I told myself. *You will be a great
man one day, just like your father. His father and
grandfather. Great men do not panic.* I sped up further,
weaving through the three lanes of traffic on the
interstate.

"Joseph! For God's sake, slow down!" Alison
shouted over the whoosh of wind through the open
window. "You're going to get us killed—or stopped by
the police. Then what? You don't even have your
driver's license, do you?"

"You have your cell phone?" I shouted back without
answering her question. She knew that I had no wallet.
When she pulled her phone from her handbag, I said,
"You must call my Aunt Marguerite."

"But I don't speak French!"

"*Bon Dieu*, Alison! She's American! Tell her you're with me. Tell her what's happening. That we're followed." I gave Alison the number, repeating it when after a moment's hesitation, she began punching it in.

I listened as she spoke into the phone. "Yeah. I'm with him right now," she insisted after twice telling my aunt who she was. "No, he can't come to the phone. That's the whole point! He's driving at an insane speed down I-95. We're being chased by some nut jobs in a green car. Joseph thinks they're the same men who killed Philippe and kidnapped him." She listened for a moment, then ended the call. "She said you have to lose them. She'll call you back in fifteen minutes."

"I cannot lose them on the highway," I said. "I must get off."

"There's an exit coming up. I know the area. I used to go horseback riding here with my—my mom. There's a bunch of back roads. If the car following us misses the exit and has to come back, they won't know which road we've taken. Only… it's on the right."

We were in the left lane.

It was true. Three years ago, in Israel, I had taken a driving course especially for this kind of situation, but I had never needed to use any of the techniques I had learned. I did not wish to kill myself, Alison, or anyone else.

"I see it," I said as the exit came into view. "Hold on." Looking for a safe passage through the traffic and thinking, *Dieu merci, at least it's not rush hour,* I turned hard right.

Car horns blared. Alison screamed as we shot across two lanes and onto the exit ramp. I took the curve as fast as I dared, hanging onto the steering wheel with all my strength as the car fought the laws of physics. Slowing down, I turned right on the first country road, left on the third. When it appeared that we were not followed, I pulled over on the side of the road.

"Oh my God," Alison gasped. "Oh my—sweet Jesus—sorry—Oh. My. God!" She let go of the bar above the door that she had clutched with her right hand and glared at me, her fists now clenched in her lap. "What the hell were you thinking? You could've gotten us killed!"

"I'm sorry," I said. My voice came out in a croak. My hands were slippery with sweat. I wiped them on my jeans and put them back on the steering wheel to stop them shaking. I cleared my throat and added, "I had to lose them."

"Why? Do you seriously think they'd hurt us?"

I considered this for a moment. "If my cousin Gregory is still in control of things, they would not dare to hurt me. At least not seriously. But you…" I gave her a long look. "If he suspects you know my secret, I do not know what he would do to you. And if he's no longer in control—"

"What? What do you mean?"

"Gregory only wished for me to go public about who I am, but when Philippe was killed, he panicked. The four other men in the house… I think they're hired men. Mercenaries, yes? I heard them argue once. They were worried that I know about Philippe and the fire. That I can identify them. This is the reason I ran when I had the chance."

"Oh. Oh!" Alison clasped her hands to her cheeks. "Oh my God, do you think they'd try to kill you to cover everything up?"

"*Oui*. I think this is possible." I put the car back into Drive and pressed gently on the accelerator. We moved forward at a more reasonable and less dangerous speed. I took another left and then a right. I had no idea where we were, but at least we had lost the green car.

Alison's cell phone rang. She looked at the number, shook her head at me, and answered it. "Hey, Dad. What is—what?" Her voice rose sharply. "Seriously? Are you sure they were looking for—?" She paused while her father spoke. "Joseph. Yeah, I know."

So, he knows who I am now… and certainly that I'm wanted. Merveilleux!

Alison lied through her teeth, telling her father that of course she had not seen me again. That she was on her way to New York City with Roxie. She promised to be careful in the city and ended the call. "The police spoke to my dad at the hospital. He told them the truth: that he left you at the bus station and didn't know anything about you."

Her phone rang again about a minute later. She answered but held the phone up out of my reach. "It's your aunt. I'm not giving it to you until you pull over."

I stopped the car again and took the phone.

"Joseph. I don't know how to tell you this, but… Gregory is dead," Aunt Marguerite said to me in her American-accented French. Her voice was thick and trembled with emotion.

"What?" I exclaimed in the same language. "How can this be?"

"I just spoke to Emily in Scotland. She said her husband was found dead this morning in the house he was renting in New Haven."

I swallowed and forced myself to breathe. "The

house where he took me. How?"

"He… I'm afraid he was shot."

"Shot? Are you sure? Philippe was stabbed."

"Yes, I'm sure. The police told Emily. Be careful, Joseph. Very careful. Gregory's side of the family didn't condone the actions he took. He acted alone against their wishes. He wanted to make the bloodline public, and he got involved with some bad people in hopes of being able to persuade you to do so. I don't believe he meant for things to go the way they did. I'm afraid it's the men Gregory hired who are after you now."

"Yes, I'm sure it's them," I agreed. "Don't worry, *Matante*. I'll be careful. I'll see you soon."

My hand shook slightly as I gave Alison her phone. She was watching me closely, her eyes narrow. "What happened? Joseph? What did she say to you? You look like you're going to cry."

I rubbed my uninjured left hand over my face and took a moment to compose myself. "My cousin Gregory has been killed." Then, much too late, a realization came to me. "Alison? When those men came to your house, did they touch your car?"

"Huh? I—I don't know. They were standing near it, but it was locked. I always lock it. Why?"

Without answering, I got out and started searching the hidden parts of the car, groaning as my ribs protested my bending over to look in the low places. It did not take me long to find the wee black device stuck under the rear bumper.

"What's that?" asked Alison, who had also got out of the car and hovered behind me.

"It's a… *appareil de suivi*… uh… GPS?" I said, the English term escaping me.

"You mean a tracker? Oh my—I'm so sorry! I never thought—"

"It's not your fault. I should have thought of this before." I considered turning off the device or smashing it under my heel, but when I noticed a pickup truck heading toward us, a better idea came to me. I grabbed the fast-food bag from the floor below the back seat, slipped the GPS device inside, and threw it amid the crates in the back of the truck as it passed us. Then I got back in the car with Alison scrambling to follow, backtracked, and took another road heading away from the interstate.

"I must still go to New York City," I said, "but I do not wish to return to I-95."

"Hmm. Okay. Well, if we keep going north, we'll hit US Route 1. Hang on a sec." She tapped a few things on her cell phone and continued, "Yeah! It joins I-95 near New York. It might take longer, though. Route 1 kind of meanders."

I had never heard "meanders" before but got the general idea. I looked sideways at her.

"What?" she asked, lifting her palms. She still held her phone in one hand.

"Nothing. Just… I'm sorry I made you involved in this mess. None of it should have happened."

"Don't be sorry," she said. "I involved myself when I asked you to get into my car last night. And it's okay. It's the most excitement I've had in years."

I made a rude sound in my throat but could find no words to go with it. I continued heading north, meeting only an occasional car or farm truck. We reached Route 1, stopped for gas which I paid for with the last of Mr. Mitchell's cash, and continued in relative silence toward the city. I knew Alison had questions, but I was sure they were questions I could not—or should not—answer.

We had just rejoined I-95 near the Bronx when Alison's cell phone rang. "It's your aunt again," she said.

"Answer it."

"Yeah, we just arrived in the city," she explained to my aunt. "We—wh—we can't? Why not?"

I looked sharply over at her but could not take my attention off the road in the city traffic. The last thing we needed was to have an accident. She lowered the phone and said to me, "Your aunt says a dark green car just pulled up outside her townhouse and that you shouldn't go there."

"*Merde!*" I hit the steering wheel with my fist and let out a stream of curse words in French that I was happy Alison could not understand.

While I let off steam, Alison was back on the phone. She ended the call and told me, "You're supposed to go to the country house. She said she'll meet you there as soon as she can. Probably tomorrow. Do you know where—?"

"Yes," I said through my teeth, "but I cannot take you there."

"What're you going to do?" she demanded. "Hop a bus? Throw me out of the car and steal it?"

"No! I do not know what I will do. Give me a minute to think. *Bon Dieu!* I 'ave never been in a situation like this before!" I drove around with my head thumping as if it would explode, no idea where I was going, until I found a side street where I could pull over. "Get out," I said with as much authority as I could produce. I motioned with my hand toward her door. "*Vas t'en!* You can say I kidnapped you and stole your car. I will admit it if I'm stopped by the police."

"No! No way!"

"My problems do not concern you!" I was shouting now, fear for her safety and anger at the whole situation getting the better of me. "You had some excitement, as you say. Good for you! Now go out of the damn car!"

"I won't!" she shouted back.

"Alison. Listen to me. Those men learned somehow where I'm going. Perhaps they looked in my cell phone. Or Gregory told them I might go to my aunt before they killed him. You do not know how dangerous—you cannot—" English failed me and another string of French—half of it bad words—streamed from my mouth. "*Bon Dieu! Tu ne comprends rien. Ce n'est pas le moment*—"

"Stop with the French, already!" she screamed. Lowering her voice only slightly, she added, "I don't know what the hell you just said, but if you think you sound anything like the great world leader you say you're supposed to become, you're way, way wrong. And if you think you can order me out of my own friggin' car, you can just think again!"

I let her rave. No one had ever spoken to me in such a way in my life, but she was right. I had to pull myself together. *Calm down, Joseph. Go to the country house. Take Alison with you. Keep her safe. Wait for Aunt Marguerite and work things out.*

"All right," I said when Alison had finished her tirade. She sat breathing fire and glaring murderously at me. "I will take you with me, yes? But you will not be home tonight." I hoped that she would change her mind at this revelation and decide to jump out of the car.

But no.

"Fine," she huffed, settling back in her seat. "So, let's go."

Chapter 5

The Country House
Alison

We drove around in the hectic Bronx traffic for a good fifteen minutes, searching for a way onto I-87 before finally stumbling upon it pretty much by accident, then headed north.

"So… where's this country house located?" I asked. When Joseph didn't answer, I snapped, "Seriously? You're not going to tell me? I'll see when we get there, anyway. I can read, you know!"

Joseph shot me a narrow look but a moment later said, "You're right. It's about ninety minutes from 'ere. Lake Peekskill."

"Thank you. Now we're getting somewhere. Do you go there a lot?"

"No, not a lot." Another pause. "I 'ave been there per'aps five or six times. The last time was in August, just before school began. My mother and sisters came on vacation."

Temporarily satisfied, I sat back and tried to relax as I watched the scenery change from city to suburb, to farmland, to forest-lined hills. Just as Joseph had predicted, in less than two hours we turned off the highway, made a couple lefts and rights on secondary roads, and pulled into the paved driveway of a low, log cabin-type home with a wide veranda and a stone chimney. I could see the flat, gray-blue water of the lake in question across the road.

I followed Joseph out of the car. He took a few steps toward the house and dropped stiffly to one knee. Using my car key, he pried up a random brown paving stone near the top of the driveway, removed a small plastic bag, and replaced the stone. He extracted a key from the bag, waved it triumphantly in front of him, and motioned with his head for me to follow him around to the rear of the house.

The key opened the back door. Joseph stepped inside and quickly punched in a code on the alarm console on the wall. "We will be safe 'ere," he said, turning to me.

I had the distinct feeling he was trying to convince himself as much as me.

We were in a kitchen featuring an open area with a round table and six captain's chairs, a cooking area with white marble countertops, modern stainless-steel appliances, and what looked like solid maple cabinets.

Joseph dropped the plastic bag and key on the table and threw his jacket, baseball cap, and scarf onto a chair. I left my coat and handbag on a second chair. He led me through the kitchen to the living room, an even larger area furnished with two brown leather sofas, glass-topped coffee tables, and brass standing lamps. A massive desk, complete with office computer, printer, and landline phone, stood in one corner of the room. Colorful throw rugs covered portions of the hardwood floor, and a fieldstone fireplace took up half of the outer wall.

Taking it all in, I thought, *If this is your aunt's*

country house, what the hell does her main residence look like?

"Do… make yourself at 'ome," Joseph said almost shyly. "I must make some phone calls."

"Okay, sure. Um… where's the bathroom?" I asked. I'd been needing to go for the past half hour.

He gestured with one hand to a hallway off the living room.

I used the facilities in the tidy, modern bathroom and returned to the living room, where Joseph was on the desk phone, this time speaking in English.

"I will wait for you, no worries," he said. "Yes, I will call my mother right now. Yes, *Matante*. Goodnight." He hung up, paused, then punched in another number and said, "*Élisabeth? C'est moi. Oui, ça va, je vais bien. Oui, merci… Maman?*" He continued in such rapid-fire French that it could have been Martian for all I understood.

Still, I smiled. I'd understood that first bit. *He's talking to his mom.* A sudden lump popped up in my throat; I swallowed hard and turned my attention to exploring the house in order to avoid thinking about how I would never have the chance to speak to my own mom again.

Past the bathroom, the hallway led to four bedrooms. The master bedroom held a king-size bed with a white comforter, various other solid pieces of furniture, and a private bathroom in one corner. The other rooms were smaller and less luxurious, but no less inviting. I found myself wondering which room Joseph used when he was here, and which one he would offer me.

I wandered back to the living room to find him

sitting on one of the sofas, his long legs stretched out in front of him, and his eyes closed. "Nice house," I said by way of letting him know I was there.

He let out a heavy sigh, opened his eyes, blinked a couple times, and slowly focused on me. "Yes. Uh… are you 'ungry? There's per'aps not much in the fridge except pickles and ketchup, but there's box and can foods in the cupboards. And I'm sure the freezer is full. Aunt Marguerite comes 'ere at least once a month, so she keeps the freezer on. Everything else… I must go in the cellar and open the breakers."

"Oh. Okay," I said, relieved that he seemed to know what he was doing.

He rose with a little groan of pain, absently rubbing his left hip, and limped to the first door in the hallway, which it turned out led to the service basement. He proceeded carefully down the stairs in the dark.

A moment later, the refrigerator came on with a click and a hum that startled me. But that was nothing compared to the shock Joseph gave me when he rejoined me.

"What. Is. That?" I exclaimed, pointing to the black firearm in his bandaged right hand.

"Oh." Joseph raised the gun slightly to give it a cursory glance. "It's protection. A semi-automatic pistol. Just in case . . ."

"In case?" I repeated, my voice coming out in a squeak. I hated guns. Always had. "Do you even know how to use it?"

"Yes, no worries," he said conversationally. "I 'ave 'ad some training and I practice—used to practice— often with Philippe."

"Oh. My. G—" Suddenly the hallway seemed to

swim around me. My knees went weak, and I pressed one hand against the pine-paneled wall to steady myself.

Then Joseph was at my side. He slipped an arm around my back, and I leaned gratefully against his lean but solid form. He helped me wobble to the living room, where he gently deposited me on the nearest sofa. I sat with my head between my knees until the feeling of dizziness passed.

"Are you all right?" Joseph asked when I looked up. I hadn't noticed he'd sat down on the arm of the sofa beside me.

"Um… yeah. Sorry, I don't know what happened." *Well, actually I do. An accumulation of stress and then your gun happened, but no way I'm going to tell you that.*

"Per'aps you need a wee drink of water, yes? And something to eat?" Before I could answer, Joseph had gone to the kitchen. He came back a moment later with a glass of water filled with ice cubes.

"Thanks," I said, sipping the cold water. I was vastly relieved to see that the gun had disappeared. I didn't ask where it was. "I feel better now." The ice cubes clinked against the glass as I handed it back to him. I pushed slowly to my feet, but the moment of weakness had passed. I walked to the kitchen, dug my cell phone from my handbag, and added, "I have some calls to make too."

"Of course," Joseph said easily enough.

I plopped down on a kitchen chair and punched Roxie's number into my phone. "Hey, girlfriend," I said when she answered her phone. "Has my dad called you?"

"No. Why?" Roxie asked in a low, suspicious voice. "Alison? Are you even in New York?"

"Not exactly."

"Well, what're you doing? You're not with a guy,

are—oh, you are, aren't you? I knew it!" Roxie squealed with delight. "It's about time! Who is it? Do I know him?"

"You don't," I said firmly.

"Is he cute?"

I glanced over at Joseph and couldn't help smiling to myself. "Yeah, I guess." *If you like tall, handsome, and mysterious, with a charming French accent and a lineage from heaven. Literally.* "Look... I can't explain right now, but if my dad calls you—which he probably will—you can tell him... Oh my God, go ahead and tell him I'm with Joseph." I pronounced his name the French way.

Another squeal. "Joseph?"

I ignored her. "Tell him... Joseph didn't kidnap me. He hasn't hurt me or threatened me or anything like that. He didn't do anything wrong, and he's trying to find a way to prove it."

"You're not making any sense, Alison. What on earth are you talking about?"

"I promise I'll tell you everything I can when I see you. Thanks, Roxie. You're the best best friend ever."

I hung up on Roxie's exasperated protestations, and hastily texted my dad:

—Won't be home tonight. I'm fine. Don't worry about me. See you soon. XOX—

Then, because my battery was running low and I didn't have the charger, not to mention I really didn't want to talk to my dad, Roxie, or anyone else tonight, I turned my phone off.

Joseph had been going through the kitchen cupboards, resolutely pretending not to pay attention to me, although I was pretty sure he'd registered every word. As I slipped my phone back into my handbag, he said, "You can take your car and go 'ome, Alison. I will not stop you." He pulled my car keys from his front pocket and tossed them to me.

I caught them and closed my fingers around them. They were warm from being close to his body. "No. I want to stay."

"Why do you wish to do this?" He seemed genuinely confused.

"Well… for one thing, I'm way too tired tonight to drive home in the dark on roads I don't know."

"And—?"

"And… I don't know why, okay? You've trusted me with the secret of who you are, and I guess I just to help you get out of trouble. What you said in the car about making friends? Well, I want to be your friend."

He nodded thoughtfully. "Thank you. I do not know what more to say." Then he gave me a brilliant smile, and I knew I'd made the right decision.

"So… is there anything to eat?" I asked, trying for a casual tone to lighten the mood. "Or do we order pizza?"

The smile faded from his lips but lingered in his eyes. "No pizza. I wish for people not to know we're 'ere if someone asks questions in town. There are steaks and bread in the freezer, and lots of can vegetables."

"And you can cook?"

"But of course! I'm French!" He actually winked, and I saw what his sense of humor might be when he wasn't running for his life. "No, to be honest, not a lot. Philippe was more the chef than me, but I do very good steaks on the barbecue."

I couldn't help laughing, albeit somewhat sadly. "Then I guess we won't starve, will we?"

An hour later, we sat down to microwaved veggies, crusty bread I'd heated up in the oven, and inch-thick T-bone steaks grilled to medium-rare perfection by Joseph on the back veranda barbecue.

"Now that we're sort of in this together," I ventured as we neared the end of the meal, "will you tell me who your aunt is to make you think she can help you get out of the crappy situation you're in?"

"Yes," Joseph replied more promptly than I'd expected. "Aunt Marguerite is a justice on the New York State Supreme Court. She 'as connections with the FBI and people in the French embassy."

"Oh. Right. Yeah, I guess she would." I finished my steak and looked hard at Joseph across the table. "What about your dad? You said he was the French ambassador to Israel. What is he now?"

"Dead." He said this so abruptly I dropped my fork, which clattered to the floor in a splash of green beans. He blinked hard once and went on, "'E was killed in August of last year in a bombing in a Tel Aviv market. We do not know if 'e was targeted, or if 'e was just in the wrong place at the wrong time.

"I was in France at the time. They told me that my father spotted the bomber. 'E got some people out, but 'e did not get far enough away 'imself before the bomb exploded."

"Oh. My—I'm so sorry, Joseph. I had no idea," I blurted. "I never would've asked—"

He raised a hand to silence me. "It's all right, Alison. I was not as close to my father as I would have liked to be, but I'm very proud of 'im. 'E died courageously, saving the lives of innocent people. Children." He coughed and took a gulp of his cola and looked past me out the patio door.

I retrieved my fork but didn't finish my vegetables. I'd lost my appetite. After supper, I offered to wash the dishes while Joseph got on the computer. I wanted to give him some time alone and honestly, after what he'd told me about his dad, I didn't know what to say to him.

The dishes done and my thoughts collected, I asked him if I could take a shower.

"But of course." He left the desk to fetch me a thick blue bath towel and wash cloth from the hall closet and showed me to the pale lavender bedroom with two twin beds where I could sleep.

I found everything I needed on the bathroom shelves—even a blow dryer for my hair. Once I was clean, dried, and dressed, I wandered back to the living room to join Joseph.

He wasn't there.

I discovered him sitting on the stairs of the back veranda, a red chenille throw from one of the sofas pulled around him against the cool night air, a bottle of amber liquid and two brandy glasses at his side. I sat down beside him, close enough to bump his firmly muscled thigh.

He poured some of the amber liquid into the second glass—he'd already started on the first one—and handed it to me. "Cognac. It will 'elp you sleep."

I sniffed the cognac, took a sip, and gasped as it burned its way down my throat. Back in my rebellious days I'd been a confirmed light beer girl, but I'd never touched the hard stuff. When I looked at him, Joseph was smiling at me. "What?" My voice came out in a rasping croak.

"You," he said matter-of-factly. "You're quite

incredible, you know."

I giggled and took another sip of cognac. "You think? Coming here with you today is probably the craziest thing I've ever done."

"Per'aps. But you're 'ere—and I'm glad of it." The smile faded. He poured himself another glass of cognac and took a long swallow.

I had to ask, "If it's such an important secret, why did you tell me about your family? About the Jesus bloodline, I mean?"

"To be honest, I do not know. I only felt that I must." He paused, his forehead creasing thoughtfully. "My aunt says that she will be 'ere tomorrow afternoon."

"Um… that's good. Isn't it?"

"*Oui*. It is. You… uh… you will leave in the morning, yes?"

"No!" I took another slug of cognac, exhaled fire, and glared at him. "Don't tell me you still don't trust me?" I exclaimed indignantly once I could speak again.

"No," he said, surprising me. "*Je veux dire*… Yes, I trust you. But I'm afraid for you."

"Why? What do you think's going to happen?"

"I do not know," he admitted with a shrug. "This is why I'm afraid."

Whether it was the effect of these discouraging words or the chilling breeze coming off the lake, I shivered involuntarily and shifted a little bit closer to Joseph's warm and comforting form. He smelled good, of cognac and the salty scent of his own skin.

He fiddled with the throw, draped a length of it over my shoulders, and reached across to pull it around me. We drained our glasses, and Joseph refilled them without a word.

"Have you ever shot anyone?" I asked later, my third glass of cognac in hand, my thoughts on that deadly-looking gun stashed somewhere in the house.

Joseph's head swiveled toward me, dark eyebrows raised in surprise. "No," he said solemnly, "and I wish to never do so. The gun is just—"

"In case," I finished. "Yeah, got it."

We sat there, side by side, watching the sun go down behind the pine trees in a pink and orange sky, listening to the humming of cicada and the occasional howl of a coyote, not quite together but maybe a little bit less far apart.

Chapter 6

Confessions
Joseph

I awoke at dawn after what seemed a very short night. The cognac had not helped as hoped. Between the beating I had received from Gregory's men and being hit by Alison's car, my whole left side was one large, painful bruise. I had not been able to sleep well all week. I lay there for a few minutes, forcing myself to take long, deep breaths, listening to the singing of birds in the trees outside my window and wondering what trials were in store for me today.

My thoughts turned to prayers for courage to do whatever Aunt Marguerite might say I must do. I was reminded of Jesus asking God to take the cup away when he faced arrest in the Garden of Gethsemane.

You're not facing crucifixion, Joseph, I scolded myself scornfully in French. *You're saving your life and protecting the bloodline. Get on with it.*

Finally, I rose. I removed the bandage that Dr. Mitchell had put on my right hand and took a long, hot shower while Alison still slept. I blow-dried my hair into something respectable and shaved for the first time in a week, revealing the blue-and-yellow remains of a bruise on my jaw. I swallowed several ibuprofen and dressed in clean jeans, a T-shirt, and a gray Université de Paris hooded sweatshirt that I had left here in August. I was happy to notice that yesterday's pounding headache had gone away overnight.

I made coffee, toasted slices of last night's bread, and spread orange marmalade over them.

"Hey there," said Alison, strolling out to join me in yesterday's clothes, her wavy, red-blond hair falling loose around her shoulders. She looked quite chipper considering the amount of cognac she had consumed last night. She studied me for a moment before pouring coffee into the cup I had put on the table for her and sitting down opposite me. "Hmm… I like the new look." She smiled, pointing at her own jaw. "Except maybe for the color."

I shrugged and smiled back and pushed the porcelain bowl of sugar toward her. "There's bread for toast. I'm afraid there's no milk for cereal or coffee."

"That's okay. I'm sure I'll survive black coffee." She dumped in two heaping spoonfuls of sugar and stirred her coffee for a very long time.

I could not help watching her. I had met many girls in my life, most of them beautiful and much more sophisticated than Alison, but something attracted me to this American girl. She was honest and courageous, and she did not hang all over me as if I were her ticket to the good life as some of them did. Even after I told her about the bloodline—and whatever had made me take such a chance?—she did not act differently than she had before I told her.

Authenique. Oui, this is the word for her.

"I really need to talk to my dad before he goes totally berserk and sends the police out looking for me," Alison said after breakfast. "You'll have kidnapping and grand theft auto charges on your hands on top of the rest. My cell phone's nearly dead, though. Can I use the phone here?"

"But of course. Or you can just go home to your father this morning."

She rolled her big blue eyes at me. "Do we have to go through that again?"

I gave her an exasperated sigh and shook my head. I tried to not listen as she made her call, but her voice grew loud as she explained my situation and her actions to her father without saying anything I had asked her not to say.

"I can't tell you where I am!" She was shouting now. "Stop it, Dad! I'm fine." She lowered her voice to something closer to normal. "Don't worry about—what? No! Why do you—why? Oh my God…" She lowered the phone and called to me. "Joseph? My dad wants to talk to you."

"*Pourquoi?*" I asked, crossing the living room to reach her.

"I don't know why. I told him I'm fine, but…" She shrugged. Shook her head. "He's my dad." She held the phone out to me, mouthing, "I'm sorry," and gave me an apologetic smile.

I took the phone, no idea what to say. "Uh… Dr. Mitchell?"

"John—Joseph—whatever your real name is," he began in a cold voice, sounding not at all like the kind doctor who had cared for me the other night. "What the hell do you think you're doing with my daughter?"

I do not know. Believe me.

"She's all right," I said when nothing better came to mind. "She will be home today." I gave Alison a hard look to confirm this.

"Where are you?"

"I'm sorry. I cannot tell you this. I can only tell you that I did not do what you think I did. I was kidnapped. Set up. I'm trying to—to right things, yes? Alison is helping me."

"Helping you? If anything happens to her, I swear I—"

"It will not," I assured him. *Bon Dieu, please let this be true.* "She will be home with you tonight. I promise."

Dr. Mitchell made a low, strangled sound. I handed the phone back to Alison and walked away. I did not wish to hear the rest of the conversation.

Alison came to join me on the back veranda where I was sitting, trying to settle my mind. "My dad calmed down there at the end," she said, "a little bit." She pulled up a chair beside me. "Are you okay?"

I shrugged. "Yes. I was just thinking. I'm sorry I pulled you into this—"

"Stop!" she exclaimed, slapping her hands down on her thighs. "Will you get over it? You didn't *pull* me into anything. I'm here because I want to be. Can't you just accept that and move on?"

"All right," I said slowly, surprised at her vehemence although I supposed I should not be. "I accept it."

She grinned triumphantly.

The sun having come out today, we passed the rest of the morning walking along the rocky shore of the lake. We talked easily of things like the horses Alison had ridden and the pets she had had; Beau and Belle, my two aging French spaniels back home in Carcassonne; Harry, my sister Laurence's wee cat she had named after the boy wizard. I told her that I played football—Americans called it soccer—since I was six years old, and that I played midfield on the team at Yale. I had even scored a goal in my last game.

"Seriously? That was true?" she asked, her eyebrows rising in surprise along with her voice. "My dad said you told him that was how you injured your ribs."

I shrugged, smiling apologetically. "*Bien...* the playing soccer part was true."

"I have questions," Alison said suddenly after we had walked for another minute or two.

"I expect you do," I replied, still walking. "Ask me what you wish. I will answer if I can."

She turned sideways to consider me. "Okay... Well, how do you know it's true? The whole Jesus bloodline story? And if it's true, how do you know your family is connected to it?"

"It's true." I stopped walking to sit on a large, flat rock on the edge of the water. Besides wishing to rest my left leg, which had begun to ache so that I could not help limping, this story—and how much I chose to tell of it—needed my full attention. "As I told you before, there are a number of ancient texts that speak of the bloodline. In the nineteenth century, a priest named François Bérenger Saunière made renovations at St. Mary Magdalene Church in the village of Rennes-le-Chateau, in the south of France. This is well known." I looked up at her and patted the rock beside me, inviting her to sit.

"If you say so." Alison plopped down beside me, her hands clasped together in her lap. "Go on."

I cleared my throat and looked out at the dark water of the lake. It rippled gently in the breeze. *Take it slow,*

Joseph, I told myself, *and tell her just enough to answer her questions.* "Hidden in the church, this priest found some *parchemins...* uh, parchments, yes?" As she nodded, I continued, "One of these tells stories of Jesus, of his childhood and the years before he began preaching. Two other parchments tell the *généalogies* of the two strongest bloodline families from the time of Mary and Jesus to the eighteenth century. My mother's family—St. Clair—is one of them. My father's family—de Lorraine—is the other."

"And that's how you know you're a descendant of Jesus? Because a couple old parchments have your families' names on them? They could be total hoaxes."

"They're not hoaxes, Alison."

"And one more time—how do you know?"

"The parchments discovered by the good Father Saunière came to be in the possession of my mother's family before the First World War. They're genuine."

Her eyes narrowed. "You're absolutely sure about this? Have you seen them?"

"Yes, I 'ave seen them. Read them." I gave her a long look and asked hopefully, "Do you believe me now?"

Alison blew out a breath like a puff of wind. It was a moment before she answered, "Yeah. Actually, I think I do."

I stood. "Come. We should head back. I do not know at what time Aunt Marguerite will arrive." I reached down to take Alison's hand and pulled her to her feet. We walked—still holding hands—back to the country house.

****

Aunt Marguerite arrived at two-thirty accompanied

by her driver/bodyguard, a large, forty-something Native American man called Germain.

"Were you followed?" I asked anxiously as they came inside.

"I'm counting on it," my aunt replied.

"*Pardon*?" This popped out in French.

Aunt Marguerite put down her handbag and other items, removed her coat, and turned to Alison. "You must be the young lady who's been helping Joseph?"

"Alison Mitchell," I said, remembering my manners. "My aunt Marguerite."

After introductions were over, my aunt nodded to Germain, who opened a case from one of her bags and extracted a device with wires hanging from it.

Merde, I thought with a sinking feeling in my stomach, *they wish me to wear a wire.*

"Please take off your sweatshirt, Joseph," Germain said politely, holding up the tiny microphone and wires. "I need to put this on you immediately."

"I have an FBI surveillance team with me," Aunt Marguerite explained when I hesitated. "They'll remain out of sight until needed. Joseph, there are arrest warrants out for you in two states. You're considered to be armed and dangerous. The police suspect you in the murders of Philippe and Gregory. The best way for you to clear your name is to get the men who are following you to admit to their role in your kidnapping and the two deaths. Once we have their confession on tape, the FBI will intervene. Now hurry up. They may be right behind me."

I pulled my sweatshirt and T-shirt over my head, allowed Germain to adhesive tape the electronics to my chest, then carefully put my clothing back on.

"We need to test—" Aunt Marguerite began.

"There's no time!" Alison interrupted urgently. She had been peeking out the window from behind a corner of the curtain. "Green car across the road. Two men inside."

I marched into the kitchen, grabbed the gun I had placed in a bottom drawer, stuck it in the waistband of my jeans, and pulled my sweatshirt down over it. "Go in the last bedroom. Both of you!" I commanded to Alison and my aunt, actually pushing them not too gently down the hallway. "Lock the door. Do not come out until I come for you." I laid eyes on Alison as she turned to look at me over her shoulder. "Promise me!"

"Yeah. Okay, I promise," she said in a shaking voice. Her face had gone white except for two crimson blotches on her cheeks.

I waited to hear the click of the door lock over my pounding heart before heading back to the living room. By the time I reached the end of the hallway, the front door had burst open. Germain was on his knees, clutching his stomach and looking surprised. Blood oozed from between his fingers.

"What did you do?" I demanded. I tried to go to Germain but was blocked by the men dressed in black. I immediately recognized them as two of the men who had come to my house, and who had kept me under guard in Gregory's house.

The larger man—the boss, apparently—said coldly, "We handled a complication. Now the question is, what are we going to do with you?"

I asked my own question, hoping I sounded more confident than I felt. "Who are you?"

He snorted. "Me? I'm nobody. Gregory—your

cousin, I believe?—hired the four of us to help him convince you to do or say whatever the hell it was he wanted from you. No one was supposed to get hurt. Things went south fast when that idiot roommate of yours jumped Marty. We had to improvise, eh? Then when you ran—stealing my jacket to boot, you little prick—Gregory refused to pay us. Said we had to get you back, clean things up. The other two guys gave it up as a bad job and bailed, but me and Marty"—he nodded toward the other man, who held in one hand a black combat knife dripping blood—"we're in it to the end."

"*Salaud*! You killed Gregory."

"Well, yeah, no choice. Like I said, the asshole refused to pay. And he knew who we were. He wouldn't tell us what the damn big secret he wanted from you was, but he did give up your aunt's address in New York before he died. Good job he did, eh? After that fast one you pulled on the interstate…"

Germain moaned and fell over on his side in a puddle of blood.

Where are the damn FBI? I thought frantically. *Have they not heard enough?*

"I wanted to get rid of you," the man who was not Marty went on, "but now I'm thinking you might be worth something. We could take you. Figure out exactly who you are and what Gregory wanted from you. Ransom you for whatever you're worth." He shrugged. "But first we have to tie up loose ends." He nodded at Marty. "Kill the woman. Bring me the girl. I might have some fun with her befo—"

"No!" I pulled the gun from my back and pointed it at the man called Marty, willing my hands to remain steady while my blood ran cold. "Do not move or I will shoot you." I prayed that the FBI would show up before I had to pull the trigger.

Marty had frozen at my words, but the other man chuckled. "If you really want to shoot someone, son, you don't hesitate. You just do it," he said calmly. "Like this." He pulled a pistol from his coat pocket and fired.

The force of the shot spun me halfway around and knocked me back against the wall. I dropped my gun as pain like fire exploded in my left shoulder. I staggered but managed to remain on my feet.

"Sit down," said the man who had shot me, motioning with his gun toward the nearest sofa. "Before you fall and we have to pick your sorry ass up. Go on. Do it!" he said to Marty.

I was still standing there, my right hand clamped to my bleeding shoulder, when men in dark uniforms and bullet-proof vests poured through the open door. "FBI. Don't anyone move!" shouted one of the four agents who rushed in.

The man who just shot me spun on one heel and fired off a round.

Blood and tissue sprayed from the throat of one of the FBI agents. He let out a huff and dropped on his face. The agent who had shouted rapidly shot the large man in black four times. He dropped his gun, staggered backward, and collapsed sitting on the floor before flopping over onto his back.

One of the agents ran down Marty, who promptly tossed his knife on the floor and reached his hands into the air, shouting, "Don't shoot! I'm not armed! Don't shoot!"

"Are you Joseph Lorraine?" asked the fourth FBI agent, holding his gun on me. He said my name the

American way, and I wondered briefly if he knew who I really was.

"Yes."

He picked up my gun from the floor before slowly lowered his own gun. "Where are they? The women?"

"In a bedroom," I said, remarkably calm. "I must go to them… or they will not open the door." I noticed in a dim sort of way that the left side of my body was warm and wet. There was a large bump that should not be there on my shoulder, and my left arm tingled painfully. I heard an FBI agent calling on his walkie-talkie for paramedics, men down, as I went down the hallway, and then I was at the bedroom door.

"You can come out," I managed to say quite loudly. My heart raced in my ears, and I was beginning to feel like I had just got off a rollercoaster. "It's over."

The door flew open. Alison's expression of relief changed to one of horror as her eyes fell on my bleeding shoulder. "What happened? We heard gunshots! Jo— they shot you?"

"Yes. I-I'm all right. It's just… it's my shoulder. I'm all right."

Alison pulled my hand away from the wound and clamped it back a second later. "You're nowhere near okay, Joseph! The blood's spurting every time your heart beats. That's arterial bleeding. You need to get to the hospital right now."

"They called the paramedics," I said, gesturing with my head over my shoulder. I tried to point but could not lift my left arm. "I must go—see—what's happening. Germain and the—"

"No, you don't," my aunt said. "You need to lie down. Right now." She and Alison hustled me toward the nearest of the two beds.

I did not have the strength or presence of mind to argue with them.

"Get a towel or something," Alison said to Aunt Marguerite. "We have to keep pressure on the wound." She laid me out with my feet elevated on pillows. A moment later, she pulled my hand away from the wound and pressed something soft against it.

I felt something crunch and shift in my shoulder and bit my lower lip so hard in my effort not to scream that I tasted blood, warm and thick and metallic. The lavender walls of the room swam for a moment and then stilled.

"I'm sorry," Alison said, her voice catching. "I know it hurts. I'm pretty sure the bullet broke your collarbone, but we have to keep pressure on the artery. Where are the paramedics?" she shouted.

I squeezed my eyes shut, tried to concentrate on breathing and block out the pain. Tried to think of good things. Football. My family. My future. Alison.

I opened my eyes and looked at her. She was close, sitting on the edge of the bed and pressing hard on my shoulder with both hands. She had tied her hair back, but a few loose wisps hung in her face. I could see tiny beads of perspiration on her forehead and her eyes were narrow with concern.

"They were going to kill you and Aunt Marguerite," I explained a bit breathlessly. "I could not allow this, but I hesitated… should have shot…"

"You did just fine," Alison said. "You're going to be a great man when you get—no, scratch that. Y-you already are. Great, I mean."

My aunt sat on the opposite side of the bed and took my right hand in hers. "Joseph?" she asked gently in

French. "What have you told her?"

I tried turning my head to look at her, but the movement sent an excruciating flash of pain through my shoulder and chest. This time, I could not help crying out. When I was able to speak clearly, I said in French, "More than I should have, but… it's all right, *Matante*. I trust her." I closed my eyes again. My respiration had slowed down a bit, but every breath I took made my shoulder scream. My left arm was cold, and I could no longer feel my fingers.

At some point, Aunt Marguerite left, coming back a moment later with a second towel, which Alison stacked on top of the first.

This cannot be good, I thought objectively. I closed my eyes again and tried to stop thinking altogether.

Some time later, I heard sirens in the distance, growing louder and louder until I thought they would come into the house. Then they abruptly stopped.

"It's about good goddamn time!" exclaimed my aunt, pushing to her feet and leaving the room. I heard her voice from the living room; she must have been shouting. "Come! You have to take care of my nephew in the bedroom. Hurry. You have no idea how important his life is!"

The next thing I knew, there were more people in the bedroom. I sensed bustling, hurried movements. I forced my eyes open to find two uniformed paramedics wearing blue latex gloves hovering over me. The man motioned Alison out of the way and she stood back, the sleeves of her green sweater and the hands at her sides stained red with blood. My blood.

This cannot be good, I thought again.

The paramedic removed the towels, cut my blood-soaked clothing open, and pressed a wad of bandages to my shoulder. The woman ripped the wire from my chest, taking a good amount of my chest hair with it. "What's your name, son?" she asked.

"Jo—Jean René Joseph de Lorraine. Joseph."

The man grunted and smiled absently. "Do you know what happened to you, Joseph?"

I might have laughed had I not been in so much pain. "I'm shot."

"Are you on any medications?" the woman asked. She was taking notes. "Do you have any allergies? Health problems?"

Other than being shot? "No."

They worked on me for a few minutes, taking my pulse and blood pressure, putting an IV needle into my right arm. I stopped paying attention. My head ached. The room was slowly turning around me, and the heavy copper smell of blood made me feel sick to my stomach. Knowing that it was my blood did not help. I forced my throat to work. "How are they? Germain and the FBI agent? They—"

"They're being taken care of," the woman paramedic said. "Don't worry about them. Worry about you. You need to stay calm and quiet and let us get this bleeding under control."

The man asked, "Do you know your blood type, Joseph?"

"Uh... *oui. C'est AB negatif.*" I noticed dimly that this came out automatically in French, but he seemed to understand.

"AB negative. That's rare. Are you sure?"

I sighed. Swallowed. *English, Joseph.* "Yes. I'm sure. But I do not wish... cannot..."

But the man appeared to no longer listen to me, studying the bandages on my shoulder before saying to the woman, "Pressure's not doing it. We've got to get in there and clamp this artery before we transport. Otherwise…" He shook his head.

Otherwise? Ah, Dieu…

I closed my eyes, unwilling to watch what they were going to do. *It cannot hurt more than it already does,* I thought.

I was wrong.

I moaned and sobbed, then pressed my lips together, refusing to scream like a child as they worked on my wound. Finally, they finished, put on more bandages, and transferred me, gasping for breath, from the bed to a *civière*. I had by now forgotten what I wished to say earlier.

They placed a plastic oxygen mask over my nose and mouth. The gas was cooler than the air in the room and helped with the feeling of nausea. They rolled me out of the bedroom and out of the house. My peripheral vision was now blurring, but I was aware of Aunt Marguerite and Alison walking nearby. I heard my aunt say something to the paramedics about meeting me at the hospital.

My arms were strapped into the *civière*, but I managed to raise my right hand to pull the oxygen mask down below my chin. This simple effort made me break out in a cold sweat and my heart beat faster. I felt dizzy all over again. "Alison," I said as loudly as I could, which sounded to my own ears like nothing more than a hoarse whisper.

Still, she must have heard me. She came to my side, bending down close to listen to me.

"You must go home… home to your father," I managed to say between breaths. "He worries… uh… about you."

"No way! I'm going with—"

"Go home!" I repeated, loudly enough that the woman paramedic told me to be still. "I promised your father. Leave your phone number… with my… my aunt. I will… call you… uh, when I can."

"Okay. Okay, I will," she said reluctantly. "But I'll be thinking of you. Remember that."

I smiled as best I could and gave her a wink. "*Oui.* I will."

Then the woman paramedic put the oxygen mask back on my face. I was lifted into the ambulance. After the door closed with a metallic click, we roared off down the road with the siren screaming.

Chapter 7

News
Alison

Once Joseph and the other injured men had been taken away in ambulances, I raced back into the house and straight to the bathroom. I barely made it in time to throw up in the toilet, all my anxiety and the thick smell of Joseph's blood in my nostrils coming out in heaves and sobs along with my lunch of canned beef stew. That taken care of, I pulled off my soiled sweater, tossed it in a heap in the corner, and went to work scrubbing the drying blood from my arms and hands, from under my fingernails.

"Miss Mitchell?" The sole female FBI agent poked her head into the bathroom. "Are you doing okay?"

"Yeah—no—I-I don't know," I stammered, standing there like an idiot in my bra and leggings. "I just... I have to wash."

"I understand," she said with a little nod. "I'm Agent Jensen. When you're ready, I'll need to take your statement."

"Right. Of course."

Agent Jensen returned a moment later with a white turtleneck sweater Joseph's aunt had told her I could have. I dried, pulled on the sweater, and emerged from the bathroom to find Marguerite preparing to leave with one of the other FBI agents. She and I exchanged phone numbers and email addresses, and she promised to call me as soon as she knew anything about Joseph's condition. While I'd initially found the older woman somewhat cool and detached, I'd seen enough by now to know that she genuinely cared for her nephew. I thanked her profusely, then accepted Agent Jensen's request to sit with her in the kitchen.

I told her everything I could, starting with hitting Joseph with my car Friday night and ending with what she'd seen and heard herself this afternoon. Of course, I left out everything that had anything to do with the Jesus bloodline and the fact that Joseph believed he had his destiny somewhat laid out for him.

"Thank you," said Agent Jensen, after I finished breathless and trembling with renewed adrenaline and maybe the onset of emotional shock. "I'll get in touch with you if I need anything more. You're free to go home, Alison. Do you need someone to drive you?"

"No, I'll be okay. Thanks." Before leaving, I called my dad to tell him in a bogus calm voice that I was fine and would be home in a few hours. I refused to answer his questions, promising to explain everything when I saw him.

I retrieved my sweater and stuffed it into a green garbage bag I'd plundered from beneath the kitchen sink. I picked up the cap and scarf I'd lent to Joseph, shrugged on my coat, and left the house, ducking under the yellow crime scene tape that had been strung around it just like in the movies.

The drive home was endless. I pulled over twice when my vision blurred with tears and once when I began to tremble and shiver so badly, I was afraid I would drive right off the road. The steady rain that fell for the last two hours only made things worse but finally, I made it to New Haven.

"Alison! Thank God you're home!" Dad exclaimed as I stumbled into the house just after sundown. He grabbed me by the shoulders, and I crumpled into his arms, all my tension and worry coming out of me in loud, hiccupping sobs. "Alison... Allie-cat..." He hadn't called me that in years. "It's okay, Allie. You're safe now. Good God... I knew there was something fishy about that young man the moment I laid eyes on him. What the hell did he do to you?"

"Nothing!" I cried in a whoosh of breath. I let go of my dad, took a step backward, and wiped my wet cheeks with the palm of one hand. "I told you on the phone. He didn't—it wasn't him. He—he's in the hospital, Dad." Another racking sob escaped me. "He got shot!"

"He—what?" Dad took his own step back and looked hard at me, his eyes narrowed to blue slits. "Sit down, Alison. I'm going to make us some coffee, and you're going to tell me everything."

No, I totally am not, I thought dismally, *but I'll tell you what I can.*

I washed up in the bathroom, holding a cold washcloth to my face until my eyes and cheeks stopped burning. I went up to my bedroom, where I changed into fresh clothes and plugged my cell phone into its charger. When I joined him in the kitchen, my dad had made peanut butter and jam sandwiches and set out our cups of coffee. I wasn't hungry, but I sipped the coffee and tried to tell him what had happened in a way that made sense.

"His real first name's Jean," I said, trying my best to pronounce it the French way, "but he prefers Joseph."

Dad grunted.

"He comes from an old—really old"—I fought the urge to laugh hysterically—"influential family in France. He came to Yale last year to study international law and improve his English. Last Monday he was kidnapped. The kidnappers killed his roommate, roughed Joseph up when he resisted, and set his house on fire to cover things up."

Another grunt, this one louder and decidedly filled with concern.

"They took him to a house here in New Haven. He doesn't know exactly where…" I went on, telling Dad how Joseph had escaped, how he'd been running when I hit him with my car, how he'd subsequently been pursued by two of the kidnappers.

By the time I got to this afternoon's events in the country house at Lake Peekskill, Dad had forgotten his coffee and was gaping at me, his eyes dark circles in a face gone white with what I could only guess was abject horror. Finally, fidgeting in my chair and gazing fixedly out the patio door at the empty bird feeder in the yard to avoid looking at him, I told Dad how Joseph had been shot while preventing one of the bad guys from killing his aunt and me.

Dad didn't say anything. He drained the cold coffee from his cup in two or three long gulps, got up, and carried his cup to the sink. I heard it rattle as he set it down.

I swallowed. "Dad?"

Finally, he turned to me and said in a very low voice, "He should've called the police as soon as he could. What the hell was he thinking, involving you in his problems? He put your life in danger, Alison. Do you even realize—?"

"No!" I objected, shooting to me feet. "You're way wrong, Dad! Joseph gave me back my life. I haven't cared about anyone or anything since Mom died. You have your work, which you've gone back to with a passion. But I—I've been alone with nothing, going through the motions of living when I haven't even been sure I want to."

Dad's eyes widened. "You have me, Allie-cat."

"Yeah, right." I gave him an eye roll. "When you're not at the clinic or putting in double weekend shifts at the hospital. Or doing paperwork in your office. You've totally buried your—"

"That's not fair. You know we went into debt when your mother's insurance ran out. I have no choice but to work as much as I possibly can. And you're not alone. You have friends at school. You have your pets. You have Roxie."

"Seriously?" I snorted. "Roxie's sweet and in case you haven't noticed, she's the only friend I have left, but she doesn't—she can't—understand what I've been going through—"

"And this young man can?" he asked cynically.

"He can. He does. His dad was killed last year in a bombing. He knows what it's like to tragically lose a parent. How I—how we—have to go on even though we feel like we can't possibly..." My words dissolved into dry sobs. When I recovered once again, I added, "I know Joseph lied to you about his name and how he got hurt, but he didn't lie about who he is underneath—a good, kind person who wants to make the world a better place."

Dad coughed and frowned. "You honestly believe that?"

I nodded. "With all my heart." I took a deep breath.

"Oh my God, Dad, I'm so worried about him. He was conscious when they put him in the ambulance, but I could see how the pain and loss of blood were affecting him. He was bleeding from the artery under his collarbone. The paramedics clamped it, and his aunt said she'd let me know how he was doing as soon as she could, but she hasn't called me yet. And it's been hours."

Dad's frown had deepened at this revelation. "That's a hard place to get to," he admitted. "He could lose his arm if—"

"If what?" I interrupted, my voice rising sharply. "If he doesn't bleed out first?"

"I was going to say, if the blood supply is disrupted for too long, but yes… he could bleed to death from that kind of injury."

"Thanks, Dad," I said, my heart falling like a rock into my stomach. "That's just what I needed to hear."

****

After taking a shower and forcing myself to obey my rumbling stomach and eat half of one of the sandwiches still sitting on the table, I could wait no longer. I called Marguerite on my partially charged cell phone, only to have her phone go straight to voice mail. I left a message asking her to call me back. An hour later, I left another message. And another. At midnight, I gave up and went to bed, only to toss and turn all night.

I woke shortly after seven the next morning and texted Marguerite for news. To my surprise and relief, she called me back ten minutes later.

"Yes, Alison," she said, her voice rough with worry and lack of sleep. "I got your messages, but I was waiting to be able to tell you something… something better."

The relief immediately evaporated. I clutched the

phone to my ear and blurted, "Wh-what do you mean?"

"Oh, my dear…" She let out a long, tortured sigh. "The paramedics weren't able to control the bleeding as well as they'd hoped because of the way Joseph's clavicle was fractured. He lost some six pints of blood—over half the blood in his body. His blood pressure dropped so low that his heart stopped just as the ambulance arrived at the hospital."

I made a choked sound, my knees gave out, and I plopped down on my bed. "No."

"They got it started again in the emergency room. They gave him blood and got him stabilized enough to take him into surgery. The doctors removed the bullet, repaired the damaged blood vessels and nerves, put a plate and screws in the shattered clavicle."

I realized I'd stopped breathing and drew air in a long, ragged breath. "O—kay, then. He's going to be okay?"

"Well… We were expecting him to have awakened by now. He's breathing on his own, but he's unresponsive. The thing is… there's no way of telling if he suffered any damage due to the lack of blood—oxygen—to his brain. We won't know unless—until—he wakes up."

"He'll wake up," I croaked, my eyes filling with tears. "He has to."

"He does," Marguerite agreed, her voice huskier with forced hope. "But I've called his mother in France. She's on her way. Just in case…"

Just in case. God, I hate that expression!

Marguerite collected herself and went on, "Germain and the FBI agent who was shot have also been through surgery. Germain should make a full recovery, but I'm afraid it's too early to be sure about the agent." She didn't have to tell me that the man who'd shot Joseph and the agent hadn't made it; I'd seen him picked up from a wide pool of blood and put on a stretcher with a sheet over his face. "Thank you for helping my nephew, Alison. I'll let you know as soon as I have more news. I promise."

We ended the call and I sat there for a long time with hot, silent tears streaming down my cheeks and landing, salty, on my lips. Finally, I got up and proceeded to relieve my anxiety the only way I knew how.

Dad left for work at the clinic. Happily—or not—I was on fall break for two days.

I moped around the house, took Bax for a quick walk between rain showers, played with the cats. I did laundry, only to find that yesterday's sweater remained stained with Joseph's blood. Unable to part with it because it was one of the last gifts my mom had given me, I packed it up in a fresh plastic bag and shoved it to the back of my closet shelf. I nearly jumped out of my skin when the doorbell rang mid-afternoon, afraid it was one of the other kidnappers. Or the FBI. Or…

It was Roxie. She wanted to know everything and wouldn't take "no" for an answer.

We sat down in the living room with colas and a bowl of BBQ chips, and I told her the same thing I'd told Agent Jensen and my dad. She had as many questions as they'd had—only they weren't the same ones.

I described Joseph—his looks, how he walked, how he talked, how he'd lived in various countries around the world and had come to Yale to perfect his English—while she practically drooled on herself.

"He sounds divine!" She batted her hazel eyes

dreamily. "You want to introduce me to him?"

"He's in the hospital, Roxie. Fighting for his life…"

"Well, yeah, so you said. I mean, when he's better. Do you think he has a girlfriend at Yale? Back home in France?"

I shrugged. Shook my head. "We never talked about—"

"Oh, Lordy! You have your eye on him, don't you?" She punched me on the shoulder. "Come on, admit it!"

"I don't know, Roxie. I haven't had time to think—"

"It would do you good, you know. You haven't had any fun since… well, since forever."

I knew what she was thinking: *Since it became clear your mom was dying.*

Roxie stayed for supper and once she'd got off the topic of Joseph, we talked about normal things—school, fashion, the latest big-budget movies—although I couldn't get my worries off my mind. As soon as Roxie left, I called Marguerite to learn that Joseph's condition remained unchanged. He was going to be transferred in the morning by ambulance from the county hospital to New York City's Mount Sinai Hospital, renowned for its care of patients with brain injuries. She said this like it was a good thing, but it gave me a sick, heavy feeling in the pit of my stomach.

Unable to think of anything but Joseph, I sat down at the desk in my bedroom and opened my laptop. After absently surfing Facebook for a few minutes, I Googled "Jesus bloodline" and nearly fell off my chair at the 500,000 results!

It didn't take me long to realize that the idea was much more than a modern, wing-nut conspiracy theory.

It was an ancient tradition perpetuated by various groups including the Knights Templar, the Freemasons, and a secret society—which wasn't so secret that mention of it couldn't be found on the internet—called the Priory of Sion. Joseph's *Prieuré de Sion.*

I found a multitude of apparently legitimate sites asserting that a hidden treasure, possibly including parchments, had been found at Rennes-le-Chateau, France in 1892. That the fabled Grail may not have been the cup that Jesus drank from during the last supper, but the sacred bloodline carried by his descendants. That the historical de Lorraine family was one of those connected to this bloodline. It all seemed fantastical and yet, given what he'd told me over the weekend, Joseph believed it all to be true. And I wanted to believe him.

****

Dad woke me up early the next morning and insisted it would help me if I did something constructive with my day. I spent the morning taking care of Bax, Molly, and Mister. I brushed them and cut their front nails. I took Bax for a long, mind-clearing walk. After lunch, I did some homework and studied.

I heard nothing from Marguerite that day, nor the next. In fact, I heard nothing until I opened an email from her Thursday at noon. In it, she told me that Joseph had undergone a battery of tests at Mount Sinai, including blood tests, an EEG, and an MRI, all of which seemed to indicate that his vital organs—including his brain—were functioning at an adequate level. He was showing frequent signs of dreaming: rapid eye movement, twitching, moaning. But no one could understand why he wasn't waking up. The doctors were beginning to mention that dreaded word: coma. My mom had been in a coma for two weeks before she passed away; it was a word I never wanted to hear again.

I'd gone to school these past two days, but any lingering interest I'd had for my courses went down the proverbial toilet. I skipped my afternoon class and drove around town for a while, finally ending up at the cemetery where my mom was buried. I'd used to come here all the time to talk to her, but weeks had passed since the last time…

Ignoring the soggy ground, I sat down cross-legged on the sparse grass covering her grave and words started pouring from me of their own accord. I told her everything I'd felt—and not felt—for the past many months. About begrudging Dad for how he'd gone back to his work and his life with such vigor and apparent ease after the first few weeks.

About Joseph. About the Jesus bloodline and how Joseph didn't know when or even if he should make his truth public. About his kidnapping and the subsequent events. About how I hadn't known I needed him in my life until I met him, and how now I didn't think I could go on without him.

I told her everything. I laughed a little. Cried a lot. As I slowly got to my feet, totally emptied but somehow more at peace, my cell phone rang in my coat pocket.

"Alison?" My heart skipped a beat at the sound of Marguerite's voice. "Joseph's mother just came in from the hospital. She said he woke up! He was extremely groggy, but he opened his eyes and responded when she spoke to him. She said he squeezed her hand and smiled, and although he didn't speak, she's sure he knew who she was."

"Oh. My—that's wonderful!" My eyes filled with

renewed tears, which I wiped away with the edge of my free hand.

"It is. After a few minutes he drifted off again, but the doctor said it's a very good sign."

"Do you think… um… can I come to see him tomorrow?"

"Yes, of course. I'm sure he'd like that, and it might even be good for him. Visiting hours are from nine to nine. But perhaps come later in the day, will you? They'll have to examine him and wash him and… all those kinds of things they do to patients each morning."

I tried to block out the mental image of Joseph helpless and being washed by some nurse. "Okay. I'll come after supper. Thank you so much!"

Ending the call, I placed my hand on my mom's tombstone, for some silly reason feeling as though she'd had something to do with this. "Thanks, Mom."

Chapter 8

Awakening
Joseph

I felt like I was under water. My arms and legs were so heavy, I could not move them. After a time, I heard muffled sounds in the distance. Music. Voices. I could make no sense of them. I could not see. Then I realized that my eyes were closed, and I opened them. Or tried to.

Finally, I managed it, but the light was so bright it brought tears to my eyes. I blinked repeatedly in an effort to clear my vision, and slowly things came into focus. I faced a dull white ceiling with neon lights. One of them flickered the way they did before they burned out. It occurred to me that I lay in a bed. Then I heard something like a sob and turned my head as far as I could—which was not far—to find a woman sitting in a chair next to me.

I fought to think through the fog. *I know her.*

"Joseph?" she said, her voice barely coming through the roar of the ocean in my ears. She leaned in close to me, and I listened hard to make out her words. "I'm here, Joseph. Do you see me? Do you hear me?"

Oui, Maman. I tried to speak but could not seem to form the words that were in my mind. My mouth felt full of cotton and tasted as though something had crawled in it and died. My throat hurt. My head and left shoulder throbbed so severely that I could not think past the pain.

"I'm holding your hand, Joseph," *Maman* said more loudly, as if she sensed that I could not hear properly. "Can you feel it? Can you squeeze my hand like you did last night? Do you remember seeing me?"

No. I remember seeing Philippe. Papa. Grand-père. And... but no... it's not possible, is it?

I saw that she held my right hand and realized I could feel her fingers in mine. I squeezed as hard as I could, which was not hard at all.

It was enough to bring a wide smile to her face and tears to her eyes. "That's good, Joseph. Very good."

"Ma—mm," I heard myself moan. The ocean sound was fading.

"Don't try to talk, *mon choux*, it will come." Tears were now running down her cheeks. She dabbed at them with a tissue. "The important thing is, you're awake again. Try to stay with us a little bit longer this time, will you?"

This time? I did not know what she was talking about, but I felt terrible for making her cry. *Don't worry. I'm not going anywhere. But where am I?*

I turned my head very slowly to avoid my brain sloshing out my ears and recognized my surroundings. Of course. The harsh lighting and antiseptic smell in the air should have given it away. *What happened to me? Why am I in the hospital?* The questions were piling up in my mind, but I could not seem to get them past my throat. And I was so thirsty…

A muscular man with a shaved head whom I supposed was a nurse came in, pushing a cart piled with white towels and other things. My mother kissed me on the forehead and said that she would come back after my bath.

Bath?

The following experience was so humiliating that I wished I was once again unconscious. I moaned and protested with a few slurred, rude words, which for some reason brought a big smile to the nurse's wide face. He gave me a sponge bath one body part at a time and changed the bandage over a long, stitched up cut along my left collarbone. He dressed me in a fresh blue hospital gown while I lay there like a *marionette* with its strings cut, struggling to get an idea of my condition. Clearly, I had been in some sort of accident.

An IV needle attached to a narrow tube was stuck into the back of my right hand and fixed in place with tape. A plastic clip on the end of my index finger ended in a wire running off somewhere behind me.

Thin wires were attached to round stickers on my chest, the whatever-one-called-it machine that monitored heartbeats. *This cannot be good,* I thought with some concern.

I took advantage of the nurse lifting my right arm to raise it higher, toward my face. The edge of my hand was covered with dark red scabs, but it seemed to work, and I was able to touch a tube running into one of my nostrils, also taped in place. When I swallowed, I imagined I could feel it going all the way down to my stomach.

Merde! No wonder my throat hurts.

Finally, horrified by the knowledge that I must pee through a catheter leading into a plastic bag, I closed my eyes and focused on the nurse's voice.

He spoke to me as he worked in a kind, sing-song way, as one speaking to a young child or a fool. At first, I felt a fool; I did not understand a word, but a sense of time and place gradually came back to me. It was then I realized that my mother had been speaking to me in French. The nurse was speaking English.

English? But of course! I'm in America! I came to study at Yale University. I remember…

The nurse left with his cart. I had a few minutes of peace before my mother came back, along with my sister, Élisabeth, and a *petite* woman with curly, gray hair. She wore a white coat and had a stethoscope hanging around her neck.

"I'm so happy to see you awake, Joseph!" Élisabeth said to me in French. Her cheeks were white, her eyes red and puffy. She had clearly been crying, and she looked as if she might burst into tears again at any second. "You gave me the worst scare, big brother. Don't you ever dare do that again."

I gave her a smile. "Promise," I mouthed.

The woman in white said something to Élisabeth, and I realized that she was asking her if I could speak English.

"'e does," my sister said in her heavily accented English. "Much better than me or *Maman*."

"My name's Dr. Scott," the woman said, leaning toward me. "Can you tell me your name?"

I licked my cracked lips and tried to clear my throat—which of course I could not, given the tube in it—and fought a reflex to gag. Taking a minute to wrap my mind around the English language, I whispered, "Yes," my voice hoarse. "Wa-water. Please." I made a vague drinking motion with my right hand.

The doctor smiled. "That's very good. You can have some water in a few minutes. I need to examine you first. Now… do you know who you are?"

But of course! I'm Jean René Joseph de Lorraine. Son of Marie-Chantal St. Clair and René Robert Joseph de Lorraine. Big brother to Élisabeth and Laurence. Heir to— Yes, I know who I am. But I did not think I could say all of that. "Jo-Joseph," I croaked.

Élisabeth squealed with delight and clapped her hands together.

"Joseph. Good," the doctor said. "Do you know where you are?"

Hô—pi—tal." It came out in French, but she seemed to understand.

Very good. You're actually in Mount Sinai Hospital in New York City."

New York? But Yale is in New Haven. What the hell?

"Now, Joseph, I need you to do some things for me."

Dr. Scott asked me to move my legs and my right arm and squeeze her finger with my right hand, which I did. She shone a wee light in my eyes and asked me how many fingers she was holding up. I told her. All of this seemed to please her immensely, but when it came to squeezing her finger with my left hand, I could not. My whole arm was pins-and-needles below the aching shoulder.

"Why?" I pointed with my chin toward my left arm, panic rising inside me. "I cannot…?"

Doing a poor job of hiding the concern in her face, the doctor said, "You have a broken clavicle— collarbone. You needed surgery. Let's not worry about your arm just now, okay? Do you remember what happened to you? Try to think back. Do you remember the ambulance ride? Anything before?"

I tried. I remembered being angry and frightened. Running between trees, as in a forest or a park. Fighting.

A white car.

"Car," I said, my voice low and rasping in my throat. "I think… I'm hit by a car, yes?"

"You were," Élisabeth said to me in English. "But eetz not why you're 'ere. Somezing 'appened after this."

I very delicately shook my head. The room swirled around me, then settled. "I don't re—mem—ber." I moved my tongue around in my mouth but could produce no saliva. "I… water. Please?"

"Okay. I think you can have some now." The doctor cranked up the back of my bed a bit, until I raised my right hand for her to stop. Once the dizzy feeling caused by sitting up had passed, I gestured for the water and Élisabeth held a cup with a bent straw up to my lips.

I gratefully sucked in a mouthful of water, choked, and spluttered it out all over my sister's hand.

"*Pardon*," I said with an attempt at a smile, but she only shook her head and raised the cup again.

"Take it easy," she said in French. "Go more slowly."

I did. This time the water went down correctly.

"Tell me… what happened… to me," I said to the doctor, the English coming easier with use.

"Dr. Scott thinks we should wait and see if you remember on your own," *Maman* said in French from the foot of the bed.

I looked straight at her. "Why? It is so bad?"

"No, of course not," she said quickly. Too quickly.

Even in my present condition I could see that she was lying, but I did not have the strength to argue with her. *De toute façon,* I almost never won when I argued with *Maman*.

"What is this?" I asked the doctor, touching my

working hand to the tube running into my nose. What I really wanted to do was yank the disgusting thing out.

"It's a nasogastric tube," she told me. "We're giving you medication and nutrients through it directly to your stomach. But if you continue to improve… if you're able to eat and drink tonight and tomorrow morning, I think we'll be able to take it out."

"Yes. Good." Suddenly, I was very tired. I yawned widely.

"Get some rest, Joseph," Dr. Scott said. "That's the best thing you can do right now. I'll check on you later this afternoon."

"Th-thank you," I said, my eyes closing.

"We're going for lunch," Élisabeth said, "and then we'll come back and sit—" She was still talking when I fell asleep.

****

I woke up some time later feeling slightly more myself. The roaring ocean sound was gone. My headache had dulled to the point where I could consider moving without fearing that my head would fall off.

Finding I was alone, I did just that. I was weak and shaking, but I managed to bend my knees, wiggle my toes, raise and bend my right arm, wiggle my fingers. Except for my left arm, which lay numb at my side, everything appeared to work.

In sudden panic, I reached across my chest, grabbed my left wrist with my right hand, and dragged my left arm up onto my chest. The movement sent such excruciating pain through my shoulder that I cried out and the heartbeat monitor started beeping urgently.

Almost immediately, the nurse from this morning rushed in with the doctor at his heels.

"It's all right," I gasped as they leaned over me to check on things. "I just... had... to move... move my arm. I'm all right."

The doctor turned off the machine while the nurse looked down at me, a huge grin on his face. "Well, am I happy to hear you talking like that! Not everyone wakes up as bright eyed and bushy tailed as you. But you need to try not to move, okay? Or that monitor will be screaming again." He did, however, leave my left hand where it was.

Something about his words worried me, but I had no time to think about it as my mother, Élisabeth, and Laurence came into my room.

Laurence grabbed my good arm with both hands and fell over me, sobbing into my hospital gown. "I was so afraid I was going to lose you, Joseph," she eventually gulped in French. She looked up at me, her large, dark eyes full of tears, her lower lip quivering. "I just couldn't... not after *Papa*. Please... please promise me you'll never leave us."

"I promise," I said, freeing my hand to comb my fingers through her hair, the way I used to do when she was a wee girl.

My family sat with me for a while, telling me about everything going on at home and carefully avoiding mention of my accident except to reluctantly inform me when I asked for about the eighth time that I had been unconscious for three days.

Three days. Why does this sound important?

At some point, I fell asleep. I awoke to the clattering of dishes and the smell of food to discover that it was supper time.

I was allowed to sit up to eat a bowl of clear chicken

soup and some green jelly dessert, and to drink orange juice from a plastic cup. Élisabeth wanted to feed me like a baby, but I would not allow this. I felt sick to my stomach after the first few bites, but I went slowly and managed to keep it down. *Maman* and my sisters watched me, smiling and murmuring encouraging words, hanging on my every move as if I was competing in a FIFA tournament. I did not understand what all this fuss was about but clearly, something more serious had happened to me than a broken collarbone.

After supper, Aunt Marguerite came to visit. She spoke quietly in French to my mother for a few minutes in the far corner of the room, then *Maman* and my sisters kissed me goodnight and left for the evening.

"I'm happy to see you awake and looking so good," said Aunt Marguerite, sitting down on the chair beside my bed. She spoke to me in English.

I doubted if I looked very good, unshaved, with greasy hair, and wires and tubes sticking out of me as they were.

"Joseph… can you tell me? What's the last thing you remember?" she asked, leaning intently toward me. "Think hard, please. This is very important."

"Why? Why is this so important? What happened to me… after the car?"

Aunt Marguerite's eyes widened hopefully. "You remember being hit by the car? That's wonderful. What else?"

"I remember school," I said slowly. Things were coming back to me in mixed up bits and pieces. "My house. Philippe shouting. A wee dog?" I puzzled over this image. "Falling up—up?—stairs. Where's Philippe? Has he come to see me?"

Aunt Marguerite frowned, shook her head in a way that made my stomach clench, and gestured with a hand for me to go on.

"I remember the country house. We were all there together. We went canoeing. Is that where I had my accident?"

The frown deepened. "No. That was two months ago, Joseph. Do you remember anything more recent besides the car? For instance… do you remember meeting Alison Mitchell?"

"Oh… uh, yes?" I said slowly, the name bringing an image to mind. Red-blond hair, intense blue eyes. The feeling that I cared for her and trusted her.

"She's here," Aunt Marguerite said. "Do you want to see her?"

"But of course," I said, my heart beating harder although I did not quite know why.

My aunt rose and went out to the hallway. She returned a moment later with the young lady, who looked just as I had envisioned her. Not a glamorous beauty, but pretty without a lot of makeup, done up hair, or fancy clothes. And she was not skin and bones like many of the Yale girls who followed the soccer team about. *Au contraire,* she had a roundish face and some nice curves to her body.

"Alison!" I pushed myself up a little straighter with my good arm.

"Hey there," she said, sounding very American. She sat gently on the edge of my bed, her freckled face beaming with her smile. "It's good to see you. I was so worried about—"

"I remember! It's you—you hit me with your car! I was running… and you—"

"And I hit you," she said, nodding. "Yeah. Sorry about that."

"No. You helped me. I—ah, *Dieu*, I remember." I looked past Alison to my aunt. "Gregory came to my house with men... They wished for me to go with them... uh... but Phi—Philippe..." I stumbled, thoughts and images coming too fast for my mouth to keep up. "They... one o-of them... he had a knife..." I slapped my shaking hand to my mouth as I felt my tasteless supper rising in my throat. I wondered dimly if I vomited, would it come out my mouth or the tube in my nose?

"Try to be calm, Joseph," Aunt Marguerite said. "We need you to remember, but you need to stay still, as well."

"Philippe... he's dead, *n'est-ce pas*? I remember the—there was blood. A lot of blood."

"Yes. I'm afraid so." Aunt Marguerite looked out the window, as though she didn't want to look me in the eyes.

"And what has—where is he now?"

"His body was taken home to France. He was buried yesterday." She turned toward me, and I saw that her eyes were bright with tears. "I'm so sorry, Joseph."

I swallowed hard, blinking back my own tears. I took a couple deep breaths and looked at Alison. "I remember they took me, locked me up. When I had the chance, I ran away. You helped me. I—I hid in your house. We went... uh, no... not to New York. To the country house, yes?"

She nodded and put a hand on my arm, which I dropped to my side.

"I remember drinking cognac... with you... on the

stairs."

Another nod and, if possible, an even wider smile.

"Men came... two... after us." I looked at my aunt. "They killed Germain and—"

"No, they didn't," she assured me hastily. "Germain was injured, but he's going to be fine."

But there were more... men with guns. FBI. I had a gun! I remember now...

"Shot!" I exclaimed, starting at the memory, my voice not quite a shout, but very close. *Bon Dieu! I remember. I did not break my collarbone in an accident! I. Was. Shot.* In a sudden panicked need to move, I tried to push myself around, to swing my legs off the bed, but I was too weak to manage it. Pain shot from my injured shoulder into my arm, and I immediately broke out in a hot sweat.

"Joseph! Stop it!" Aunt Marguerite shouted, while Alison held my good shoulder down in an effort to restrain me. "Calm yourself, please!"

The heartbeat monitor dutifully started beeping again.

A new nurse rushed in, looking like she expected to find me half dead.

"*Pardon*," I said thickly, still kicking weakly at the bed covers as the nurse stopped the machine beeping. "But I cannot... I need... ah, *Dieu*..." My head swam, wee black spots jittered on the edges of my vision, and I threw up my supper, such as it had been, in a lumpy, liquid mess down the front of my gown.

Bien alors. That answers this question.

The retching left me gasping for breath, my heart racing so hard and fast it scared me into silence.

"You need to be quiet," the nurse said briskly,

wiping my chin and throat with a clump of tissues. "I'll send someone in to clean you up." She straightened my legs and lowered my bed until I lay flat. Glaring at Alison and Aunt Marguerite, she said, "Mr. Lorraine can't afford to be upset at this point in his recovery. I'm going to have to ask you to leave." Looking down at me, she added, "This will help with the pain, calm you down, and help you sleep."

I noticed then that she held a syringe in one hand. I opened my mouth to object, but she had already injected the contents into my IV drip. "Say goodnight to your visitors, Joseph," she advised me. "You're going to be asleep in a few minutes."

"She's right, Joseph," Aunt Marguerite said. "You need to rest. I'll see you tomorrow morning."

"No, wait," I said as Alison stood to leave. "There's more… I saw… I need… remember… everything." I blinked, the medication already making me feel as if I was floating. I reached for her, but my arm had become too heavy to lift. "Stay."

She took my hand in hers, lacing her fingers through mine, and gave it a squeeze. "I promise I'll come back tomorrow," she said, her voice thick with the tears I could see in her eyes. "We'll talk then, okay?"

"*Oui*," I said, my voice sounding as if it came from far away. I could no longer manage to think in English. "*Demain.*"

Chapter 9

No Saying No
Alison

Marguerite called me Saturday morning to tell me Joseph had awakened calm and far more coherent than he'd been the previous evening. FBI agents were going to interview him at one o'clock, and I shouldn't plan on visiting him until much later in the day. Then Dad informed me in no uncertain terms that he was coming with me. No amount of complaining or arguing could dissuade him.

So it was that we drove together to Mount Sinai Hospital in Dad's SUV, arriving just after six that evening. Once we reached Joseph's floor, however, I asked my dad to wait in the sunroom that I'd spotted yesterday.

"Seriously, Alison?" he said, looking down his nose at me.

"Yeah, Dad. We don't know if he wants to see you, do we? Or even if he's in any shape to see anyone."

Dad harrumphed and headed into the spacious sunroom. I took off my coat, smoothed my white blouse over the top of my jeans, and walked down the hallway to Joseph's comfortable private room.

He must have a ton of money or amazing insurance. We could never afford a private room for Mom. I couldn't stop the tiny bitter thought popping into my head, but I squashed it immediately. Joseph lived in a world I'd never known and never would know, plain and simple.

I was surprised—extremely, pleasantly surprised— to find Joseph sitting in a wheelchair by the window, free of all the wires and tubes that had made him look so seriously ill yesterday. My joy quickly faded, however, when I walked closer and noticed the plate of semi- appetizing creamed meat and veggies, along with a transparent plastic glass half-full of orange juice, untouched on the table beside his bed. Then I got a look at his face and my heart almost stopped.

While his cheeks were now dry, his red-rimmed eyes and tightly pressed lips told me he'd been crying not long ago.

"Um… I'm sorry," I said gently from a few steps away. "Maybe I'll just come back later."

"No." He sniffed and cleared his throat, and waved me closer with his right hand, the edge of which was still half-covered with scabs from its meeting with the asphalt a week ago. "It's all right, Alison. Come. Sit down."

I pulled up the beige *faux* leather armchair and sank into it opposite him, not quite close enough for our knees to touch.

Apart from his expression, he looked much better than he had last evening. He was wearing checkered blue pajama bottoms, an expensive name-brand black bathrobe, and black slippers. His left arm was firmly secured beneath the open bathrobe in an industrial strength sling. From what I could see now that it wasn't covered in blood, his chest was flat and muscled and sported a sensual crop of fine, dark hairs. I dragged my eyes upward with some effort. He'd shaved—or more likely, been shaved—and his lovely thick hair, formerly almost long enough to tie back, had been washed and cut short, presumably so it would be easier for him to care for using only one hand.

"I'm so glad to see you sitting up," I said, opting for an upbeat tone. "You look way better. Nice pajamas too."

"Ah—yes. My sisters were very 'appy to go shopping for them in Man'attan last night." He made a valiant attempt at a smile but didn't quite pull it off.

"I'll bet they were," I agreed, hoping I would get the chance to meet them before they returned to France. "So… um, I guess the FBI came by?"

Joseph took a deep breath through his nose and slowly let it out. At first, I thought he wasn't going to answer. Then he nodded and said, "They came with Aunt Marguerite and 'er lawyer. They asked for my statement. I told them everything I remember until I was shot. After that, I… *bien*... things are a wee bit messed up, you know?" He was silent for a moment, and I saw the acute pain of recollection in his chocolate eyes.

When he spoke again, his voice was thick with emotion. "The man called Marty killed Philippe and set the house on fire, and 'e almost killed Germain. The big man the FBI called Alec told me at the country 'ouse that 'e killed Gregory. 'E shot me. 'E killed that FBI agent and—yes," he said at the horrified surprise that must have showed on my face. "They told me this morning, 'e died last night."

"Oh. God." My words were hardly more than a murmur. My stomach turned and I clutched the arm of the chair to steady myself.

"Aunt Marguerite and you could 'ave been killed

too." Joseph took another long breath, this one coming out in a labored huff. "All because of me."

"No!" I exclaimed. I leaned closer and grasped his good hand between mine. "Joseph, you're wrong. All of that was because your cousin hired some horrible, crazy thugs to try to force you into doing something you didn't want to do."

"Yes, per'aps this time, but... there are so many things you do not know, Alison."

I gave him my most piercing stare. "Then tell me. You said you trust me."

He shook his head. Gently extracted his hand from mine and stared out the window at the red and orange tops of the maple trees across the street.

I waited him out, tapping my foot impatiently but forcing myself not to say anything. Finally, he pressed his hand to his forehead, took yet another deep breath, and began. "*Bien*... Philippe and I are—were—best friends since I'm six years old and 'e's eight. We did everything together. 'Is father was my father's *aide-de-camp*. A sort of assistant and bodyguard, yes?" He turned to look at me. "After I began my studies at the *Université de Paris*, I received some... uh..." His forehead creased as he searched for a word, gave up, and said in French, "*menaces.*"

"*Menaces*? You mean threats?" I caught my breath as he nodded. "From whom? Your cousin Gregory?"

"No, not 'im. The family de Lorraine is associated with the legend of the sacred bloodline since many years—centuries—yes?"

I gave a nod but didn't want to interrupt to tell him I'd Googled this.

"Most people know nothing of this, but there are

some who follow it. *Bon Dieu*, this will sound quite mad to you, but there is a group of people who believe the biblical Antichrist will come from one of the bloodline families. They—"

"What?" I gasped. This seemed so ludicrous I nearly burst out laughing, but one look at Joseph's grim face choked the laughter off in my throat. I clapped my hands to my cheeks and blurted, "They think you're the Antichrist? You can't be friggin' serious!"

"Unfortunately, yes. It's not as if they spend all their time stalking me, but occasionally some person goes mad. I was targeted at a foot—uh, soccer—match in Paris four years ago. Someone tried to shoot me. They missed, and fortunately no one was injured. The shooter was arrested and questioned, and we learned that the Antichrist movement is genuine. After this we were more careful, you know? And Philippe became my bodyguard." Fresh tears welled up in his eyes and he hastily wiped them away with his good hand. "*Pardon*." He said this the French way.

I'd dropped my hands from my face to rest them on my thighs. "It's okay to cry, Joseph. You lost your best friend. God knows Dad and I cried rivers for my mom."

He sighed. "Yes, I know. But I 'ave cried enough. Now I must decide what to do next."

I shook my head and shimmied my chair closer. My right knee bumped his, and his expression softened a bit. "No. Now you have to concentrate on getting better so you can face the next lunatic who wants a piece of you."

"*Oui.*" His eyes narrowed. "About getting better… No one will tell me, but I think I 'ave more than a broken collarbone. I was unconscious for three days. They will not let me walk on my own. And to be honest, I think if

I try… I will fall on my face."

"Well, yeah. You were shot, after all," I said, trying to avoid telling him what I was pretty sure he wanted me to tell him.

"But of course. Per'aps the bullet did more than break some bone, yes? I know you know, Alison. I saw it in your eyes last night. You were afraid for me. I broke my ankle playing soccer when I was eleven years old, and no one was so worried about me. I will find out eventually. Why not just tell me and get it done with?"

I groaned. "Oh. My. God. You really are going to be a great leader one day. There's no saying 'no' to you."

This time, he managed a crooked smile. Waited patiently, like someone who was used to getting his own way.

Oh, what the hell. Like he said, he's going to find out eventually, anyway.

"The bullet—or the fractured bone, I don't know which—nicked the artery below your collarbone," I explained reluctantly. "The paramedics couldn't clamp the artery properly because the bullet was in the way, and you lost a lot of blood. So much that your heart stopped before you reached the hospital. They got it going again—obviously—" I giggled like an idiot as pressure escaped me like steam from a boiling kettle. "But Joseph… you almost died."

"I died," he said with a nod, as if he'd come to a realization.

"Almost."

"No. I died," he repeated in a level voice. "I remember… I thought it was a dream, but now… I think it was not."

Okay, then. What did Marguerite say about brain

Donna Marie West

damage caused by blood loss?

"Don't look at me this way," he said sharply, and I saw a hint of the usual sparkle in his eyes. "Yes, I was confused when I woke up. I 'ad trouble putting my thoughts together. Trouble with my English. But I'm all right now. I'm not even on morphine anymore because I 'ad to 'ave all my 'ead when I talked to the FBI today." His eyes narrowed in thought. "You said I lost a lot of blood. Did I receive a transfusion?"

"What? Of course you—oh, I know what you're getting at."

His eyes opened wider, and he gave me a steady look.

"Don't worry. Your body's making more of your own blood as we speak. In a few weeks, the bloodline will be safe inside you. Didn't you learn anything in science class?"

He nodded, then gave an audible sigh of relief.

"My dad came with me today," I said in hopes of getting back on a neutral topic. "He's waiting in the sunroom if you want to see him. You know, the visiting room?" I added, seeing his forehead crease in incomprehension. "Are you allowed to leave your room?"

"I do not know. Yes, why not? But… uh…" He gave a rueful look down at his immobilized arm. "You will 'ave to push."

"No problem. Um… don't you want to eat your supper first?" I gestured with my head toward the waiting plate of food.

He gave it a long, unenthusiastic look. "No. Per'aps later."

"It'll be cold later."

- 102 -

He waved this away as unimportant. "It's cold already."

"Okay, then. Let's go." I released the brake on Joseph's wheelchair and started to wheel him out of the room. "Wait a minute." I went into the bathroom, ran a washcloth under cold water, and brought it back to him.

"Thank you," he said. He wiped his face and throat with the cloth, rubbed it over his hair, which proceeded to stand up in little spikes in front, and handed it back to me to put away.

My dad was sitting on a sofa looking impatient, but he rose with a tight smile when we arrived. "Joseph," he said politely, sitting again as I plonked down beside him. "How are you doing?"

"Better, thank you, Dr. Mitchell," Joseph replied, equally polite.

The air between them was so rife with tension, I expected it to start crackling any second.

"Well, that's good." Dad muffled a cough against the sleeve of his cardigan. "Alison tells me you talked to the FBI today?"

"Yes."

"So, have you been cleared of all the charges against you?"

"Yes, I'm cleared," Joseph replied pleasantly with a discreet glance at me.

"Well, that's good. Do you know if you'll be in the hospital for long?"

"I 'ave no idea. I 'ope not."

Joseph really does need to work on pronouncing his "H"s, I thought, and a nervous giggle bubbled out of me.

Dad and Joseph both looked at me.

Then Dad pressed on, and I wished I'd left home

without him. "What will you do when you get out?"

"I do not yet know exactly, but I 'ope to return to my studies at Yale."

"Really? I'm surprised to hear that."

"Why?" asked Joseph, a challenge in his rising voice. "With respect, Dr. Mitchell, you know nothing about me. You do not know what I 'ave been through in the past or what I wish to do with my future."

"I know you're an entitled rich boy who's probably never worked a day in his life. Who got an innocent girl involved in his muddled personal drama and put her life in danger," Dad declared. "My daughter—"

"He didn't, Da—" I began, but the daggers Joseph shot me with his eyes shut me up.

"Yes, this is true," Joseph said stoically. "I put Alison in danger. But I did not intend it, believe me."

"Whether you intended it or not, if something had happened to her… If I'd lost her…" Dad's bravado broke down and he swallowed hard. Shook his head. "You probably think I'm being very hard on you, but I don't know what I'd do without her, Joseph. I just don't know."

"Dad…" I reached over and took his hand. It was warm and a bit damp, and it was trembling. "Please."

"I understand," Joseph said, his tone solemn now, but his voice strong. "I'm sorry about my part in what 'appened, but I would not—never—let anything 'appen to your daughter."

Dad blinked.

I gaped, my mouth hanging slightly open at this declaration. God only knew where the conversation might have gone next if last night's very business-like Nurse Allen hadn't burst into the sunroom.

"Mr. Lorraine! I've been looking all over for you," she chastised him. "You haven't eaten your supper. You shouldn't even be out here!" She gave him a long, critical gaze. "You've had much too much excitement for today. Too many visitors." She gave Dad and me scathing looks, as if we should have noticed this and remedied the situation.

"I'm all right," Joseph insisted.

"Well, we'll see how all right you are. If you don't eat, you'll end up being fed through a tube again. Is that what you're after? Now, the physical therapist is waiting for you in your room."

Joseph frowned up at her. "I already saw 'im this morning."

"You want to get back on your feet and get that arm working?" Nurse Allen demanded. As Joseph replied yes, of course he did, she added, "Then you'll see him again tonight."

"Go on, Joseph," I said, standing up. "Do what you have to do to get better. Eat your supper and get some rest."

"Come back tomorrow in the afternoon," he said to me. "I... I must talk to you."

"I will, no problem," I assured him. *And don't worry, I won't be bringing my dad.*

Nurse Allen wheeled Joseph away toward his room.

Dad and I left, stopping for supper at the nearest fast-food joint before hitting the highway. We talked a little bit, but mostly I kept to myself, lost in my own swirling thoughts.

Roxie was right the other day. I have to admit it, I don't only have my eye on Joseph, I'm falling for him. Probably have been since that first evening when he got in my car. And why not?

Why not? Maybe because I have no clue if he has a girlfriend here or in France. Or both. No clue what—if anything—he feels for me.

Maybe because as good and kind as Joseph is, Dad's right too. Joseph was raised with a silver spoon in his mouth, heir to the bloodline of Jesus Christ himself and destined to do great things with his life. I'm a nobody who's lost most of my friends while mourning my mom, barely able to get through high school and as of this moment probably on the verge of failing my first semester of college. We have nothing in common, and yet I can't shake this bizarre feeling of connection I have with him...

Chapter 10

Picking up the Pieces
Joseph

I spent half the night thinking about what I had experienced—as far as I could get it clear in my mind—between the time I was shot and the time I awakened in the hospital. I had to tell someone before the memories became more mixed up or faded away altogether—or before I went mad trying to make sense of them.

But I could not imagine telling *Maman* or Élisabeth. Or Aunt Marguerite. Philippe, to whom I had always told everything, was gone. I did not have the heart to speak to his father, who was a second father to me. That left Alison. I had wanted to tell her last evening, but I had held back. I was afraid I would send her screaming away, wishing never to see me again. Finally, I prayed about it. I was still praying as I fell asleep.

Dieu merci, I was making progress physically. At my therapy session this morning, I was able to walk back and forth across the room several times without becoming dizzy or losing my balance. I was able to use the bathroom—a huge and welcome improvement over the catheter-and-bedpan situation earlier in the week. While my left hand was still faintly numb, I was able to feel a pen dragged along my forearm. I could lift my arm a few inches, bend and straighten my elbow, and move my thumb and fingers, even though my left shoulder and upper chest were a mass of aching blue-and-purple bruises. Fainter green-and-yellow areas covered my ribs and thigh on the same side, but at least these were no longer painful. My collarbone hurt like hell at the slightest movement of my shoulder, but my headache was gone. I had refused all pain medication except ibuprofen since yesterday, although I thought I would perhaps buy a case of these when I left the hospital.

Dr. Scott came to examine me after my physical therapy and finally gave me some concrete answers to my questions.

She explained that the muscles in my arm had been deprived of blood for some period of time, causing the persistent tingling sensation. That the nerves behind my collarbone had been damaged, causing the partial paralysis. But she had good news too: the actual shoulder joint had not been injured. There was no infection, and circulation appeared to be returning to normal. The repaired nerves would hopefully regenerate themselves in time.

"Hopefully?" I asked, my throat closing around the word.

The doctor looked at me over her glasses. "Well, yes. I'm afraid it's going to take some time and hard work on your part to regain full use of that hand."

"All right. I can do this," I told her, breathing again. "I play soccer at Yale. I have plans for my life. I will not have a disabled hand."

Dr. Scott's gray eyebrows shot up. "Then I'm sure you'll make a full recovery. Look, Joseph… you're a very lucky young man. You seem to be mending extraordinarily quickly. Your strength and balance should improve day by day. If you feel good when I see you tomorrow—and you're eating well and not vomiting—I'll think about signing your release forms on Tuesday. Do you have somewhere to go? Needless to say, you shouldn't be alone for the next few weeks."

"Yes, I—I will speak to my aunt," I said, while another possibility brewed at the back of my mind. "Thank you for your concern and for the good news."

When Fred—the man I had first taken for a nurse but since learned was what Americans called a patient care technician—came to wash and shave me, I insisted on doing everything myself. It was important for me to prove to him that I could do it. Perhaps more important still, to prove it to myself.

Aunt Marguerite, my mother, and my sisters came for lunch. I wished to walk with them to the cafeteria, but they all immediately protested that it was much too far. Then Laurence begged me to let her push me in my wheelchair, and I gave in. I could not refuse my baby sister anything.

Once we arrived in the cafeteria, with our trays of salad, soup, and sandwiches on a table, I told my family that I hoped to leave the hospital on Tuesday. As expected, Aunt Marguerite said she would make arrangements for me to stay at her townhouse. She also told me that the New Haven police had recovered from Gregory's rented house my wallet, cell phone, wristwatch, and silver Cross of Lorraine pendant that had belonged to my father and his father before him, which I had worn every day since *Papa*'s funeral. I almost wept with joy at the thought of retrieving this item—not simply a memento of the origin of my family name in the northeast of France, nor of my father, but an ancient symbol of much, much more.

Maman announced that she and my sisters would be

leaving the next day. This was not a surprise. I knew that the girls had to get back to school. I told them I needed some clothing and personal items, having no idea what might have survived the fire, and Élisabeth promptly offered to go shopping again. She fished her phone out of her bag, and we made a list of what I would need in the next few days, with many enthusiastic suggestions from Laurence.

My sisters gleefully rushed off to shop, and I had serious worries about what I might end up wearing tomorrow.

Maman and Aunt Marguerite remained to discuss grown-up issues with me: the house insurance, getting me a new passport, finding me a bodyguard. Whether or not I should return to France to recover.

"I don't wish to return to France. Or remain here in New York City," I told them firmly in French. "I wish to return to Yale as soon as I can. And I don't need another bodyguard. Gregory is dead, and the men who took me are dead or arrested. The threat is over."

"Joseph," Aunt Marguerite said with a little tut-tut as if I had uttered an idiocy, "for your family, the threat is never over. Besides that, you won't be able to manage on your own until your arm is healed. How long will that be? Weeks? Months? And what about your house? It will be a while before it's ready to be lived in again."

"Yes, I know. I've been thinking about all of this. I… Well, you've met Alison—"

"I have not," said my mother, looking like this was the very next thing on her must-do list.

"Stay this afternoon and you will, *Maman*. She should be here soon."

She was. I saw her walk into the cafeteria, hesitate

when she spotted us, then square her shoulders and march straight to our table. She looked nice in jean leggings, boots, and a long, black sweater. And I was happy to see that today she was alone.

I introduced Alison to my mother, who examined her up and down as though appraising an antique of questionable provenance.

"My sisters went shopping for me," I said, switching from French to English for Alison. "I need clothes and things. The doctor said I can probably leave the hospital on Tuesday."

"That's wonderful!" she exclaimed, dropping onto the chair beside me. "What—um—where are you going to stay?"

"*Bien*... You know, I wish to talk to you about this," I said, ignoring the shocked stares from my mother and my aunt. "I learned at an early age that if I want something, I should ask politely for it. So, I will ask you: would it be possible for me to stay at your home until I'm able to be on my own? Perhaps a few weeks? I will of course pay rent, groceries, and whatever else..." I finished with a shrug of my good shoulder.

Alison's face had gone bright pink all the way to her ears as I spoke. Now she let out a sort of strangled giggle and asked, "What about your aunt? Friends at Yale? There must be someone, maybe one of your soccer teammates or... or a girlfriend... who could take you in?"

I noticed the brief hesitation before she said "girlfriend" and could not help smiling. "I have gone out with a lot of girls, but I do not have a girlfriend. As for friends... yes, perhaps," I admitted, "but to be honest, I have some trust issues at the moment."

"Oh. Yeah. I can understand that," Alison said, suddenly looking quite happy. "Well, I'm pretty sure you know that if it was up to me, I'd say yes right away. We have the room. But it's—I—I mean, it's my dad's house. You—I have to ask him."

"I understand," I said as casually as I could, while my heart beat a bit faster, "but I'm thinking… it's close to Yale, you know, and your father's a doctor. Just in case…"

And of course, you're there. This is more important than you can imagine.

Alison ran her hands through her loose hair, looking like she just might pull some out. "What does your family have to say about it?"

"I did not ask their permission," I replied. "Aunt Marguerite will have me at her home, of course, but since I wish to go back to Yale, it's not the ideal solution."

"Wow. Okay, well, let me call Dad. If he doesn't drop dead of shock on the spot, I might have to do some fancy talking to convince him."

"I'm sure you will," I agreed, my hopes dropping considerably.

Alison punched the number into her cell phone, got up, and strolled around the cafeteria as she talked to her father.

"Are you sure about this, Joseph?" my mother asked in French. She leaned across the table toward me. "She seems a nice enough girl, but really, what do you know about her?"

"I know more than you think, *Maman*. And she knows things about me."

My mother's face went white as the tablecloth. "What? Don't tell me you told her—"

"Not everything," I said. "But enough. I had to give her a reason to not call the police on me when she saw me on the news. And… I cannot explain why to you right now, but I trust her."

"Oh, *mon Dieu*," she mumbled, fanning herself with her napkin. "Do you understand what you're risking, Joseph? Truly? For yourself as well as that innocent family? For all of us?"

"Yes *Maman*, believe me, I do." *Even more than you know*.

Judging from Alison's raised shoulders and the agitated gesturing of her free hand, I suspected that things were not going well with her father. Eventually, however, she dropped her phone into her handbag and came back to the table. Then a smile broke out on her face. "He said yes!"

"He said yes?" I repeated her words. "Just like that?"

"Well, no. Not just like that, but the thing is, we sort of need the money."

"*C'est vrai*? I thought doctors in America make a lot of money."

"Well, yeah, they do, but—" She took a long breath and then the words tumbled from her mouth. "Dad took a medical leave of absence when my mom got sick. But she was sick for a long time, and both his leave and her insurance ran out months before… before the end. He took a second mortgage on the house and invested it in some new company his dad's best friend's son was starting up. But the company flopped, and Dad and Granddad lost everything they'd put in.

"Dad went back to work a few weeks after Mom died, and even though he's doing a ton of overtime, it'll take him years to recoup what we lost. I offered to get a fulltime job, but he won't have it. He says as long as I live under his roof, I have to abide by his rules. He wants me to get a degree and have a chance at a good, solid career. So, here we are…" She sighed. "He's going to make you sign papers promising you'll pay your rent every week, keep your room clean, respect our rules, and… um, keep your hands off me." She rolled her eyes. "I'm sorry, Joseph. It's just… he's—"

"Your father. It's all right, all of it. I will do whatever he asks."

Of course, my mother wished to know more about Alison and her father, so we sat there drinking coffee, exchanging some facts and innocent stories of our lives and exhausting *Maman*'s limited English, with Aunt Marguerite or me interpreting when necessary. I thought that after a while, my mother looked less panic-stricken than she had earlier at the prospect of my going to Alison's house.

Laurence and Élisabeth came back loaded with shopping bags and silly grins on their faces. Clearly, Aunt Marguerite had told them about Alison, because they immediately knew who she was. Élisabeth said hello. Laurence's face went bright red, and she clasped a hand over her mouth to muffle her giggles.

My sisters clearly enjoyed showing me the T-shirts, hooded sweatshirts, jeans, sweatpants, underwear, and slip-on sneakers they had bought. They had even bought an I-Pod, which they promised to fill with some of my favorite music and give me tomorrow morning. Élisabeth wasted no time in becoming friends with Alison and before they said goodbye, they had exchanged phone numbers and email addresses, and

Élisabeth had shared the Facebook page she held under an alias.

We decided that Aunt Marguerite would have her driver—an Italian fellow called Roberto who would replace Germain until he could return to work—drive me to New Haven on Tuesday afternoon, if in fact Dr. Scott signed my release forms. I should go directly to the police station to collect my things and find out what had become of my car before disembarking at Alison's house.

It all sounded good to me. I was not going to have the chance to talk to Alison alone today, but I would take my first opportunity once I was out of the hospital.

****

By the time I sat in the passenger seat of Aunt Marguerite's white town car Tuesday afternoon, I was exhausted and wondering seriously if I was ready to leave the hospital. Monday had been almost restful aside from the physical therapy sessions. I had managed to meditate twice with the intention of bringing healing energy into my body. I had listened to some music and flipped through channels on the television for an hour before finding a movie that almost put me to sleep. Tuesday morning, however, had been one long rush of therapy, blood and urine tests, X-rays of my collarbone, and a final examination by Dr. Scott, who warned me against any physical effort that might rip out the stitches holding the blood vessels beneath my collarbone together, with potentially fatal consequences.

The physical therapist had given me exercises for my arm and hand and advised me to find a good therapist in New Haven as soon as possible. The occupational therapist had shown me how to get out of and into bed without straining my shoulder, how to put on and take off my sling, and how to dress and undress using only one hand. To be honest, this was all going to take some practice.

Roberto programmed the address of the New Haven police station into the town car's GPS system. I sat back in the comfortable seat, asked him to wake me when we arrived, and closed my eyes. I did not expect to actually fall asleep but the next thing I knew, Roberto was shaking my knee and telling me to rouse myself.

We were parked outside the police station. The distance to the front door seemed daunting, but I told myself that if I could not walk across the street and up about ten steps, I should still be in the hospital.

"You want me to come with you?" Roberto asked. Before I could even answer, he had jumped out of the car, hurried around to my side, and opened my door.

I accepted his help getting out of the car but insisted on walking on my own. Roberto nodded and followed at my elbow, ready to lend assistance if I should falter. He was only a few years older than me, but someone had trained him well.

By the time I got to the top of the stairs, my feet felt as if they were made of cement, my heart pounded against my ribs, and my T-shirt was stuck to my back with sweat. I gritted my teeth against the pain in my shoulder and hung onto the door handle to remain upright while everything swayed around me.

After a moment, the world steadied. When I felt strong enough, I nodded to Roberto, who pushed the door open for me. I managed to walk in a straight line to the front counter, where a young policewoman looked at me with a question on her face. I gave her my name—

Joseph Lorraine, pronounced the American way—and explained that I had come to collect my things.

"I need to see some ID," the policewoman asked automatically.

"Uh, yes. My ID is in my wallet, which you have," I replied.

"I'm sorry," she said, certainly following to the letter some rule in the police rule book, "but I can't give you anything until you prove to me that you are who you say you are."

I really did not feel up to having an argument today. "Please, Officer"—I squinted to read her name tag— "Spencer. My name is Jean René Joseph de Lorraine." I pronounced it the French way this time. "Two weeks ago, I was kidnapped. My home was burned. I escaped from the place where I was held against my will. I was shot. I died—almost," I added quickly. "I have just left the hospital to come here for my things. I have nothing… My ID is in my wallet. You will see my photo, and if this is not enough… we can call the FBI, yes?" I stopped, gasping for breath, closing my eyes for a second against the wave of dizziness that hit me but just as quickly passed.

Roberto stepped forward, introducing himself as a personal aid to New York State Supreme Court Justice Marguerite Lorraine and showing the police officer his own ID.

Officer Spencer gaped, took an audible breath, and said she would be back shortly.

I looked longingly over at the waiting room chairs, but I was afraid that should I sit down, I would not be able to stand up again, so I stood there, my good arm resting heavily on the counter to steady myself, and waited.

Finally, after a period of time that seemed hours but was probably about ten minutes, Officer Spencer returned with an older African American officer and a flat cardboard box. Inside the box were my wallet, cell phone, wristwatch, pendant, and—a pleasant surprise—set of keys.

"Sorry about the delay, Mr. Lorraine," the older officer said. "These things come from the house where you were held. Mrs.?— Justice?— Lorraine identified them the other day as belonging to you. Your car's in the back lot. You can take it as well."

"Yes, all right," I said, although to be honest I barely heard him through the pounding of blood in my ears. "Thank you. I think I cannot drive my car today, but I will send someone for it as soon as possible."

I signed the necessary paperwork and slipped the two-inch-long Cross of Lorraine on its silver chain over my head, dropping it down inside my clothes. I looked through my wallet to find that everything except the cash was there—French national identity card and driver's license, Connecticut driver's license and gun permit, student visa card, Yale student ID card, credit cards. I shoved my wallet along with my other things into the right-hand pocket of my hoodie.

"Just one more thing, Mr. Lorraine," the same office added. "We have a copy of the statement you gave to the FBI, but in case we want to talk to you again, please let us know if you plan on leaving town."

"No worries, I will not go anywhere," I assured him.

It took all my remaining strength to put one foot in front of the other all the way back to the car. Once there I collapsed, panting, into my seat. Roberto fastened my seat belt for me and closed the door. Before he took his seat, however, I asked him to get something for me from beneath the driver's seat of my own car. It must be there since it was not in the box with my other possessions; a miracle the police had not found it.

His eyes widened in surprise, but he nodded, took the keys from me, and obediently left on his errand.

I sat back and closed my eyes in an effort to relax and slow down my heartbeat before all those stitches tore and the fatal consequences Dr. Scott had mentioned came to pass.

Roberto returned soon enough. He opened my door and handed me a pistol identical to the one I'd had at Aunt Marguerite's country house.

"Thank you," I said. I checked that the gun was loaded and locked, fumbling a bit as I had only one hand, and shoved it down into the pocket of my sweatpants.

If I find myself again in a situation where I need to use this, I will not make the mistake I made last time. God forgive me, but no one else near me will die if I can help it. Next time… I will not hesitate to fire.

Chapter 11

Surprises
Alison

I went to class Tuesday morning, but I hurried home at noon after Marguerite texted me to say that Joseph should be arriving mid-afternoon. The house was clean, and the guest room was ready for him. I was somewhat worried he would have trouble with the stairs, but there was no way my dad would give up the master bedroom he'd shared with Mom for twenty-four years. I hadn't even bothered to ask.

Dad was—of course—at work at the clinic, but he'd promised to be home as soon as possible. He'd instructed me to call him immediately should Joseph say or do anything untoward. I'd had to refrain from laughing in his face.

I was alternately watching out the window and distracting myself by browsing Élisabeth's Facebook photos from weekends in Switzerland and Scotland on my cell when a white luxury sedan pulled into the driveway behind my car. I hurried outside to help as Joseph emerged awkwardly from the car, and his driver started pulling shopping bags from the trunk.

Joseph looked like he'd come straight from the gym in navy sweatpants and a white hoodie; only his left arm in its sturdy black sling suggested this wasn't the case.

"Hey, I'm so glad to see you!" I exclaimed. "Here, let me help you with those." I took a couple bulging shopping bags from the driver.

I kept a watchful eye on Joseph as we hauled everything into the house. I was happy to see he was no longer limping, although he looked a tad green around the gills and seemed at moments unsteady on his feet. In spite of this, he insisted on carrying two bags in his good hand. We took everything upstairs to the guest room where Joseph had spent the night a week ago Friday. It felt like a month had passed since then.

Joseph thanked the driver, who left for New York, and sank with a groan onto the bed. His face had gone pale, and I could see his bad hand trembling slightly in its sling.

"Are you okay?" I asked, suddenly worried that he'd left the hospital prematurely.

He looked up at me and let out a long sigh. "Yes, I'm all right. It's just... I feel as if I 'ave been in bed for a week, you know?" He gave me one of his charming, crooked smiles.

Oh God, even with the short hair and sling, he's nearly irresistible.

"Do you... um, do you want help putting your stuff away?" I asked, just to have something to say.

"No, thank you. I think I can do it."

"Okay. Well, there's a bathroom at the end of the hall. You can put your... you know, bathroom things... in there. I'll use the one downstairs."

He nodded. "Thank you. I think... I will rest for a while before I come down."

"No problem. We usually eat around six."

"I will not be late," he said, giving me a wink.

But he was. He finally showed up downstairs looking somewhat rumpled at seven-thirty with profuse apologies for falling asleep after putting his things away.

"Don't worry about it, Joseph. It's totally understandable," I told him. "Do you want something to eat? I made meatloaf; there's lots left over."

He gave a nod. "Yes, please. If it's no trouble."

"No trouble at all." I warmed up a plate of meatloaf and mashed potatoes in the microwave and put it on the table with ketchup and a bowl of coleslaw. "Do you want some milk? It's good for your bones."

Joseph's forkful of meatloaf stopped halfway to his mouth. "Yes, all right," he said, one side of his mouth curling up.

"What?"

"Nothing. It's just… I think I 'ave not drank milk since I was a wee boy."

I felt my cheeks flush and replied defensively, "Well, it's good for your bones."

"So you said." He bit down on his lower lip in what I took as an effort not to laugh.

My cheeks boiling, I poured us each a glass of cold, low-fat milk and sat down to join him. I sipped my milk and watched him eat and drink, take his antibiotics and a couple too many ibuprofens from bottles he pulled from his pocket. I couldn't help asking myself, *Now that the drama and excitement are over and he's no longer on the run, what will he think of ordinary American domestic life? What will he think of me?*

After Joseph ate, I sent him to see my dad in his office as Dad had requested. They spent nearly an hour in there, but eventually came out together. Joseph looked relaxed and pleased with himself. Dad looked rather stunned, and I wondered what exactly had transpired.

Joseph said he couldn't stay on his feet a minute longer and excused himself to go to bed. When I pressed him, Dad said they'd come to agreements about everything and that Joseph could stay as long as he needed to, provided he followed the house rules. He concluded, rather grudgingly, that Joseph appeared to be a decent young man after all. I agreed wholeheartedly, thinking, *You have no idea.*

****

Since I didn't see Joseph before I left for school the next morning, I left him my cell phone number and a note on the kitchen table telling him to call me if he needed anything. He didn't call, but he was waiting for me when I got home that afternoon. He said he'd spent the day on his phone, basically letting people know he was still alive and reasonably intact. He'd talked to administrators and his professors at Yale about getting back to class and making up this week's missed midterms as soon as he was able. He'd talked to his friend Michael from the soccer team, and he'd cleared things up with the insurance and restoration companies so that repairs could begin on his house. He'd even made an appointment for tomorrow to see a physical therapist at the rehabilitation clinic my dad had recommended. He had the nagging feeling he'd forgotten something essential but couldn't for the life of him think what it might be.

He was dressed to leave the house in blue jeans and a burgundy sweatshirt. He asked me if I would go with him to the police station to pick up his car, admitting that he wanted to be sure he was no longer having dizzy spells before trying to drive. Of course, I jumped at the chance. I called a taxi, which Joseph offered to pay for if we stopped at his bank so he could get some cash, and I helped him pull his new black jacket on over his bad arm.

Less than an hour later, we were walking into the compressed gravel lot behind the police station. After passing two rows of cars, Joseph stopped abruptly.

"Wait—what—that's your car?" I exclaimed, gazing at the slightly rain-spotted but still magnificent dark blue sports car in front of us. I looked at the manufacturer's emblem and my mouth fell open. "No way! A Mercedes-Benz? I—I can't drive that!"

Joseph's eyes narrowed. "*Non*? Why not?"

"Seriously?" My voice came out in a screech. "This thing costs like, twice as much as my dad's SUV and my car together. I'll totally have a nervous breakdown worrying about denting it. Or scratching it. Or somehow screwing it up."

"I'm sure you will do none of these things," Joseph said in a maddeningly calm voice. He gave me a confident smile and handed me the electronic smart key.

"Oh my God," I muttered under my breath, "if I'm dreaming, please don't wake me up!"

We got into the two-door coupe, which at least no longer had that new car smell. Joseph gave me a few pointers and asked me to drive him to his house.

"Right now?" I asked, still reeling from the shock of sitting in the gray leather driver's seat of such a lovely car. "Are you sure?"

"Yes. I need to see it. I cannot wait any longer."

I grabbed the leather-covered steering wheel, drew in a deep breath, and slowly let it out. "Okay then. Just tell me where to go."

Despite my misgivings, I managed to drive Joseph's car to his house fifteen minutes away in Short Beach without crashing it or passing out from anxiety.

My heart dropped to the pit of my stomach at the sight of the once-white, two-story colonial home a block from the beach. The loose ends of the torn yellow crime scene ribbon surrounding the property fluttered in the breeze.

I stood rooted to the spot beside the car while Joseph took a few hesitant steps toward the house for a closer look. The front of the house was cracked, burned, and blackened, the windows and front door gone and boarded up. There was a four- or five-foot-wide hole in the roof covered with thick clear plastic. Even though the fire had taken place over two weeks ago, the odor of smoke and wet charcoal still lingered in the air.

"Oh. God. Joseph, I'm so sorry," I blurted, stumbling to join him. Without even thinking, I took his good hand in mine and gave it an encouraging squeeze. "Do you think you can save anything?"

"The insurance company thinks no, not a lot. The fire was in the living room and the room above it. My bedroom," he added with a grimace. "There's water and smoke damage too. The restoration people will come this week and then I will know more if something can be saved."

"Well, that's good news, at least."

"Yes, I suppose." Since I wouldn't let go of his hand, Joseph tugged me along with him as he slowly walked around the house. The rear part looked to be in much better shape than the front, with windows and the veranda intact.

There was a gray-and-black lump of something on the veranda, pressed against the smoke-stained sliding door. At first, I thought it was a mat or discarded piece of carpet. Then it moved. "Oh my—what's that?" I asked, stopping to point.

Joseph's face went chalk white. His jaw dropped and he pulled his hand out of mine to rub it across his forehead. "*Ah, Dieu*, it's the wee dog."

"What? You have a dog? Why didn't you tell me you—"

"I forgot," he said under his breath. Then he explained, "It's not our dog. She appeared 'ere a few days before the fire. We asked the neighbors, but no one knew where she came from. She would not allow us to touch 'er at first, but we gave 'er food and water out on the deck. She finally came in the 'ouse that Monday afternoon. I never thought... *Merde*! With everything that 'appened to me, it went out of my mind, you know?"

As he spoke, we made our way slowly up the eight stairs to the veranda. I noticed two stone-ware bowls in one corner half-filled with scummy water. No food.

The filthy little dog yipped and struggled to her feet. She made a valiant effort at wagging her tail, then wobbled and sank onto her haunches, her meager reserves of courage and energy spent.

"Oh my God—she's just a puppy, Joseph," I said, my heart in my throat. "And she's starving. Look, you can see her little hip bones and all her ribs."

"Yes, I see," he said, sounding like he wished he didn't.

"She probably hasn't had much of anything to eat since... since that night when you..." I got a hold of myself and rushed on, "We have to go home, get a cage, take her to the refuge where I used to—"

"No!" Joseph said sharply.

"What do you mean, no?" I demanded, my voice

rising with sudden anger and disdain, and the next words popped out of my mouth before I could stop them. "Don't tell me you're afraid you'll get your car dirty? We can't leave her here! Look at her, she needs to see a vet as soon—"

Joseph held up his hand to silence me like I was his lowly subject and said in his I'm-going-to-be-a-great-man voice of authority, "We will not leave 'er 'ere, Alison. There's a blanket in the boot of my car. We will wrap 'er in it and take 'er straight to the vet, yes?"

"Oh! Yeah. Okay." *Good job, Alison, speak before you think, why don't you? Idiot!*

Joseph overlooked my little tirade and asked me to stay with the puppy in case she tried to flee while he fetched the blanket. A minute later, he was back.

He draped the blanket gently over the puppy. She gave one half-hearted yelp, then watched us silently, her odd-colored eyes—one brown, one blue—wary as I tucked the blanket around her and cautiously picked her up.

She smelled like Bax after a roll in the ditch behind our yard and weighed next to nothing. I carried her easily back to the car, apologizing all the way to Joseph for the way I'd jumped down his throat. We got the dog, still in the blanket, settled in the back seat. Joseph turned and marched up the front stairs, scooped what would turn out to be a soccer magazine and some bills from the smoke-stained but still intact metal mailbox, and returned to the car. He tossed the mail onto the passenger seat and slid awkwardly into the back seat beside the puppy. I helped him with his seatbelt, got in the car, and drove to the veterinary clinic where I took my own pets.

Joseph was murmuring a string of sweet nothings in

French to the puppy. I glanced over my shoulder a couple times to see him gently stroking her head. She seemed to have given up all resistance and now lay quietly in the blanket, probably warm and dry for the first time in over two weeks.

I parked the car in the lot behind the clinic. We got the puppy out and I carried her inside, straight to the reception counter.

Roxie was on her Wednesday afternoon shift at the clinic. "Alison!" she exclaimed, her green eyes falling on the bundle in my arms. "What have you got there?" Then she spotted Joseph at my elbow, and her eyes nearly popped out of her salon suntanned face. "Is that—is he— oh, Lordy!"

"Yeah, Roxie, that's Joseph. Joseph, my best friend Roxie," I said hastily to the two of them.

"You didn't tell me he got out of the hospital," Roxie said through her teeth.

I didn't tell you he's staying at my house, either. I didn't tell you a whole lot of things.

"I promise I'll explain everything to you later, but right now, this puppy needs to see a vet."

"Oh. Um. Right," said Roxie, getting back to business. "We'll have to open a file for it. Um... under your name?"

"Yeah, I guess." The puppy wriggled in my arms; I held her tighter to prevent her slipping out of the blanket and landing headfirst on the floor.

"No," said Joseph, stepping up to the reception counter. "My name. Joseph Lorraine." He said it the American way.

"O—kay then," Roxie said, typing on the computer while she continued to gape at us. "What's the dog's name?" "

"*Fleur*. This is French for 'flower.' "

"What?" Roxie and I asked in unison. I added, "You gave her a name?"

"Philippe did," Joseph admitted. "'E wished to keep 'er. 'E named 'er for the... uh, the *moufette* in the children's movie, you know? Bambi?"

"Bambi? You mean he named her after the skunk?"

"*Oui*, because... she's too dirty to see now, but she 'as a wee white stripe on 'er back." He looked at Roxie, and she practically melted. "Please. The dog needs to see a vet. The cost is no matter."

"Right," Roxie croaked. "Hang on." She disappeared into the depths of the clinic and came back a moment later to direct us to examination room two.

Fatherly Dr. Ford, who had been my vet forever, needed an assistant's help to examine Fleur. It was clear the puppy hadn't been handled—or had been mishandled—before showing up at Joseph's place. Joseph explained that she was a stray he'd been feeding. That she'd been left alone while he was in the hospital recovering from an accident. Dr. Ford glanced at Joseph's immobilized left arm beneath his open jacket and nodded sympathetically.

"The dog appears to be a border collie," the vet said at the end of the rather rock-and-roll examination. As thin and weak as she was, Fleur had found the strength to fight the vet all the way, bolting from the examination table the moment he'd finished with her. She was currently cowering under the stool in a corner. "About four months old. She's not dehydrated, which is a good thing, but she needs to be given some quality food. Washed. Vaccinated and de-wormed. Treated for fleas.

Tested for heartworm, the parvovirus, and other possible health issues. Then she needs to be socialized." He gave Joseph a long look. "That's a lot of expense and effort for a stray dog. Are you planning to keep her afterward?"

"Yes," Joseph said without hesitation. He looked at me. "At least I can honor Philippe this way."

"I'm sure he'd be happy with that," I said over the lump that suddenly popped up in my throat.

"Yes, I think so, too," he agreed with a sort of sad smile. "May I bring 'er to your 'ome until I can move back to mine?"

"Of course," I said. "Bax might like to have a doggy friend."

Dr. Ford suggested leaving Fleur for the night and picking her up tomorrow afternoon after all her tests and treatments were done. Joseph agreed and told Dr. Ford to do whatever he felt was necessary. We helped the vet assistant round the puppy up to take her to a comfortable cage in the overnight ward.

Joseph paid for today's visit with a credit card.

Roxie completed Fleur's file with Joseph's cell phone number and the address at his house. Then she beckoned me to the counter with an index finger as Joseph walked toward the door. "You and me, girlfriend," she said in a low voice. "Friday night. Seven o'clock. Our usual place. And bring Joseph."

"I'll come," I whispered back, "but I don't know about Joseph. You have no idea what he's been through lately. He might not feel like going out."

Roxie gave me an exasperated eye roll. "Whatever. Either way, you have some serious explaining to do."

Chapter 12

Evening Out
Joseph

With only one working hand, everything was a slow, frustrating chore. Washing and drying myself. Dressing. Making my bed. Opening the jars of peanut butter and strawberry jam. *Dieu merci,* I was right-handed. I did not know how I would have managed had I not been.

I was a wee bit worried about driving, but I had not had a dizzy spell since yesterday morning when I rose from bed too quickly. I assured Dr. Mitchell and Alison that I was strong enough to go alone to my physical therapy treatment and, in fact, I was.

The therapist, a middle-aged and clearly competent man called Colin, first asked me about my injury. Then he put my shoulder, arm, and hand through a gentle but painful series of exercises. My collarbone still hurt when I moved my shoulder, but the pain was less than it had been. My control of my arm was improving. What worried me most—scared the hell out of me, actually—was that I could not yet properly feel or use my fingers. When I lifted my arm, my hand flopped like a dead fish.

"Can you tell me," I said, pointing with my chin to my hand resting limp on my thigh, "how long will it be this way?"

Colin replied with a nod and a hopeful smile.

"Nerves regenerate at the rate of about one inch per month, so depending on the extent of the damage, you may start seeing improvement in a few days to a few weeks. It's important you continue physical therapy, do your exercises every day, several times a day. When you're able to go without the sling, I suggest you get a wrist brace at the drug store. That'll support your wrist until you have more strength in it."

I agreed to do this, thanked Colin, and made another appointment with him for the following Monday morning. From there, I drove to the pharmacy for a supply of ibuprofen and to the university bookstore where I bought new textbooks. I grabbed a roast beef wrap and an espresso at the café counter inside the shop. Lastly, I went to the nearby electronics store to buy a new laptop and school bag. Since my laptop had been in my bedroom the evening of the fire, I was quite certain that it was lost. Back at Alison's house, I called the veterinary clinic to ask how was Fleur doing. I was told I could pick her up between four and six that afternoon.

After that I took a nap—a nap!— waking up to sounds downstairs and Alison's voice as she said cheerful hellos to Bax and the cats. I did the exercises Colin had taught me, freshened up in the bathroom the Mitchells had left for my use, and went downstairs.

Alison cheerfully agreed to go with me to the veterinary clinic to collect Fleur. This time, we took her more practical four-door car with her once again driving.

The vet told us with a smile that except for being half-starved and harboring fleas and worms but no heartworms, Fleur was in good health. She had been bathed, treated for the parasites, and given her vaccines. I paid the bill and before the puppy was brought out, I bought puppy food, two stainless steel bowls, half a dozen small rawhide chew bones, and a couple rope tug-toys in the boutique adjoining the clinic.

Fleur was now a recognizable black-and-white border collie with a crooked stripe along her back. Alison put the leather collar I had bought on her, but it was clear that the wee dog did not know how to walk on a leash. In the end, Alison picked her up and carried her to the car. I put the bag of supplies in the boot of the car, and Alison placed Fleur on the blanket from my car that we had spread on the back seat. I sat in front but kept looking over my shoulder at the dog.

Fleur was nervous, whining and scrambling frantically back and forth on the seat. Getting her into the house and settled in the basement was quite an adventure, but this was eventually done. We took the cats' litterboxes from the basement and placed them temporarily in the first-floor bathroom to avoid conflict between the felines and Fleur.

Alison began making supper with frozen chicken wings, frozen vegetables, and fresh, whole potatoes. I helped as much I could, setting the table and putting the potatoes to cook in the microwave. As silly as it sounded, I was happy to be even this useful.

We ate alone as Dr. Mitchell would be at the clinic until nine o'clock. Alison told me about her day, and I told her about mine. She invited me to supper with Roxie tomorrow night if I felt up to it. I told her I would look forward to it. All the while, however, I was trying to figure out how to bring up the other subject that had been in the back of my mind for days now.

The opportunity came later that evening. We were downstairs with Fleur, gently handling the puppy and showing her that we would not hurt her and making good progress. We sat on the sofa with Fleur lying quietly at our feet, a rawhide bone hanging from her mouth, clearly exhausted from her day.

"Alison?" I began. "Do you remember in the hospital, when you told me I almost died, and I told you that I had?"

Alison's eyes grew wide. She looked around the comfortable rec room as if searching for a place to hide. Finding none, she nodded and turned toward me.

"I must tell someone." I cleared my throat with a cough and wondered, *Why is this so difficult?* "It may sound as if I 'ave lost my mind, but it happened. I remember it clearly."

I saw her throat work as she swallowed. She nodded again. "Go on."

"*Bien alors...* After I was shot, I remember you and Aunt Marguerite tending me. The paramedics. I was so much in pain. I do not remember a lot of the ambulance, until... suddenly I felt no more pain. I was floating, yes? Above a young man on a *civière*. His chest was covered with blood and bandages. The paramedics rushed him into the hospital. I followed as if I was attached to the man and I saw... he was me."

I stopped to put my thoughts in order and found I was gripping my knee so hard with my good hand that it hurt. I tried to relax and went on, "Doctors and nurses worked urgently. I heard them talking. Shouting. They said, 'We're losing him.' They used the... uh, *défibrillateur*? I do not know this word in English." I looked at her and was surprised to see tears in her eyes.

"Defibrillator," she said, her voice no more than a whisper.

"Ah, *bien*. They shocked my body. I saw it jump in the air. One. Two. Three times. I thought, *I'm not ready to die. I have too many things to do.* Suddenly, I felt terrible pain, and everything went black. I fell back into my body, you see?" I blinked. My hand was wet with cold sweat. I wiped it on the thigh of my jeans.

Alison reached over and placed her hand on mine. "It's called a near death experience," she said. Her voice trembled. "I've seen a couple TV shows and movies featuring it, but I can't say I've given it much thought. Or believed in it—until now."

"You believe me?"

She shrugged. Sighed. "It's about as believable as anything else you've told me."

I wanted to hug her. Instead, I said, "Thank you. I was afraid you would think me mad."

"You don't have to worry about that, Joseph." She squeezed my hand and looked closely into my face. "That's not all you remember, though. There's more, isn't there?"

"To be honest, yes. But I think…" I slid my hand from under hers and rubbed my palm over my face. "I think this is enough for one night, you know?"

She nodded and smiled, a beautiful smile reflecting a beautiful soul. For the first time, I imagined that perhaps she… we… But no, this was too much to hope.

We gave Fleur an evening meal and went upstairs. Alison took Bax out for a walk. She did not ask me to join her. I supposed she wanted to be alone to think over what I had told her and to be honest, I could not blame her. Dr. Mitchell came home and after eating his supper, he offered to examine my shoulder and arm. Saying he was pleased to see the movement in my arm and the condition of the incision, he made an appointment with me Tuesday afternoon at the medical clinic to take out the twenty-three stitches. This was welcome news, as they had started to itch annoyingly.

I waited for Alison to come in and told her goodnight. I went to bed confident that my life was now getting back on track and slept all night without waking or dreaming.

****

Friday morning, I called my friend Michael to ask where we were in class and told him that I hoped to return to school next week. I called the restoration company and was told where they had stored the items salvaged from my house; they would give me a key if I came by their office. I told them I would go there tomorrow. Finally, I called my mother to let her know how I was doing.

I spent a lot of time with Fleur, letting her out alone in the fenced-in back yard and sitting with her in the basement while I configured my new laptop, downloaded the programs I needed, and read my textbooks in an effort to get my head back into school mode.

I took another nap late in the afternoon and woke up feeling strong enough to face an evening with the girls. I took a long look at myself in the bathroom mirror. The bruises and scrapes from my fight with Gregory's men and being hit by Alison's car were gone from my face. My hair was much shorter than I liked, but I told myself that it would soon grow. The black-stitched incision along my collarbone was surrounded only by faint splotches of green and yellow. All in all, I supposed I looked quite good for a man who had died not two weeks ago. I showered and shaved and dressed in jeans and a black shirt Élisabeth had bought for me. With a lot of fumbling, I managed to button my shirt, but I gave up trying to tie the laces on my sneakers. I swallowed my pride, carried my shoes downstairs, and asked Alison to please tie them for me.

She gave me an easy smile and tied bows in my shoelaces as if this was the most natural thing in the world. Then she asked if we could take my car to the restaurant, informing me that Roxie would lose her mind when she saw it.

I said yes, of course, and let Alison drive to a sketchy-looking pizzeria in the old part of New Haven. We met up with Roxie inside and sat at a booth beside a window. I had serious doubts about the quality of the food here but kept my mouth shut for the sake of a peaceful evening.

The girls had dressed up in flimsy, off-the-shoulder tops, short skirts, and nice shoes, and put on enough makeup to look several years older than they were. At first, I assumed they wanted to impress me, but then I grasped the truth.

But of course, I thought with a smile as they flashed what were certainly fake ID cards and ordered light beers. *They are not yet twenty-one.* I showed my own legitimate ID and asked for a glass of the best French red wine the place served.

The weary-looking, middle-aged waitress stared blankly at me for a few seconds. Then she said she would see what she could find, dropped menus on the table, and shuffled off toward the kitchen. I opened my menu and read through the lists of house specialties and side dishes. The heavy fragrance of tomato sauce and cheese made my mouth water. For the first time since I was shot, I was actually hungry.

We ended up deciding to share two pizzas—pepperoni and Hawaiian—and side orders of French fries and onion rings.

The waitress brought our drinks and took our orders. I thanked her and winked. For a moment, she just stood there looking baffled. Then she flushed to the ears and gave me a wide smile, showing white but crooked teeth.

Roxie laughed as the waitress walked away, her shoulders a wee bit straighter and her step a wee bit lighter than they had been. Alison, who was sitting to my right, leaned close to me and whispered that I had probably made the waitress's entire week.

We spent the next two hours in pleasant conversation while the girls took turns cutting my slices of pizza for me, refilling our glasses several times during what turned out to be a surprisingly good meal. I told the girls some stories about growing up in France and the boarding schools I had attended in Scotland and Switzerland. I learned that they were both in the psychology program at New Haven University, Roxie one year ahead because Alison had taken that time off after high school. Alison related her side of recent events to Roxie, causing Roxie to choke on a French fry and gulp beer when she got to me staying at the Mitchells' house. I learned that Alison had just turned twenty years old on the first of August, and that she had not had a boyfriend in over a year. All good as far as I was concerned.

We shared our favorite music and photos on our cell phones, and suddenly the evening took on a surreal sensation. It was all I could do to not leap from my seat when I saw the images Alison had of her mother, who looked remarkably like an older version of her daughter. And remarkably like—

It's not possible, I told myself, looking down at my lap to hide my face. *Just a coincidence.* But I was enlightened enough to know that it was not a coincidence. Then I noticed something else equally unexpected and even more disturbing. Alison's skirt had hiked up her leg, and I saw a series of faint, thin lines along the top surface of her left thigh. Most of them were white, but two of them were quite red. Fresh. Having seen something like them before in a refugee camp, I immediately knew what they were. I could barely refrain from asking her about them on the spot.

I sipped my wine, looked at the rest of Alison's photos, smiled, and managed to collect myself without the girls noticing anything unusual—I hoped. When photos of the refugee camp known as "the Jungle" near Calais in the north of France came up on my cell phone, I told them how Philippe and I had worked as volunteers there for the two past summers. Roxie seemed surprised to hear this, but Alison did not, and I recalled that I had mentioned something about it as we drove to New York City. Alison asked me if I would return there next summer and I said no, Élisabeth had told me it was closed just ten days ago.

I sent the girls Facebook friend invitations, which they both immediately accepted. By the time we moved on from beer and wine to desserts and coffee, I realized I had for a short time forgotten about being kidnapped, shot, and burned out of my home. Despite my arm hanging in a sling, I was beginning to feel normal again.

Over the girls' protests, I insisted on paying for our

meals. It was the least I could do after everything Alison had done for me.

"Oh, Lordy, that's yours?" Roxie squealed when we left the restaurant and headed to our cars. "Oh please, please, take me for a ride in it! I've never been in such a beautiful car before. Please!" she begged, batting her eyes and making praying gestures at me.

"Yes, all right, I will take you," I told her, half-laughing and thinking that Alison had been right about Roxie going mad over my car. Turning to Alison, I said, "It will not be long. Just around a block or two." I looked around the dimly lit parking lot and noticed two men— one white and one black—hunched over drinks on the terrace. It was difficult to be sure in the near dark, but I thought I perhaps recognized them as the third and fourth men from my cousin's house. "Wait for me inside, yes? Just in case." I waited for her to go back into the restaurant before getting in my car.

Roxie plopped into the passenger seat, still bubbling about my beautiful car and how much money did I have to be able to afford such a thing? Knowing how many beers she and Alison had had to drink, I did not bother to answer. As we pulled out into the street, however, she calmed down all at once and said, "You saw them, didn't you?" While I wondered if she meant the suspicious men or something else, she pressed on. "The cuts on Alison's leg? Don't bother saying you didn't. I was sitting right across from you. I saw the look on your face when you noticed them."

Bon Dieu, this was not all I noticed . . .

I realized then that I had made a serious mistake about Roxie. She came across as wild and silly, the stereotypical "dumb blonde," but she was clearly not silly. Not at all.

"Yes. I saw them," I admitted reluctantly.

"You know what they are?"

"Yes. I think so."

"She started when her mom got sick. She hasn't cut herself in months, though—at least not as far as I know." Roxie glanced at me as I looked to my right to make a turn, and for a second our eyes met. "I know she cares about you. A lot. And I'm willing to bet you like her too. Whatever kind of relationship the two of you have or might end up having, just be careful not to hurt her. She lost her mom last year, you know that? She doesn't need any more heartache... And Joseph?"

"Yes?" I replied, my eyes on the road.

"Please don't tell her I told you anything. She'll be totally pissed. Well, at me, anyway. I doubt she could get very mad at you."

Oh, I'm quite sure she could, I thought, but instead I said, "Yes, all right. No worries. I do not wish to hurt her or make her angry. Or upset her in any way." *Although I may end up doing all those things if I'm not careful.*

Roxie suddenly burst into a fit of giggles.

"Wha—what is it?"

"You!" She stopped laughing and blurted, "Alison told me you were more than a pretty face and a delicious accent and oh, Lordy, was she ever right!"

Chapter 13

Revelations
Alison

I smelled bacon before I got halfway down the stairs Saturday morning.

"Good morning," I said, shocked and awed to find Joseph, dressed in jeans and a navy-blue hoodie, standing at the stove with a spatula in his good hand. His left arm hung at his side. Then I saw the plates of food on the counter. "What—you made French toast?"

"But of course," he said, turning toward me with a pleased expression on his face—and a wink. "What do you expect? I'm French."

"I thought you said you don't cook."

"I said I do not cook *a lot*," he corrected me. "But *pain perdu*—this is what we call it at 'ome—is quite easy, you know?" He gave me one of his charming, crooked smiles, melting me.

I poured myself a cup of fresh dripped coffee, piled bacon and French toast on my plate, and sat down at the table.

Joseph joined me a couple minutes later with his own plate and cup.

"So—no more sling?" I asked as I poured maple syrup over my breakfast.

"Unfortunately, yes," he admitted, "but I will try to

go without it a bit more every day."

After breakfast, Joseph put on his sling and jacket, then left to see to his affairs. From what he told me, this included checking on progress at his house and shopping for clothes to wear to school. I would've gone with him if he'd invited me. But he didn't, and as much as I wanted to invite myself, I hesitated to intrude on his private affairs.

Dad had left for his weekend shift at the hospital before I came downstairs. Alone for the morning, I took care of the dishes. Then I stripped the beds, found Joseph's pile of dirty laundry on the floor of his closet, and hauled it all downstairs to wash. I couldn't help noticing that his clothes were all expensive name brands, and I reminded myself once again that Joseph came from a different world than mine, where even though my dad was a doctor, a stack of hospital bills, two mortgages on the house, and a poorly advised investment meant shopping liquidation sales or discount stores for the foreseeable future. I wondered if he and Philippe had had a housekeeper or whether they had deigned to do their household chores themselves. I realized that I still barely knew Joseph at all but God, how I wanted to know him.

I spent some time with each of the dogs in turn, thinking that we should introduce them to each other today. When Joseph returned mid-afternoon loaded with shopping bags from high-end stores, he agreed.

We let Bax and Fleur out together in the back yard and watched them carefully, ready to separate them if it became necessary.

It didn't. After five minutes of circling each other and engaging in mutual butt-sniffing, Fleur rolled onto her back with her belly in the air, a typical position of submission.

Bax barked, jumped around a little bit, and took off running with Fleur on his heels.

"I think they will become friends," Joseph said. His smile was coming easily today.

"I think they already have," I agreed with a giggle. "So… um, how did things go this morning?"

Joseph's smile faded. "I got the key to the storage place, and I went to see… to be honest, all I 'ave left are things from the kitchen—dishes and such. Everything else—furniture, clothes, books, electronics—are ruined." He shrugged—with both shoulders, I noticed. "I regret the loss of the books, but it's no matter. It's all insured. I will buy new things when I move back in."

"I'm sorry you couldn't save more," I said, feeling vaguely sick to my stomach at the thought of losing everything in my house. Of course, the New Haven house was only his temporary, part-time home and probably hadn't contained anything irreplaceable, but still… "Do you know how long it'll be before you can move in?"

"I went to my 'ouse. They're finishing repairs on the roof and will next work inside." He looked up at the heavy gray sky that threatened to drench us at any minute. "They said per'aps a month for the rest. You will be stuck with me until then." The smile came back, then disappeared again. "Alison, I must tell you. I… uh, I noticed something last night."

My stomach sank a little further, but I tried to sound nonchalant. "Really? What?" As if I couldn't take a good guess.

"*Bien*… to be honest, two things." Joseph motioned with his head for me to come. He turned and walked away to sit on one of the plastic lawn chairs on the patio.

I followed to take my own chair beside him, dismayed to see that my hands were shaking ever so slightly with dread. I had a pretty good idea about what he was going to say.

"I… uh, I saw the cuts on your leg last night, Alison," he said carefully. He looked down at my left thigh, even though my jeans covered the evidence.

"Oh. Yeah," I said with a sigh. "I figured you might have. I can explain, though…"

"You 'ave no need to explain. I think I understand. It's a way to relieve unbearable pain with… pain that is more bearable, yes?"

He was totally right, but I had to explain, nonetheless. "When my mom got sick… I felt so bad, so guilty, because I'd been such a wild, disrespectful teenager. Sneaking out at night. Drinking. Going with boys—the wrong kind of boys. She was so good to me, so understanding. When Dad would yell at me or ground me or threaten me with boarding school, she would try to talk to me, to understand me. She got me the volunteer job at the animal shelter because she knew how much I love animals. We went horseback riding together every couple weeks. But watching her get sicker and sicker, just withering away… I couldn't stand it. I had to find a way to relieve the pain, some way other than going out and doing the stupid, self-destructive stuff I wanted to do. So, I-I cut myself. Over and over. I mean, I guess that was self-destructive too, but not as much as booze or pills. I kept it up for a while after she died, but I eventually stopped."

He leaned slowly toward me, and I could see by the little creases at the corners of his chocolate eyes that he truly cared. "What made you stop?"

"I don't quite know. I'd been so depressed and angry for so long. But finally, I started to feel a little better, like maybe there was something to live for. I was ready to try. I pulled myself together and registered for classes. I felt like I might be getting my life back on track."

"And then I came along and upset you so badly that you cut yourself again," he said with a remorseful shake of his head. "Ah, *Dieu*, Alison, I'm afraid I may make things worse for—"

"No!" I interrupted him, desperate for him to understand. "No, it's not you, Joseph. It's me. I was so worried about you when you were unconscious in the hospital. I couldn't imagine losing you, and I tried to relieve my anxiety the wrong way. But I won't do it again. It—it didn't help anyway." I gave him what was probably a pathetic attempt at a smile. "So… what was the other thing you wanted to tell me?"

Suddenly, he looked like he would rather do anything else. He shifted in his chair and gazed past me at the dogs. After a minute or two he cleared his throat with a cough and looked at me. "It's about your mother."

My jaw dropped, and my arms crossed defensively across my chest without my even thinking about it. "My—what about my mother?"

"*Bien alors*… while I was unconscious in the 'ospital, I… I went somewhere. My soul, you know? Call it 'eaven or the astral plane, or whatever you wish. But I saw things. People…" He paused, swallowed a couple times. Blinked. "I saw my body on the bed in the emergency room, the doctors and nurses working on me. I saw your mother, Alison. I did not know it at the time, until… when I saw your photos on your phone last night.

I recognized 'er at once. She… uh, she came to me. She spoke to me."

My vision blurred as my eyes filled with tears. "She—what? What did she say?" I croaked. I sniffed rather indelicately and tried to concentrate on his words.

"She said that someone I care about needs me as much as I need them, even if I do not yet know this. She said that it was not my time to die. That I must return to my body and consider in what direction I wish to take my life." He shrugged. Shook his head. "When I woke up in the 'ospital I thought it was a dream, but then I saw you and I realized it was not. And I remembered the woman said… she said, 'tell my Allie-cat I love 'er. That I watch over 'er always.' Allie-cat is you, *n'est-ce pas*?"

I nodded, hot tears spilling from my eyes and running down my cheeks. "She used to call me that all the time. She—" But I couldn't go on. I flung myself from the chair and bolted blindly across the back yard until I reached the rose garden my mom had loved, where I stood with my face in my hands, sobbing uncontrollably.

At some point, I sank to my knees in the grass. Bax came to see me, nudged me with his cool, wet nose, then left me again for Fleur's more enjoyable company.

Though my eyes were squeezed tightly shut in an effort to stem my gradually slowing tears, I sensed the presence of someone to my left.

The air shifted and a strong arm wrapped itself around my shoulders.

I turned my head, cracked my eyelids apart, and looked into Joseph's chocolate eyes, narrow now with concern. He was kneeling beside me, close enough that our hips bumped together.

"Please forgive me," he said. His voice trembled with suppressed emotion. "I 'ad no intention of making you cry. I only wished for you to know what—"

"Tell me the rest," I said over the lump in my throat. I pressed my palms to my eyes, wiped my wet cheeks with my sleeve, and shifted a bit to face him.

He withdrew his arm from my shoulders and rubbed his hand across his mouth.

"I know there's more," I said. "To begin with, the someone my mom said needs you. That you need—" I paused to put my thoughts in order. "She meant me, didn't she?"

"Per'aps," Joseph said evasively. "I do not know for—"

"Seriously?" I exclaimed, the remainder of my grief exploding out of me in anger. "We're going to do this again?"

"No. *Mon Dieu*, Alison, I do not know 'ow to tell you—"

At that moment, the sky opened up with a rumble of thunder and rain fell in a sudden torrent, sharp and cold against our hands and faces. We scrambled to our feet, rounded up the dogs who wanted to race around in the rain, and hurried into the house without saying another word to each other.

It was more than half an hour later, after we'd rubbed down the dogs with towels and changed into dry clothes, that we sat down in the living room, each of us taking one of the two armchairs. Or at least I sat. Joseph stood again almost immediately to pace back and forth across the room.

"Come on, spit it out," I said in frustration. "It can't be that bad." When he didn't respond, I added, "I promise I won't freak out or get mad. Joseph… please."

At that, Joseph stopped. He gave me a long, tortured look and sank into his chair again. He took a deep breath in and out through his nose and began, "*Bien alors…* while I was wherever I went while I was unconscious, I was not alone. My father came to me. My grandfather. And my many-times great-grandfather Charles de Lorraine, who was Grand Master of the *Prieuré de Sion* in the eighteenth century. They spoke to me of my family, 'ow for a very long time, men and women in the bloodline families 'ave married… you know… between the families… to keep our lineage as pure as possible. It's not pure, of course, but we tried. Since I'm sixteen, it's arranged for me to marry Gregory's daughter, Isobel. She's yet only seventeen, but in a few years, yes? Except that per'aps now this is not possible."

I sat there wordless, feeling like I was having a bad dream and hoping I would soon wake up. I even pinched myself on the arm but no… I was, unfortunately, very much awake.

Joseph went on. "They showed me things. Visions, you know?"

"Visions?" I managed to ask. "Of what?" I felt sick and weak, and I really didn't want to hear whatever he was going to say next.

"Many things. Events from the… from my… uh, my past lives, yes? And events in the future, possible futures that may or may not come to pass." His expression clouded, as though he was considering whether or not to tell me more. "I learned that I should not be the one to speak the truth of our family to the world. This role will fall to my son, but this may go one of two ways. If I marry Isobel or someone else in a bloodline family out of obligation but with no love, my son will grow up to bring chaos and division to the world. 'E will be the one some people will call the Antichrist."

"Oh. My. God," I muttered under my breath. Forget pinching. If I could have cut myself to bring me out of that moment, I would have. Immediately.

"But if I marry for love... if my son is brought up with love, 'e will become a great man who will unite the Catholic Church with many nations and bring peace to the world. Do not ask me 'ow 'e will do this. I 'ave no idea. I only know that my role is to prepare the way as I 'ave done in the past, as when I was the man that 'istory calls John the Baptist. When I baptized Jesus 'imself in the Jordan River at the beginning of 'is ministry."

"Wh-what? You're saying you were... you saw Jesus?" I could barely choke the words out.

"But of course. 'E was my cousin, you know. Back then..." He paused as if to collect his thoughts, while I pondered how the hell to process this little tidbit of information. "I was shown 'orrible scenes of poverty and war and beautiful scenes of abundance and peace. No," he corrected himself, " 'shown' is not the good word. Somehow, I was there, in these places. I saw and 'eard and smelled everything. And I was told... the choices that I make in this lifetime will determine the destiny of the man who is next in line."

He looked straight across the room at me. His eyes were bright with tears and something else. Passion? Truth? Insanity?

I fought the urge to laugh hysterically and run screaming from the room.

"I know you think it's all per'aps a dream, yes?" Joseph concluded. "I'm imagining it or making it up, or

I 'ave simply lost my wee mind."

Or all of the above, I thought, but I couldn't bring myself to say it.

"I ask myself the same thing many times since I woke up in the 'ospital. I 'ave no answers." He ran his fingers through his hair, making it stand up in front. His hand trembled noticeably. "I only know that I 'ave this in my 'ead and on my shoulders. And I must do the good thing… *Bon Dieu, je ne sais plus quoi faire.*"

He pushed wearily to his feet and walked away. I heard him go upstairs, his steps slow and heavy and near the top, somewhat uneven.

I sat there stunned for a few minutes, my ability to suspend disbelief stretched to its limit. Then without any conscious thought, I followed him upstairs. I meant to go to my bedroom but was drawn in spite of myself toward his.

The door was closed, but not firmly. I could hear Joseph's voice, low and sort of droning, through the two-inch crack between the door and the frame. *Is he on his phone? Who's he talking to?*

I carefully pushed the door open a little bit wider, just enough to see that Joseph wasn't on the phone. He was on his knees beside the bed. I couldn't see his face, and I couldn't make out a word he was saying, but I could hear enough to know he was speaking French. To know he was praying. And I could tell by the frequent hitches in his voice that he was weeping.

I quietly closed the door and tiptoed away to my room. I curled up on my bed with the teddy bear my mom had given me for my seventh birthday in my arms. For the first time in over a year, I said my own prayers.

Chapter 14

Secrets and Lies, Truth and Trust
Joseph

"Where are you going?" Alison's voice rang out sharply behind me just as I reached the front door.

I took a deep breath and slowly let it out through my nose. After clearing my throat, I turned to her. "To the New Haven Homeless Shelter."

She stopped in her tracks a few feet away. "Wh-what? No, Joseph! I know I wasn't very receptive yesterday when you told me... well, you know what you told me. And I don't blame you for not coming down to supper last night. I only ate a bowl of cereal, myself. I told my dad I thought I was coming down with a cold to explain that away. But you don't have to go! You—wait..." She took the last steps to reach me. Her eyes narrowed to blue slits as she looked me up and down. "You don't have any bags with you."

I shook my head. "No. I'm not leaving, Alison. Every Sunday when I have no soccer game, I volunteer at the shelter. I think I will not be much good for serving meals or washing dishes today, but perhaps I can find some way to be useful. Talk with people. Sometimes this is the thing they need most, yes? Someone to talk to. Someone who listens to them."

Alison's jaw had dropped open. She shut it now with

a *click* of her teeth and said, "Oh. Right."

"I fed the dogs and put them out in the back yard. I left you a wee note on the kitchen table. I need to be away from here for the day. To think. Please try to understand."

"Don't worry... I totally get it. Well..." She fidgeted and rubbed her hands together. "Will you be home for supper?"

"But of course." I gave her what I hoped was an encouraging smile. I knew that I had shaken her badly last night and probably given her a valid reason to think me mad. I did not know what to say or do next, but I held out hope that someone today could give me some insight. "I'm sorry, I really must go. I told them I will be there at nine o'clock."

"Um, right." Alison frowned, her forehead creasing with doubt or concern. As I turned to leave, she blurted, "What do you want to eat?"

I shrugged, noticing that I was now able to do this with both shoulders. "I'm sure anything you make will be delicious, Alison. Thank you." I left then without looking back, even though I could literally feel her eyes piercing the back of my head all the way to my car.

I spent a pleasant enough morning at the homeless shelter, where I had celebrity status due to my exotic French accent and the fact that I played soccer for Yale University. I shared the judiciously edited tale of my kidnapping with about a dozen residents who knew me from previous visits. I taught a handful of children how to count to twenty in French and some of the older men how to say a few words of love. I drifted from one family-sized cafeteria table to another, listening to heart-breaking stories of what had brought people here. Where they hoped to go next. I was humbly reminded that despite my current dilemma, I had a family who loved me and more money than I could ever need—things that most of these people would only have in their wildest dreams.

After lunch of vegetable soup and tuna sandwiches, a young Franciscan priest called Father Thomas, who often stopped in at the shelter, gave a short, non-denominational talk—I would not call it a sermon—and spend the afternoon with anyone who needed to speak with him. Today, this included me.

"Joseph! It's been a while!" Father Thomas took a long look from my sling to my face. "What happened to you? I saw something on the news a couple weeks ago. You were suspected of arson and... *murder?*"

"Ah, yes," I admitted. "To be honest, Father, it's a long story, but I would like to tell you, if you have time."

"Of course, I have time. Do you want me to hear your confession?"

I resisted the urge to roll my eyes. "No. When I wish to speak to God, I speak to Him. This is... something else."

"Oh. Of course. And please... how many times have I told you before? Call me Thomas."

We collected cups of coffee and a plate of cookies and sat down at an empty table in the far corner of the cafeteria. I told Thomas everything I could about my kidnapping, about Philippe's death and how I regretted missing his funeral, about the events at Aunt Marguerite's country house. I told him about Alison and the part she had played in my life these past few weeks. About my near-death experience and subsequent visions of Alison's mother and my own ancestors. I did not, of course, mention previous lives, the Jesus bloodline, or the possibility of my future son becoming the Antichrist, but I did admit that I was afraid my revelations had been too much for Alison.

"Www-ow," said Thomas, drawing the word out with a lot of "W"s once I had finished my tale. "That must have been something of a shock to her, to be sure. You care about this girl, don't you?" he asked a moment later over the top of his cup.

"I do," I admitted, "more than any girl I've met. I feel as if… I do not yet know her very well, but I feel that she could be the one, you know?" I looked hard across the table at him. "Or perhaps you do not."

Thomas nodded slowly and gave me a regretful smile. "I do. I had a girlfriend before I became a priest. We were deeply in love. I only took my final vows after Chelsea—my girl—was killed in a car accident."

I almost dropped my cup of coffee. "Ah, *Dieu*. I'm sorry. I had no idea."

"Of course, you didn't. But you see, I do understand what you might be feeling, Joseph. Do you know if … That is, does she feel the same way about you?"

"I do not know. I think yes, she cares for me." I recalled how she had insisted on coming to New York City with me. What she had told me at the country house. The way I sometimes caught her looking at me with a wee smile on her lips. "But as a friend? More? I'm afraid perhaps I told her too much. Frightened her."

"You told her the truth as you understand it?"

"But of course."

"Well, then. I can't tell you what to do, Joseph, but I can tell you I sincerely believe that any solid relationship must be built on truth and trust. Secrets and lies will only cause you pain and sorrow in the end."

Secrets and lies. The story of my family's life. Merveilleux.

We continued to talk easily about things that were not so confusing or painful. We had several interests in common, such as a love for soccer and our desire to help the needy, despite the fact that he was a priest in what to me was a false religion. I told him about working at the refugee camp in Calais and before that, at a homeless shelter in Tel Aviv. I only realized that I had stayed much longer than intended when I noticed the aroma of roast chicken coming from the kitchen and the increasing number of people strolling into the cafeteria.

Merde! I will be late for Alison's supper. Again.

I bid a hasty goodbye to Thomas, who reminded me that he was at St. Francis Church most mornings and evenings should I need to speak with him again before next Sunday.

I drove at some speed back to the Mitchells' house with Thomas's words about trust and truth and a dozen things I might say to repair my *lien* with Alison running through my mind. As I turned onto Ridge Road, a gray van with tinted windows drove by in the opposite direction. I immediately had an uneasy feeling that I had seen this vehicle before, but I could not recall where or when. I arrived at the house to find Dr. Mitchell's SUV already in the driveway.

When I opened the door, Fleur came to sniff me and rub against my legs. Despite my hurry, I stopped to give her a good pet and scratch her ears. I washed up in the downstairs bathroom and joined Alison and her father in the kitchen just as they were sitting down to their meal.

"I'm sorry I'm late," I apologized as they both shot

rather exasperated looks at me.

Without a word, Alison rose to serve me a plate of beef goulash on noodles and a bowl of green salad, then sat again.

"This is very good," I said after taking a couple bites of the beef. I was relieved to see a smile come to Alison's face.

"Seriously? Thanks. It's one of Dad's favorites."

"Mmm… one of mine now too."

We had a casual exchange of stories about our day. Alison had clearly spent most of the afternoon cooking. I wondered if she had kept herself busy to avoid thinking about what I told her last night.

After a homemade dessert Alison called "apple crisp," Dr. Mitchell excused himself to go do paperwork in his office. I helped Alison put the dishes in the dishwasher. After starting it, she turned to me, her arms crossed in front of her. "Joseph? I have to ask you about what you said last night…"

"Yes?" I said cautiously.

"Do you really think you saw my mom when you were unconscious?"

I hesitated to answer but could think of nothing to tell her except the truth. "*Oui*. I do."

"And you think she said—what? That we need each other only we don't know it yet?"

I did not answer. She looked like she wanted to say more, and so I waited.

After a moment, she continued, "Do you believe it? I mean, do you think it was real? Not a dream or hallucination caused by lack of oxygen to your brain, or medication, or whatever? Maybe you saw my mom's photo in my bedroom when you were hiding there and then later, your mind grasped that image." Her eyes narrowed and she stepped away from me. "Or maybe you just have a really unique way of hitting on girls."

I was shocked and disappointed that she would think this, although perhaps I should not have been. "*C'est vrai*? You truly think this?"

"I don't know what to think, Joseph. How can I even know if everything you told me about the Jesus bloodline is true? I mean yeah, I saw stuff about it on the internet—"

"You told me you believe me."

"I do. I mean, I really want to, but I—"

"This is good," I interrupted her with a smile and the first pleasant words that popped into my mind, as the sound of footsteps in the hallway brought Dr. Mitchell into the kitchen.

"Just thought I'd make some coffee," he said, giving Alison a long look. He poured coffee and water into the coffeemaker and then looked at me. "I meant to ask you how your arm's doing?"

"A little better," I told him. I slipped my arm out of the sling and showed him how much I could move it. "Only my hand does not yet work much," I added, removing the sling with my good hand and dropping it onto a chair.

"That should improve in time. Don't forget your appointment with me on Tuesday."

"I will not forget," I assured him. "You may be certain of this."

Ten minutes later, cups of coffee in hand, Alison and I went downstairs with the dogs at our heels. We each sat at one end of the sofa, turned slightly toward each other. "Go on," I said after an awkward silence. "You wish to say…?"

"Oh. I was saying I saw the whole *Holy Blood, Holy Grail* conspiracy theory thing on the internet, but I don't see what it has to do with you. I mean, there are some obscure mentions of the de Lorraine and St. Clair families back like, centuries ago. But I still don't get how you can be so sure your family—and you—are connected to Jesus. Something's missing in the story you've been trying to sell me, and I want to know what." She stopped, it appeared, for lack of breath.

Molly, the wee three-color cat, had jumped up onto my lap while Alison spoke. I stroked her soft fur while I thought things over and, coming to a decision, I said, "You're right. I've not told you everything." I looked closely at Alison as I wondered whether I was about to make the biggest mistake of my life.

She waited, perhaps not patiently but in silence.

I thought of what Thomas had said about secrets and lies. Truth and trust. Finally, I began, each word taking me closer to the point of no return. "After he found the parchments in his church in Rennes-le-Château, *le Père Saunière* told his bishop about them. The church paid him to destroy them, but he did not. Instead, he gave them to his maid and closest friend, Marie Denarnaud. It's believed that she never revealed the secret, but this is not true. She showed the parchments to her friend, a man called Antoine St. Clair, because his family name was on one of them. Antoine fought in the First World War with my great-grandfather Joseph Marc de Lorraine. Believing they would soon be killed, Antoine told Joseph of how their families were named in two of the parchments. He told also of another parchment that spoke of … not the place, but… a riddle, yes? It told where the tomb of Mary and Jesus could be found if one solved the riddle."

I paused at the sound of Alison's gasp. "The two men did not die, and after the war they remained close friends. Joseph bought our house in Carcassonne, not so far from Rennes-le-Chateau, and moved his family there. He and Antoine retrieved the parchments from Marie Denarnaud, and they began to search. Eventually, they solved the riddle and discovered the tomb."

I shook my head before the question escaped her lips. "I cannot tell you where it is. To be honest, I do not exactly know. But in the tomb they found treasures from the Holy Land and two… uh, *cercueils*…" I searched for the English word but came up with nothing. "The box one is buried in, you know?"

"Coffins," Alison said helpfully, her voice barely more than a whisper.

"Yes! Coffins. They removed some wee bits of bone from the coffins as proof that they found the tomb."

When Alison said nothing, I continued, "The Vatican knows of the Rennes-le-Chateau parchments because of Saunière. It does not know he did not destroy them, and it does not know of the tomb or the bones or… uh…" Years of conditioning prevented me spilling the whole story, even though my heart told me I could trust her. "It does know that my father's family has for many years—centuries—collected proof connecting us to the Jesus bloodline. It—"

"And that's why your family's so rich?" Alison's eyes widened and her jaw dropped. "It is, isn't it? The church is paying you to keep your mouths shut about finding what you believe is proof that you… oh my…"

"*Oui.*" I let out a long breath, suddenly feeling

ashamed although I had done nothing wrong. "Since many years, the church pays our family a large amount of money to … uh, as you say, keep our mouths shut."

Alison pursed her lips and took a minute to absorb this. "How much money?"

"*Bien…* presently it's about eleven million euros a year."

Another pause.

I gave her a long look. "No one outside of the secret knows about these things, Alison. Except now you."

She blinked. Sat up straighter. "Don't worry, Joseph. I'll keep it—your secret, I mean."

I nodded. "I know."

We sat in silence for perhaps a minute. Then Alison said, "About the money. That is… what do you do with it all? I mean, besides buying colonial houses and expensive cars and going to Yale?"

"Ah, *mon Dieu.*" I rubbed my good hand over my face. "We give a *dime*—ten percent, yes?—back to the Church each year. We give much to charity. We invest some. The rest is put in Swiss bank accounts for future use."

She shook her head. Strands of her hair fell in her face; she pushed these impatiently away with one hand. "I don't get it. You said it yourself; you live a life of wealth and privilege. Why do you—or anyone else in your family—bother to have a profession? To work in a position that could—and did in your dad's case—get you killed? Is it all just a *façade*?"

I smiled at her use of the French word. "No, it's not a *façade*. Since many generations, my family is working for peace and justice. We were active in the French resistance during the First and Second World Wars. My father went into politics and became ambassador to Israel—*bien*, you know this. Élisabeth will become a doctor and work with *Docteurs Sans Frontières* or *la Croix Rouge* to help people who are in need of medical care around the world. Laurence… she did not wish to go away to school, and our parents did not force her. She goes to school in Carcassonne where there is a disabled boy in her class. Some of the other children are not nice to him, you know?"

"Kids can be pretty mean sometimes," Alison said, nodding.

"Yes," I agreed. "I learned this when I went to school in Scotland with not much English. Laurence made friends with this boy, Samuel, a very nice, very smart boy. As well as taking over the antique shop, she now wishes to make an *orphelinat*… uh, an orphanage, yes?" As Alison nodded again, I continued, "an orphanage where disabled children might receive the love and care they need and deserve."

"That's really sweet of her."

"Yes, it is. Perhaps she and Samuel will do this together." I sighed and shifted slightly more toward her. "*Bien alors*… about the money. It does not assure us any standing inside of France or elsewhere. But it's true, money is power, and so we place ourselves in positions of influence. Preparing for my son, although of course we did not yet know this. As for me… I've seen poverty and I've seen violence. I will do everything I can to bring peace to the world, and I will… I suppose I will work to prepare the world for the arrival of my son."

Alison's face had paled while I talked. She swallowed and said, "So maybe those crazy Antichrist people aren't such nut jobs after all? They might be right? Not about you, but—"

"No!" I exclaimed so sharply that Molly, startled, leapt to the floor. "My son will not bring division and destruction to the world. I will see to this—one way or another."

"Wh-what does that mean?" Alison asked. "Joseph?"

"I do not— There are many things I do not yet know. I do know that I frightened you. I did not intend this."

"You didn't scare me," Alison corrected me. "It's just... when you told me about my mom, it brought all the pain of losing her rushing back. And then the rest... I didn't know what to make of it. Of you."

"And now?"

"Now... well, I told you before I believe you. And I do. I mean, you'd have to be a total pathological liar to have made it all up. And obviously you were kidnapped and pursued. And shot."

"Yes." I pushed to my feet and wandered around the room for a minute or two. I stopped in front of the sofa and looked down at her. "You also told me before that you wish to be my friend. I suppose what I need to know now is... do you wish to be more?"

For a second, she looked as if I had asked her to close her eyes and jump from the top of the *Tour Eiffel* with me. Then, very slowly, she nodded. Pushed to her feet. Looked into my face. "I knew that first night when I brought you home that you were someone special. I don't know how or why." She looked away, then back at me. Smiled at last. "Whatever the reason, I felt a definite connection like I've never felt with anyone before. So... yeah, I want us to be more than friends."

At this moment, I wished to lean close and touch

her. Kiss her. I refrained for a few seconds out of concern that I would, in fact, frighten her. Then I gave in to my impulse, put my hand on her arm, and kissed her quickly on both cheeks, the French way. Her skin was soft, and she smelled vaguely of coffee and the cinnamon in the apple crisp.

Her eyes widened. She blinked. The color in her cheeks had risen from pale to crimson. "I-I… um…" she stammered, "I guess this changes everything."

"*Oui*," I agreed as I felt my smile grow wider. My heart raced in my throat. "It does."

Chapter 15

Good Things
Alison

I'd at first been shaken by Joseph's declarations—and who wouldn't be?—but they'd erased any lingering doubts I'd had concerning his story about the Jesus bloodline. And any doubts about his feelings for me. As I lay in bed that night, the shock of learning what I'd learned gradually faded and I fell into a deep, dreamless sleep.

I awoke Monday morning bursting with a *joie de vivre* I hadn't felt in years. I jumped out of bed, pulled on my bathrobe, grabbed some clothes, and dashed downstairs to shower. I emerged from the bathroom with dry hair and dressed for school in time to join Joseph and my dad in the kitchen. They seemed to be engaged in rather serious conversation over their bagels and orange juice, but they shut up tight when I walked in.

"Morning, guys!" I bent to give my dad a kiss on the cheek. I wanted to do the same to Joseph but refrained for fear of giving both of them heart attacks. "What are you talking about?" I added cautiously as I sliced a bagel and popped it in the toaster.

"School," Joseph said at the same time as Dad said, "Yale."

"Hmm." I sat down a few minutes later with my own plate and glass and peered at Joseph. He looked good—

freshly shaved and wearing a gray turtleneck sweater above black jeans. "So, you're going to school today?"

"Yes. I must see the physical therapist this morning, then I will go to school," he replied. "But I must see about cutting my course load. I think I'm not able to make up everything I 'ave missed in four courses this semester. Not with my arm like this." He glanced down at his left hand resting in his lap.

"But then… won't it take you longer to get your degree?"

"I suppose it will. But it's no matter if I finish one year or the next," Joseph explained casually. He gave me that charming, crooked smile of his. "I will just 'ave to stay in America a wee bit longer."

"Oh. Yeah, I guess that's not such a bad thing." I spread jam on my bagel and immediately took a bite to avoid grinning like an idiot. I said to myself, *Here's this insanely handsome, filthy rich French guy with a humanitarian leaning and the biggest family secret in the world. He could have any girl he wants, but it seems he thinks I could be the one for him.*

Another bite of bagel. A sip of juice. *Do I think he could be the one for me?*

A gulp of juice. *Hell yeah!*

Dad left for the clinic after breakfast. Joseph and I had some time before his therapy appointment and my morning class, so we took the dogs for a short walk.

Joseph was quiet, even subdued, and I didn't try to rouse him. I assumed he had things on his mind—his arm, his studies, maybe what on earth he was going to tell his family about me.

I wondered what I was going to tell my dad too. His opinion of Joseph might have risen considerably in the last week, but I wasn't at all sure how he would react to learning that Joseph and I were growing closer. So much closer…

"That was a nice walk," I said as we reached the front stairs of my house. "Fleur's getting way better about being on the leash."

"Yes, she is," Joseph agreed. "She will become a good dog." His expression clouded, and I suspected he was thinking of Philippe. For better or worse, Fleur would be a constant reminder of his best friend's death. Then he looked off to our right and his eyes narrowed; little creases appeared between his brows.

"What is it?" I asked, following his gaze down the street.

"The gray van," he said, pointing with his chin to the vehicle parked by the curb four houses down. "I 'ave seen it before. I—I think I'm watched."

"Watched? But who would—oh! Not the men from your cousin's house?" I hurried to open the door, get us inside, and lock the door again.

"Yes, the two men who did not come to Aunt Marguerite's country 'ouse." Joseph said, confirming my worst fear. "But I will not let them take me again."

I straightened from unsnapping Bax's leash. "Why would they even try? I mean, they don't know about your bloodline or any of that, do they?"

"No, I do not think so." Joseph dropped to one knee to take off Fleur's leash and give her ears a rub. "But they per'aps 'ope to kidnap me for ransom, yes? As the other two did."

I slapped a hand to my cheek. "Oh. My. God. We have to call the police, Joseph. Tell them you're being followed."

Joseph glanced at the clock on the mantel above the living room fireplace. "I must go to my physical therapy, and you must go to school. If we see the same van when we come 'ome this afternoon, we will call the police."

I wanted to argue, to insist we call the police immediately, but I could see his point. I couldn't afford to miss this morning's class any more than he could afford to miss his appointment.

"Okay," I said, "but be careful. Please."

"But of course," he said smoothly, making me wonder suddenly where that pistol he'd had at the country house was now.

Assuming it was in an evidence locker somewhere but realizing I didn't really want to know, I didn't ask.

We gathered up our school bags and left the house at the same time. Joseph drove away first, but the gray van didn't move. I waited a couple minutes before pulling into the street.

Looking back after I'd driven a block, I discovered to my horror that the suspicious van was following some distance behind me. I clutched the steering wheel, my heart pounding, and drove straight to the University of New Haven. When I looked back for the umpteenth time a block from school, the van had disappeared.

Maybe it wasn't following me after all, I thought, letting out the breath I'd been holding for much too long. *Maybe it was just someone visiting one of the neighbors, heading in the same direction as me when they left. A total coincidence.*

I kept telling myself that as I parked and headed to class.

"Hey, girlfriend!" Roxie called out, catching up to me outside the dining hall entrance after class. "You've been avoiding me!"

"No, Roxie, I haven't. I just had a lot—"

"Don't worry, I get it," Roxie said with a grin. "If I had Joseph Lorraine staying at my place, I'd be incommunicado, too."

"It's not like that," I objected but really, what could I say? "Okay, you're right," I admitted once we'd sat down with our lunches. "Things between Joseph and me are… well, complicated to say the least. But they're good. I think we're becoming, you know… more than friends."

Roxie stared at me with a forkful of potato salad stalled halfway to her mouth and exclaimed, "Seriously? You think you—?"

"We're taking it slow, okay? God, Roxie, Joseph nearly died two weeks ago. Relax a bit, will you?"

Roxie took her bite, chewed it slowly. Swallowed. "You're absolutely right, which leads me to an important point: does he have an available friend? Someone on the Yale soccer team, maybe? Because I'm totally over Bruce and getting pretty lonely."

I laughed and promised her I would ask him when the opportunity arose.

I got home first that afternoon and was relieved to find there was no mysterious gray van in sight. I barely had time to wash up, feed the dogs and cats, and put a frozen lasagna in the oven before Joseph came in. I heard him go upstairs and come back down a couple minutes later.

He was practically beaming when he joined me in the kitchen.

"So… things are going okay for you?" I asked as I felt my own face break into a wide grin. Whatever had been on his mind this morning had apparently been resolved.

"Yes. Do you need 'elp with something?"

"No. Supper's in the oven. Tell me, what's up with you? You look like you're going to break into cheers or something."

"Some good things," he said. "I went to my physical therapy and discovered I can now do this." He no longer had the sling but wore a black neoprene brace on his wrist. Now he reached his left arm out in front of him, grasped the salt shaker on the table, lifted it a few inches, and put it down again. His fingers appeared stiff and weak, but they were definitely working.

"Oh, Joseph, that's awesome!"

"It is," he agreed, still grinning. "After my therapy I went to Yale and spoke with my dean. I'm able to cut two classes which I will take in the next term. I still must work 'ard to pass my two remaining classes, but I think this is something I can manage. Then I went to see my 'ouse. The men are working on it, and they believe I will be able to move back in in two weeks."

"Oh, that's good," I said, feeling much less excited at this news. "I'll miss you."

"No worries," he assured me. "I intend to see you as much as possible."

"That's good to know." I tried my best to sound a tease but didn't quite get there.

Joseph put his good arm around my waist and gave me a quick peck on one cheek, then stepped back to look at me with those soft chocolate eyes.

Is he shy? I wondered suddenly. *Or just cautious? He said he's been out with lots of girls, but who knows, really?*

I stared at him for a few seconds. "Oh my God, Joseph!" I burst out, half-laughing. "Don't tell me you've never had a girlfriend before?"

"Yes, of course," he snapped, looking quite insulted. "What do you think of me? I 'ave 'ad girlfriends, but…" He paused. Looked somewhere over my right shoulder.

"But—what?"

He dragged his eyes back to mine. "To be honest, I never allowed myself to grow too close to them. I always thought I would marry Isobel, you know?"

That made me catch my breath. "Do you love her?"

"No!" He said it so quickly I knew he hadn't even had to think about it. "Never. It was always something I just assumed I must do for my family. For the bloodline, yes?"

"But not anymore?"

"Not anymore. You know what I told you. About my… visions. The bloodline does not matter to me anymore, at least not as it used to. What matters now is… *Mon Dieu*, Alison, I'm sorry. I do not even know 'ow to say this."

"Say what?" I blurted. "Just spit it out, Joseph. Do you care about me or n—"

His arms—both of them—came back around my waist and he pressed me against his chest. He smelled very faintly of his expensive aftershave—I'd seen the bottle on his dresser when I picked up his washing. He cut off my words with a kiss on my lips. A brief but passionate, totally real kiss that left no doubt as to its meaning. Once we parted, we simply stood there together, my head resting against his good shoulder, his pulse beating hard and steady beneath my ear. I could've stayed like that forever, but all too soon he stepped back, a little grimace of pain crossing his face as he dropped his bad arm to his side.

"Oh my—are you okay? Your shoulder?" I asked, hating the thought that he might have hurt himself by embracing me.

"Yes. No worries," he said easily. He took my left hand in his sound right hand and gave it a hearty squeeze. "Everything's good."

And in that moment, I had to agree. Everything was very good.

****

The rest of the week was, as they say, smooth sailing.

Joseph got his stitches out on Tuesday and was given a clean bill of health by my dad, who admitted to being amazed at how quickly Joseph was recovering. He made good progress through two more physical therapy sessions and started back to class at Yale with hopes of writing his mid-term exams before the November recess ten days away.

I applied myself to improving my own dismal grades and in fact spent most of my time in Joseph's company studying or working on assignments, while he did the same. We finished up every evening around midnight with decafs or chamomile tea, cookies, and goodnight kisses. Not very good for my waistline, which had begun to concern me, but wonderful for my morale.

Especially the kisses.

We finally took a much-needed break Saturday afternoon when Joseph invited me to see the Yale soccer team's next to last match of the season. I eagerly agreed and asked if we could invite Roxie after telling Joseph what she'd said the other day about wanting to meet a guy.

Joseph grinned and said, "But of course," the way only he could say it and promised to introduce Roxie to his friend Michael, who had recently broken up with his girlfriend.

We picked Roxie up in Joseph's car—with Joseph driving this time—and headed to the stadium, where Joseph's team beat Princeton two to one in a nail-biter that ended with all the Yale fans screaming on their feet.

Joseph had called Michael that morning to make plans, and we met up with him outside the locker rooms after the game.

Michael Taylor, star Yale defender, was a rugged, handsome African-American with neat dreadlocks and a killer smile. Joseph introduced us, Roxie went predictably gaga, and the next thing I knew, we were all having supper at the award-winning sushi place in downtown New Haven.

While Roxie and Michael were deep in their own conversation about movies and sports, Joseph and I got to know each other better. I told him all about my childhood in New Haven, the string of casual boyfriends and bad influences I'd had throughout my teen years, the way my love of animals had kept some bits together when my mom's illness and death caused my life to fall apart.

"So, after all the bad boys and rowdy crowds I went with, you can understand why my dad was apprehensive about having you around. Not that he thought you were bad," I hastened to add, "just that he didn't know you. And—"

"And one is afraid of what one does not know," Joseph finished, sounding like a philosopher.

I giggled. "Well… you have to admit the way we met was pretty unusual."

"It was," he agreed.

He drained his glass of sake and poured himself another one from the bottle on the table. He went on to tell me about his life—not the bloodline, nor what it was like to be ridiculously rich, but the life of a boy who loved playing soccer, who learned English in Scotland while being teased mercilessly by his classmates, and who so wanted to know his father better that he attended his last two years of high school in Tel Aviv so he could be with him. The son who loved his mother and the brother who would do anything for his younger sisters. The young man who liked mocha cake, red wine, and furry animals, and who was afraid he would never be able to play soccer again because of the injury to his arm.

"Seriously?" I asked, surprised. I couldn't help looking down at his left hand resting by his hip. He no longer wore the sling, and he was using his hand more day by day, but it was nowhere near normal function yet. "Do you really think you won't—I mean, with time—?" I reached over and slipped my fingers between his.

"It's silly, I know," he admitted. "What does soccer matter compared to everything else in my life? But I cannot 'elp thinking about it."

"You'll get better," I told him in an encouraging tone. "One hundred percent. You have good genes, after all. The best."

That got a smile out of him. He clenched his fingers weakly between mine.

"You couldn't do that a week ago," I reminded him.

"Yes, I know. You're right. I probably worry for nothing. It's just… watching the game today made me realize 'ow much I miss it."

Michael's ears had perked up at the mention of soccer, and he looked across the table at Joseph. "You'll get better, man. You'll be back next season, you'll see. We need you."

"You won today," Joseph pointed out.

"Yeah, but did you see us? We struggled. Marco's nowhere near as fast and agile as you."

The guys very responsibly stopped drinking when our main course ended, since they were both driving. Roxie and I splurged on Spanish coffees while Joseph and Michael ordered Japanese desserts and regular coffee. We didn't protest when the guys paid for our meals.

We eventually left the restaurant with plans to double date next weekend—Roxie and Michael had hit if off that well—and Michael offered to drive Roxie home.

As Joseph backed his car out of its parking space, I heard the squeal of tires and the long, loud honk of a horn pressed by an angry driver. I peered out my side window and managed to catch sight of a vehicle speeding out of the parking lot, while Michael's Jeep idled in the lane between the rows of parking spaces.

My cell phone rang in my handbag.

"Did you see that?" Roxie screamed in my ear when I answered it. "Some idiot in a van totally cut us off! If Michael didn't have some awesome reflexes, they would've hit us for sure!"

"A van?" I felt the color drain from my face. My hand holding the phone went cold. "What color?"

"What—I don't know. Dark. Blue or gray, maybe. It had dark windows. Who the hell cares? The driver's an ass, that's all I know!"

"I'm glad you're okay," I said, ending the call as Michael's Jeep rolled at a reasonable speed toward the street. I turned to Joseph. "Oh. My. God. Did you see that?" As he shook his head—he'd been looking the other way—I went on, "It was a van. It cut off Michael's car and took off. Joseph… Roxie said it might have been gray. It might have been the van. That van."

I could make out just enough in the shadows inside the car to see that Joseph looked concerned. After several endless seconds, he let out a heavy sigh. "If we see the van near your 'ouse again, or anywhere near me, as at Yale or someplace, I will call the police."

"Promise me, Joseph." I clenched my hands into fists on my thighs to stop them shaking. "Promise."

"Yes, all right," he said solemnly. "I promise."

Chapter 16

Recess and an Invitation
Joseph

I had meant it when I promised Alison that I would call the police if I saw the gray van again, but I did not see it the following week. To be honest, it could have driven past me a dozen times without my noticing it, I was this focused on my own life.

I studied like a mad man all day Sunday and every spare minute I had the next four days in preparation for writing my two mid-term exams on Friday—my last chance before the fall recess at Yale. When I was not studying, I was in class or physical therapy. I took time to eat, sleep, and wash, only because my body could not function without these necessities.

Finally, Saturday arrived. I awoke shortly after eleven o'clock, still exhausted but feeling a weight had been lifted from my shoulders. My exams had gone better than expected the previous day, and I was reasonably certain that I had managed passing grades. They would be far below my usual results but given the circumstances, I would happily accept them. I took a long shower that revived me considerably, shaved, and ran some gel through my hair in hopes of looking somewhat presentable. I dressed in jeans, a golf shirt, and the navy cardigan that Laurence had chosen for me and went downstairs to find Alison and her father making lunch for themselves.

"Good morning, sunshine," Alison greeted me with a smile. She looked nice in dark jeans and a white cashmere sweater that I instantly recognized. "In two more minutes, it'll be afternoon."

"Yes, I know. I slept very late." I said good morning to Dr. Mitchell and turned back to Alison. "Where did you get this sweater?" I asked, pointing in the general direction of her chest.

"Your Aunt Marguerite gave it to me at the country house after mine got messed up," she replied. "She said I could keep it."

"Ah, yes," I said, realizing that "messed up" meant "covered in your blood."

"I gave it to her last Christmas, but it looks better on you."

"You think?"

I smiled. "I would not lie to you about something like this." I went to the counter to pour myself a cup of coffee. "If you still hope to go to the soccer game at Harvard, we must leave soon. It's over two hours' drive to Cambridge."

"I do. Totally," she replied. "Roxie wanted to come too, but she called this morning to say she has to work at the vet clinic today. She said she stills wants to… um…" She hesitated, glanced at her father, and finished, "double date with us tomorrow night."

Dr. Mitchell cleared his throat rather loudly, glanced from his daughter to me and back to her, and I wondered what—if anything—she had told him about our relationship. But he did not go red in the face or start steaming from the ears, so I supposed he was not going to forbid Alison and my being together. As though he could do this if he tried.

Alison fried some more eggs and bacon for me. After we ate, we left in my car for Harvard University. I drove for an hour, managing with some effort to grasp the steering wheel with my left hand for short periods of time. By the time we stopped at a donut shop for coffee and snacks, however, my collarbone was shooting sparks into my shoulder and my arm tingled painfully all the way to my fingers. I reminded myself that this was good; as Colin had explained to me, these were signs that the injured nerves were healing. However, when we came out of the restaurant, I swallowed my pride and asked Alison to drive.

"Seriously?" She sounded incredulous, but her face beamed. "If you really want—"

"I do," I assured her.

"Okay then!" She opened the driver's side door and I slipped into the passenger seat.

We drove without incident to Cambridge, talking sporadically about everyday things, simply getting to know each other better. I felt oddly free, sitting beside the girl I was becoming increasingly convinced would one day be my wife, and knowing that she knew my deepest secret. Most of it, at least…

At the Harvard University stadium, we joined a group of people wearing Yale colors and cheered our team on from the bleachers. We were disappointed in the end, though, as Yale lost another close game three to two. I could not help wondering if my presence on the field might have made a difference, and I decided at this moment that I would play again next year no matter what it took.

After a short visit with Michael and a couple of the other guys after the game, Alison and I drove home—Alison once again behind the wheel—where I directed her to Branford, just east of New Haven, and my favorite French restaurant.

"Ooh, this is adorable!" Alison exclaimed after we were greeted by the owner, a distinguished American man named Albert—pronounced the American way despite his best efforts at a French accent—who led us inside the intimate bistro.

"Yes, it's a nice place," I agreed. We sat at a corner table with a white lace tablecloth and two flickering candles. "But wait until you taste the food. *Magnifique!*" I said with a kiss to my fingers, the French way.

We had a leisurely and delicious four course meal that included appetizers of duck confit, green salad with a house dressing, and racks of lamb with roasted potatoes. Our conversation was casual—soccer, movies, music, even American politics—until as we waited for our desserts of *crème brulée*, I asked Alison why she had helped me that first night. Why she had insisted on coming with me the next day, even if it was dangerous. I still perhaps sought reassurance that she would be one hundred percent with me no matter what happened.

"I didn't realize it would be dangerous at the time," she reminded me, draining her glass of the red wine I had ordered. The waiter had not asked for her ID—perhaps an advantage of my being on a first-name basis with the owner—and we had drunk two glasses each. "But even if I'd thought about it, it wouldn't have mattered. I wanted to be with you."

"Yes, you told me this before. But if it's still dangerous?"

"Do you really think it is?" When I did not answer, she added, "It still doesn't matter. You know what? I never believed in love at first sight, and I didn't realize it at first, but I guess that's what it was, Joseph. From the moment I picked you up in the street, I knew I had to have you in my life. I never thought you'd feel the same way." She looked straight across the table at me, her eyes narrow. "You—do you—?"

"I do," I said. "I also did not believe in love. Not true love as we see in the movies. My parents' marriage was arranged by our families. Yet"—I searched for the good words—"I do believe now that I'm falling in love with you since that night in the country house. When we sat outside together, you know?"

"I know," she said, and her cheeks went deep pink in the soft light of the candles. "You were so sweet to me that night, and I knew there was more to you than I knew—even if I already knew quite a bit."

"I feel the same way," I admitted, suddenly feeling quite hot, myself.

Mon Dieu—my thoughts came in French—*let this not be a great mistake. I do not wish to betray my family or the bloodline, but I do not wish my son to become the Antichrist. And I wish to know love. Real love, not the kind of forced love my parents had. Is this so wrong of me?*

It could not be wrong when it felt so right, I decided as we left the restaurant some time later. I slipped my good arm around Alison's waist, pulled her close to me, and whispered in her ear, "Your coming into my life the way you did is a miracle. I truly believe this. I will not let you go—unless you wish it."

"Never," she said. We reached my car and she

turned to me, throwing her arms around my neck and burying her face against my chest. "You're stuck with me now."

****

"*Bonne fête*, Joseph!" Alison greeted me cheerfully Wednesday morning.

I stopped pouring coffee into the coffeemaker and stared at her, the wee coffee scoop still in my hand. "Wh—how do you know this?"

She grinned. "Élisabeth, of course. I talked to her on Facebook. She told me how to say 'Happy Birthday' in French."

"You're *merveilleuse*!" I said, giving her a long kiss on her soft, full lips. We had done quite a lot of kissing these last few days. That was *merveilleux* too.

"You'll have to wait till tonight for your birthday present, though," she said, still grinning like the cat that swallowed the canary.

"No! I hope you did not spend money on me, Alison," I scolded her, wishing her to not spend money on something she could not afford. "I have no need of anything and if I do, I can buy it for myself, yes?"

"Actually, you need some winter clothes. A coat and boots," she replied smartly. "Don't think I didn't see you shivering on the bleachers at the soccer game on Saturday. But don't worry. I didn't spend any money. Well, not much anyway."

I sighed, knowing that I would not get more out of her. "*Bien alors…* I will wait, then." I finished making the coffee, and we sat down together to eat breakfast.

Alison left for school—the University of New Haven did not have the same week of recess as Yale—and I went to my physical therapy session.

Colin and I agreed that I had made good progress, even since my session on Monday. When I asked him, he said he thought that I could resume my previous activities, as long as I was careful to not push myself too hard.

This was all I needed to hear. After my therapy, I drove to the local gun and hunting store to buy ammunition for my handgun, which I had long since returned to its place beneath the seat in my car. I went to the shooting range where Philippe and I had always gone and did some target practice for the first time since my kidnapping. It took me some time to figure out how to best hold the gun with my left wrist still in the brace and my fingers weak, but after much trial and error, I found a hand position that did not affect my aim too badly. Actually pulling the trigger was another matter.

I summoned the voice of Tad, the Israeli soldier who first taught me how to use a gun. The voice of Philippe, who had always been a steadier shot than me. I thought of the parchments and the wee bits of bone that could change the world, sitting away in a Swiss bank safe deposit box. I thought of my family and all the sacrifices we had made for centuries to keep our sacred bloodline hidden and safe. I thought of Alison and how she made me feel. I thought of the boy yet to be conceived who may well hold the future of the world in his hands. The prospect of firing a gun at another human being made me feel sick to my stomach. I considered myself a humanitarian, hopefully one day a leader. I was not a fighter, but I resolved to do anything necessary to protect myself and those who depended on me.

And those I love. I will not let them down again.

Though my arms—especially my weak left arm—

ached from the effort of firing one hundred rounds after doing basically nothing for a month, I drove to my house to check on the progress there. The repairmen had finished working on the exterior and were now working inside. The foreman told me the work should be completed in another week. I would have to buy new furniture, curtains, and everything else, of course, and I thought I would very much enjoy doing this with Alison. If she was anything like Élisabeth, she would jump at the chance to go on a shopping trip.

Back at the Mitchells' house, I put the dogs out in the back yard. I swallowed some ibuprofen, took a shower, and put on clean jeans and my white, button-down shirt as the clothing I had worn to the shooting range carried the faint metallic smell of gunfire. I got on my laptop to talk to Élisabeth and Laurence on Facebook. They wished me *bonne fête* and asked me how I was celebrating my twenty-three years. Realizing that I would soon have to tell them about Alison and me, I promised to celebrate with them when I came home for Christmas vacation.

I was also going to have to tell *Maman* that I would not marry Isobel—if she even thought this was still possible after what had happened with Gregory. But not today. Today I told her about my decision to cut down my course load, about Fleur, about how my arm was getting stronger all the time.

I brought the dogs in and brushed them, spending extra time with Fleur, who was growing more comfortable with my contact every day. Now she sat happily thumping her tail on the floor while I forced myself to use my left hand, dropping the brush several times in the process and cursing under my breath in

French each time before resuming the task.

Alison came in at supper time with a square box that looked as if it came from a *patisserie* hanging from a ribbon in one hand and a bottle of red wine I suspected she had purchased with her false ID in the other. Her book bag hung over one shoulder; she let it fall to the floor with a thump and headed for the kitchen with me following at her heels like a puppy.

"Go away," she said with a giggle. "Go up to your room. Come back in five minutes, okay?"

"Are you sure you do not need some help?" I asked, teasing.

"Positive. Now go!" she repeated over her shoulder.

My cell phone was ringing where I had dropped it on my bed, Aunt Marguerite calling to wish me happy birthday. I had spoken to her several times since moving in here, but not in the past week. We talked for ten minutes and when I ended the call, I assumed it was safe to go downstairs.

Alison was in the kitchen. The table was set for the three of us, but there was no sign of food anywhere.

I sniffed the air. "*Bien alors…* we will not eat tonight?"

"Of course we will. Supper's on the way," she said, again with that cat-and-canary look on her face. "Okay. Élisabeth told me you love American-style Chinese food, so I ordered—"

"You did?" I exclaimed. "I do. I have not eaten this since months."

"So I figured. I didn't know what to get you that you wouldn't buy for yourself, and then I thought, the way to a man's heart, you know?"

"*Pardon*?" Clearly, I did not know.

"It's a saying. 'The way to a man's heart is through his stomach.'"

"Ah, *oui*." I grinned and patted my stomach. "This is a very wise saying."

Dr. Mitchell arrived a few minutes before the restaurant delivered a large paper bag containing a variety of Chinese specialties, including all my favorites that Alison admitted she had learned from Élisabeth.

We had an enjoyable meal during which I told Alison and her father many things about Europe and Israel. When Dr. Mitchell mentioned that he had always dreamed of visiting Paris, I invited them to my mother's house for Christmas without a second's thought.

I could not help myself laughing at the look of total surprise on their faces. Especially Dr. Mitchell.

"Why would you extend such an invitation, Joseph?" he asked. "Yes, I realize you have the money, but… why?"

I stopped laughing and looked at Alison, who shrugged, no help at all. "Dr. Mitchell, I… uh, I believe I'm in love with your daughter. I wish to show her— show you both—my country and my home. Share that part of my life with you."

The poor man stared at me as if I had two heads. "In love? You—I'm sorry, but I just don't see someone like you with a nice girl like my daughter."

"What—how can you say this?" I objected, hardly believing my ears. "Alison is—"

"I know what Alison is! And I know what you are."

I swallowed hard and my heart missed a beat before proceeding to thump in my chest. "You know—?"

"I've spoken with your Aunt Marguerite, Joseph. I know you're the eldest son in a very wealthy French family who inherited a fortune when your father passed away. You've been educated in the most exclusive boarding schools. The University of Paris. Yale. No expense spared. You'll never have to work a day in your life although for some reason, apparently, you want to. Your car is worth twice as much as our two cars together. You could have any girl you want. Royalty. Celebrity. What happens when the next beautiful or famous girl comes along? What makes you think an ordinary Connecticut girl with no status and no money will satisfy you?"

"Ah, yes. I was afraid it would come to this," I said, although I was immensely relieved that he really did not know anything at all. I looked across the table at Alison, who had gone crimson all the way to her ears, and turned to her father at the head of the table. "To be honest, I've never met anyone like Alison. She's a strong, beautiful young lady and… and you have it the wrong way around, Dr. Mitchell. I'm the lucky man that she wants to be with me. If you cannot see this… I'm sorry, but we will be together whether you approve of it or not."

Dr. Mitchell's face had gone blank as he listened to me. His mouth opened and closed and opened again, as if he wanted to say something but could not find the words. Finally, he got hold of himself and said, "Please understand me, I only want what's best for my daughter."

I wondered suddenly if he knew about her cutting herself to deal with the loss of her mother. I suspected that he did not. He did not know his daughter as well as he believed he did.

"I also want the best for her," I assured him, "and the best for me, as well."

And the best for the entire world, if it comes to this.
Perhaps one day I will be able to explain this to you...

Slowly, Alison's father turned to look at her. "Do you have anything to say about this?"

"I do," she replied with a quick glance at me. "I know my choice of boyfriends over the years wasn't always smart—in some cases, it was totally stupid—but Joseph's different. He—he's the best thing that's ever happened to me. What we have... it's special, Dad. Joseph—he's special. I love him."

Dr. Mitchell looked sideways at me. He took a deep breath and let it out in a long sigh that I took for one of resignation. "Special, huh? You'd better take care of her, Joseph. Be there for her more than I have these past couple years. I failed—"

"Dad," Alison said softly.

"You were right, Alison," her father continued with a shake of his head, "when you said I buried myself in my work after your mother passed away. It wasn't just for the money. It was the only way I knew to deal with my grief. Every moment I spent in this house reminded me of her. Of how I'd never see her again. It still does... but I left you alone with your own pain, and I was wrong to do that." He looked straight at me then, a long, steady look this time. "I haven't seen Alison as happy as she's been these past few weeks since before her mother got sick. Don't think I haven't noticed."

"She makes me happy as well," I said. "And please, you must not worry. I will take care of her."

"And I'll take care of Joseph," Alison spoke up. "It goes both ways, you know." She dabbed at a tear in the corner of her eye with the edge of her paper napkin and smiled at me.

The tension that had made the air between us so hot and heavy that I could feel my shirt sticking to my back seemed to fade and grow cooler.

I took a deep breath and slowly let it out through my nose. "My invitation still stands. I would very much like for you to come to France. Perhaps…" I paused, uncertain how they would take this, then plunged ahead. "To be honest, I think perhaps it would be a good thing for both of you. A way… not to forget your grief, of course, but a way to heal, yes?"

After a long moment of silence, Dr. Mitchell took a deep drink of wine, draining his glass. He cleared his throat, looked at Alison, and said, "I do have quite a bit of vacation time coming to me. If you'd like, Allie, I guess we could take Joseph up on his offer."

Alison's face broke into a huge smile. "Seriously, Dad? I'd like that more than anything. I mean, if you'd come with us." She looked at me, her eyes sparkling like round blue diamonds. "You really want us to come for Christmas?"

"But of course. I would not have offered if I did not."

We cleared the table together and Alison brought out the mysterious ribbon-wrapped box, which held a tall, round cake with *Bonne Fête Joseph* written in red on the dark chocolate frosting. The cake was mocha, of course.

The evening finished on a pleasant note, with glasses of brandy and cups of coffee, and a game of chess in the rec room between Dr. Mitchell and myself. We spoke of many things, generally getting to know each other better, and although I was clearly a better chess player than the good doctor, I allowed him to win.

Chapter 17

Taken
Alison

Thursday was Thanksgiving Day. I'd thought ahead on my last run to the supermarket and bought a frozen turkey, which had been thawing in the refrigerator since Monday. For the first time in three years, I felt like I had something to be thankful for.

"You're not the only one around here with important ancestors, you know," I told Joseph over a late breakfast of his delicious French toast. "When I did a family tree project back in high school, I found out that one of my several-times-great-grandfathers on my dad's side came over here on the *Mayflower*."

Joseph didn't know anything about the pilgrims or the history of American Thanksgiving—and why would he? As I prepared the turkey with my mom's mushroom stuffing and got it in the oven for the required five hours of roasting, I told him all about the *Mayflower*, Plymouth Rock, and the reason why Americans celebrated Thanksgiving the way we did.

"This is a nice tradition," he observed when I was done. "In France we 'ave the *Jour de la Victoire* on the eighth of May, when we celebrate the end of the Second World War and the liberation of France. And of course, we 'ave our *Fête Nationale* on the fourteenth of July.

This is a wee bit like your Fourth of July, yes?"

"Got it," I said, grinning at this mundane glimpse into Joseph's life.

It was drizzling rain, so we spent the day indoors, playing with our pets—surprisingly, Mister and Fleur had become fast friends—listening to some of my favorite music that Joseph wanted to hear and surfing the net. He showed me the website for his family's antique shop on the ground floor of their breathtaking eighteenth-century stone house outside the walled city of Carcassonne.

He pulled out the silver pendant he wore on a chain from beneath his sweater and told me it was the Cross of Lorraine. He explained that not only did it represent the region of France that gave his family its name, but it was an ancient symbol of the Knights Templar, the powerful organization that for centuries had known about and protected the secret of the Jesus bloodline. This particular piece had belonged to his two-times-great grandfather and had been passed down to the eldest or only child through the generations.

Roxie called and after asking Joseph his plans for the long weekend, I agreed that we would meet her and Michael for supper Saturday at our usual pizza place.

My dad had volunteered to work a shift at the hospital, but he came home for supper with a heart-warming tale of having saved a choking toddler's life. It was yet another thing to be thankful for.

I spent Friday and Saturday shopping with Joseph— home furnishings, which would be delivered when his house was ready, and clothes, shoes, winter coat, and boots, which we lugged home with us. Money being no object for him, I ended up with a couple bags of new clothes myself, gifts from Joseph that I tried to refuse, but in the end accepted with promises to pay him back with home cooking after he moved back to his own house.

We washed up, changed into some of our new clothes—gray jean leggings and a long blue sweater-coat for me, dark jeans and a black cashmere turtleneck for Joseph—and headed to the restaurant for a relaxing, conversation-and-wine-filled supper with Roxie and Michael.

The following day, Joseph invited me to go with him to the New Haven Homeless Shelter. The opening of an envelope he gave to the middle-aged woman in charge nearly caused her heart failure. She flushed crimson to the tips of her ears, threw her arms around his shoulders, and held him for a good thirty seconds while thanking him profusely and assuring him that God would bless him for giving such a generous Christmas donation to the shelter. Gritting his teeth slightly against the pain I assumed her embrace caused his bad shoulder, he told her God already had, his tone solemn despite the happy situation. After that, I helped out in the kitchen with a handful of other volunteers while Joseph visited with the older men, playing chess and talking about God only knew what. Well, I knew what he wasn't talking about…

After our lunch of—what else?—turkey, mashed potatoes, and cranberry sauce, there was a non-denominational Thanksgiving-themed service delivered by a thirty-something-ish priest whom Joseph told me was his friend, Father Thomas.

After the service, Father Thomas spoke to a few people privately, then gradually drifted over to us. "So, Joseph, is this your young lady?" he asked with a subtle smile in my direction. He was several inches shorter than Joseph, with curly, reddish hair and the brightest green eyes, none of which I supposed I should be noticing in a priest.

"Yes, she is," Joseph said and introduced us properly.

Father Thomas asked me to please call him Thomas, while I wondered what Joseph had already told his friend about me. About us.

We chatted for a few minutes about our respective Thanksgivings, and then Father Thomas said he had some visits to make to people who were homebound over the weekend. "If you want to talk—unofficially, that is— we could meet up later at the little family restaurant down the street from St. Francis Church," he suggested.

We took him up on the offer and joined him at six o'clock at the restaurant in question. Thomas had changed from his priest's clothes into jeans, a dark green wool turtleneck, and black overcoat, and now looked more like one of Joseph's fellow Yale students than a member of the Catholic clergy. I found this made it easier to relate to him, for some reason.

We had a leisurely meal of salad, pasta, and soft drinks—in deference to my under-age status—for which Joseph once again insisted on paying and would not take "no" for an answer. We enjoyed a nice conversation that by the time dessert and coffee rolled around had deteriorated somewhat into an animated debate between Joseph and Thomas about the Catholic Church's brutal treatment of heretics such as the Cathars and Templars over the centuries. Joseph took the side of the heretics, of course, while Thomas tried to defend the mostly indefensible actions of his Church. I was impressed by the fact that Joseph, although he didn't believe in Church doctrine, was quite well-educated on the subject. I also realized that all the secrecy, subterfuge, and outright lies about the existence of the Jesus bloodline had literally kept members of his family alive and safe for the past seventeen hundred years.

****

My dad left for the clinic Monday morning as usual. Joseph headed out at nine to run some errands he declined to elaborate on, promising to be home for lunch. It was our last day of holiday before classes resumed, and we wanted to spend the afternoon together.

A couple minutes after Joseph left, the doorbell rang. Expecting he was back, sheepishly admitting he'd forgotten his key and maybe asking me to join him wherever he was going, I pulled the door open without looking first, to find myself facing a bulky African-American man with close-cropped hair. I realized with a start that I'd seen him somewhere before. More than once.

"Excuse me, miss," he said with a polite tip of his head. "I lost my dog, eh, and I believe… you might o' found her?"

"No, sorry," I said with a shake of my head. "I haven't found any dogs around here." My inner alarm was going off, and I moved to close the door.

"It would've been a few weeks ago, down by the water." The man raised a hand to block the door and said, "There, I think that's her, the black and white one. Hey there, girl!"

I looked over my shoulder to see that Fleur and Bax had crept up behind me. My dear, loyal Bax was flattened to the floor, his eyes narrowed to brown slits. A most unnerving low growl escaped from deep in his throat. Fleur just stood there, tail between her legs, no evidence of recognition in her demeanor.

I had no time to figure out why, but alarm bells rang in my head. In rising panic, I tried to push the door closed but the man took a step forward, blocking it with his boot.

At that moment, a gray van pulled up into the driveway beside my car. A second man, Caucasian, bearded, and wearing a navy blue baseball cap pulled down to his eyebrows, jumped out and raced up behind the first man. I turned to run for safety inside the house, but the first man grabbed me by the arms in an iron grip.

Fleur and Bax raced forward, barking at my heels. I screamed, struggling and kicking as hard as I could with my slippered feet at my captor's shins, and for a second, I thought I might get free. Then the second man stepped in. He reached up to my face with a white cloth in his hand, which he pressed over my nose and mouth. I smelled a faint, sweet odor and tried to hold my breath but couldn't for long. My fingers and feet began to tingle, and I grew too weak to fight. I felt like I was falling sideways, and then everything went black.

I woke up lying on my side on a cold metal floor in what had to be the back of the van. My hands were tied together behind my back, my ankles were bound with duct tape, and there was a strip of tape over my mouth. My heart was racing, I felt dizzy and nauseous, and the bumping of the vehicle over what must have been a rough road didn't help. I was terrified that if I threw up, I would choke to death on my own vomit.

I closed my eyes and tried to concentrate on breathing slowly in and out through my nose. Dressed only in jeans and a tee-shirt, I was starting to shiver. After what seemed like forever but was probably somewhere between twenty and thirty minutes, the van rumbled to a stop. I opened my eyes in time to see the black man who had come to my house fling open the back doors.

Without a word, he scooped me up over his shoulder while I squirmed and grunted and tried to scream through the tape. He carried me around the back of what looked to be a farmhouse surrounded by rain-soaked, neglected fields, waited for the second man to unlock the door, and deposited me inside on a kitchen chair.

I immediately pushed to my feet but wobbled dizzily and dropped back hard on the wooden chair. The white man gave me a look plainly meant to intimidate me. "Miss Mitchell… I'm going to take the tape off your mouth now so you can answer some questions. Don't bother screaming, there's no one close enough to hear you."

I mumbled beneath the gag, nodded, then cried out as he yanked the tape off my mouth, taking half the skin on my lips with it. Tears welled up in my eyes, and my vision blurred. I took a deep breath of dry air rank with stale cigarette smoke, and my stomach heaved. I turned my head to the side and threw up my breakfast on the yellowed linoleum floor beside my feet.

"Good goddamn, what'd you have to go make a mess for?" the black man asked of me.

"What do you want with me?" I demanded, my voice ringing with courage I didn't feel. "I'm nobody. There's no reason—"

"We don't want you," the same man said. "It's him we want. Your boyfriend."

"Joseph Lorraine," added the second man, as if he thought I didn't know who his partner was talking about. "What do you know about him?"

"I know he'll find me," I spat out. "He'll come for me and you'll be friggin' sorry when he does!"

The men looked at each other. The white man gave me a menacing grin. "That's what we're counting on," he said, and something in his voice chilled me to the bone. "In the meantime, you just sit nice and tight. We don't want to hurt you—not unless you give us reason to."

He nodded to the black man, who scooped me up again, carried me upstairs wiggling and screaming to be released, and put me down on a bare twin bed in a faded pink bedroom. He turned on his heel and left me alone in the room, but only for a moment.

He came back carrying a long, black-handled kitchen knife. I screamed and scrunched back against the headboard, my heart racing so fast and hard it threatened to burst from my chest, preparing to kick out with my taped-together feet as soon as he got close enough.

"Relax, Miss Mitchell," he said in what he probably—mistakenly—thought was a soothing voice. "I'm not gonna hurt you. I just want to cut that tape off o' you." First, he cut the tape around my ankles. Before freeing my hands, he warned me, "You be a good girl now, and everything will go according to plan. Don't do anything silly like trying to escape. You'll see the window is boarded up, and I'll be lockin' the door."

From the doorway, the white man added, "We'll just let some time pass, enough time that your Joseph starts to worry, eh? Then we'll be back to see you."

Suddenly, I remembered where I'd seen the black

man before: the terrace at the pizza place, that first time I took Joseph there. The burger place near the University of New Haven. Had I seen the white man too? Probably, but I couldn't recall where.

"You've been following me," I said, hoping I sounded more accusing than terrified.

"We've been following the both of you," the white man said, "figuring out the best way to go about things. Finally, we decided it would be easier to take you. Lure him to us, rather than trying to take him by force."

"But why? Why do you want him? What's he to you?"

The man chuckled, then grew serious. His gray eyes searched my face from beneath his cap. "Well, that's the question, isn't it? How 'bout you tell me? We got it already that he's something—someone—special. But what exactly? What's his secret—and what's it worth?"

Despite my terrifying predicament, I couldn't help thinking, *Thank God they don't know. They don't know who Joseph really is.* I swallowed what little saliva I had and choked out what I hoped was a credible reply. "H-he's a Yale student from France. His family has some money. I-I don't know any more. I don't know any secrets."

The white man took a couple steps closer to my bed. "So, Miss Mitchell… can I call you Alison? How much do you think you're worth to him? What would he do to see you safe? Would he give us enough money for us to spend the rest of our lives in luxury on some tropical island? Or enough to… let me see… change places with you so we can figure out why he's so important and how much he's worth to his own family?"

I licked my raw lips with the tip of my tongue but

said nothing.

"Well, then... you turn that around in your pretty little head for a while, why don't you? When you have an answer, you let us know and we'll give your boyfriend a call." He left the room with the black man behind him.

This time I heard them lock the door.

Oh God, I've got to get out of here! I immediately leapt from the bed and rushed to the window which was, just as I'd been told, firmly nailed shut and boarded up from the outside.

I pounded on the window frame. Screamed my lungs out. Crossed the room and pounded on the door. Screamed some more. Finally, exhausted and in tears— although I had no idea when they'd begun—I sank down on the bed, pressed my hands to my eyes, and sobbed.

But my moment of despair didn't last long. I wiped my wet face with the bottom edge of my tee-shirt, noticing for the first time the pillow and sleeping bag on the bed.

They planned this, I reminded myself. *Prepared the room for me. How long do they think they'll keep me here?*

I looked around the room. It was sparsely furnished with little girl appointments: dresser, chest of drawers, and bedside table, all lacquered white just like the headboard on the bed. I got up and opened the closet. It was empty; not even a hanger remained, and I noticed the entire room smelled musty, as though it hadn't been used in a while. I wondered how long the men had been living here, preparing for today.

I stretched out on the bed and tried to picture everything turning out well. Joseph would pay whatever the men asked—of course he would, he didn't care about his money—and they would let me go. They would flee to the tropical isle of their choice, and we would never hear from them again. Joseph and I would eventually get married and live happily ever after, producing a son who would bring peace to the world.

But who was I kidding? I knew it wouldn't be that simple. I was sure these were the two men who'd skipped out of the original kidnapping deal when Joseph escaped from his cousin Gregory's house. Even if they didn't know what Gregory had wanted with him—and it seemed they didn't—they knew Joseph was someone who was worth something. They'd said that much themselves.

What will I tell them when they come back? I can't let them know about Joseph's family and the Jesus bloodline. And what will Joseph say—do—when they call him? I don't want him to risk his life to save me. But he will. I know he will, because he's a good person. Because he loves me and because he wants to save the world.

Seven hours later, I'd gone over half a dozen scenarios in my head and still had no clue what I was going to say to the men about Joseph. I only knew that I couldn't tell them the truth. On top of that I had other, physical concerns. The nausea that had come from shock and whatever the white man had shoved in my face to knock me out had passed long ago. It was warm enough in the room, at least, but I was hungry, I was thirsty, and I seriously had to use the bathroom.

"Hey! Let me out!" I yelled, pounding on the door once again. "Come on! Open the door! I need to get out!" I kept this up non-stop for a good five minutes until finally I heard heavy footsteps in the hallway.

The key rattled in the lock, and the black man opened the door.

"I have to go to the bathroom," I told him. "You don't want me to make a mess in here too, do you?"

"Bathroom's downstairs," he said after considering this for a moment. "Don't try anything funny," he added, "or we'll be givin' you a bucket to go in."

I wondered suddenly if he had a gun. The thought was nearly enough to make me pee right then and there, and I pressed my thighs together until the distressing urge passed. "I-I won't," I stammered. "Just please let me—"

He stepped aside and nodded for me to precede him downstairs.

After finishing up in the vaguely disgusting bathroom and splashing cold water on my face, I was escorted into the kitchen by the same man. "Sit down," he said with what sounded almost like a touch of compassion in his voice. "Go ahead and eat."

I noticed there was a can of cola and a sandwich on a stoneware plate on the table. I wanted to refuse, but I knew my body needed the nourishment. For half a second, I wondered if the sandwich might contain an unwanted additive, but I honestly didn't see how poisoning or drugging me would advance their stated agenda. I sat and ate the bologna sandwich and drank the cola.

"Now you've had some time to think," said the white man, a cigarette hanging between his lips, "have you got anything better to tell us about your boyfriend? Something that might actually be of interest to us?"

I shook my head. "I barely know him," I declared. "I suppose he'll give you whatever money you ask for, but I only met him when—"

He slapped me backhanded across the cheek, so suddenly and so hard that my head snapped sideways. I heard my neck crack with the force of the blow. "We know how you met him!" he shouted, that disgusting cigarette wagging up and down with every word. "What we don't know is what he told you about himself."

I pressed a hand to my stinging cheek. Choking back sobs—I was determined to be strong in front of these ignorant thugs—I said, "I told you everything I know. H-his family in France is wealthy. His cousin Gregory had him ta-taken over s-some family quarrel. I don't know what it was about. I asked him a bunch of times, but he refused to tell me. I… I don't know anything more."

God, if they believe that I deserve an Oscar!

The man frowned like this wasn't what he wanted to hear but apparently, he believed it. After a moment, he said to his partner, "I've had enough of this shit. We're wasting time. He's probably called the police by now. They may already be looking for her." He nodded and the other man suddenly raised his hand.

I squealed and recoiled in my chair in anticipation of another blow, but then I saw he held a cell phone.

"Give us his phone number," the white man said. The older of the two men, it seemed he was also the boss.

Staring at the phone in the black man's hand, a terrible sinking feeling came over me. *Oh. My. God. I don't know Joseph's cell phone number!* "I can't," I said over the sound of my own pounding heart. My voice shook despite my effort to remain defiant. "I mean, he has a cell phone, but I-I don't know the number."

"Good goddamn!" the black man exclaimed, slapping his empty hand flat to his forehead. "Don't you ever call the guy? He's your boyfriend, ain't he?"

My stomach heaved; the bologna sandwich threatened to come right back up and make another mess on the floor. I swallowed hard and said, "If you've been watching us like you say, you know he's been staying at my house. I haven't had much need to call him."

The men looked at each other for a moment. They evidently hadn't thought of that. *Idiots.*

The boss ran his fingers through his slicked-back, graying blond hair. "Give us your home number then. You do know that one, don't you?" As I nodded, he went on, "I'll ask for Joseph. If your old man answers, I don't want to hear a peep out of you. Got it?"

I nodded again, gave him our phone number, and prayed that Joseph would answer.

Chapter 18

Forty-eight Hours
Joseph

Having decided to be honest with Alison and tell her where I had gone this morning, I returned from the shooting range to find the Mitchells' front door unlocked and the house empty but for the wee furry creatures. I knew before I saw Alison's keys and phone in the glass dish on the hall table that something was very wrong.

"Alison? Are you here? Alison?" I called out, hurrying through the house with my heart racing in my throat. I threw open the back door and marched out into the yard with the dogs at my heels. "Alison!"

I immediately recalled the times we had seen that suspicious gray van, the times I had seen the same man or men at a restaurant, store, or other location. Perhaps it was the trauma of being shot and unconscious, of having visions of my past and future, or simply denial on my part, but I had not recognized them as the third and fourth men at Gregory's house. Yet of course they were.

Merde! They watched us all this time. You should have called the police when Alison wanted you to, Joseph. This is your fault!

I returned inside and walked more carefully through the house, searching for signs of a struggle or any clue that Alison might have left behind. I found her handbag on the dresser in her bedroom, and the coat and boots she had worn outside for the past week in the foyer closet.

These as well as her phone and keys told me that she had not gone willingly. I sat down on the sofa with my boots and jacket still on, Fleur pressing her body against my legs. I felt paralyzed, uncertain what to do. I assumed that there would be a phone call but so far, my cell had not rung in my pocket. I pulled it out just to be sure, but no. No missed calls. No texts.

Call Aunt Marguerite, Joseph. She will know what to do.

I called her and left an urgent message for her to call me back. *Dieu merci*, she did so almost immediately. I explained the situation, but she told me that she had no authority in Connecticut; she could not help me this time. I must call the New Haven police and make a missing person report. They would contact the FBI if they felt it necessary.

This I did. I took off my jacket and boots and changed into clothes that did not smell of the shooting range and then simply paced anxiously throughout the house for an hour, until a police car pulled up in the driveway and two uniformed officers came to the door.

I was dismayed to recognize Officer Spencer, who had not believed I am who I said I am that day at the police station. I hoped she would now believe what I had to say—or at least the other officer, an older Latino-looking fellow called Estevez would.

I told them everything I could about Alison's disappearance and how I suspected that men involved in my own recent kidnapping had taken her. Officer Spencer eventually wiped the "not him again" look from her face and said she remembered something of my own case. They both seemed to take my report today seriously. They did, however, have some awkward questions:

Had Alison and I been having problems? Recent arguments? Why was I kidnapped the first time? Why did I believe the same men were now responsible for Alison's disappearance? Who was I that I should be involved in such things?

I gave them what I hoped were believable answers about coming from a wealthy family involved in French politics and possibly having enemies who hoped to use Alison to reach me. This was of course all true—to a point.

Finally, apparently satisfied, Officer Estevez asked for a picture of Alison. I recalled the framed photos of her and her mother in her bedroom and went to get one for them.

"Are you going to look for her?" I asked, handing Officer Spencer the photo.

"We'll put out a BOLO and—"

"A what? I do not know this word."

"A BO—LO," she repeated with a roll of her eyes. "It means 'be on the lookout.' "

"You need to stay here," Officer Estevez told me. "Call all of Alison's friends and next of kin, ask if they've seen or heard from her. There's no reason to suspect this is a kidnapping until you—"

"But it is!" I interrupted, thumping the wall with my fist. "*Bordel de merde*! She did not leave on her own with no shoes, no coat, no phone, and no handbag."

"Then you need to wait here in case the kidnappers call," he continued pointedly. "I understand that you're worried, but please try to remain calm, Mr. Lorraine. You won't be any help to us if you go off any which way. We'll check out the address where you were held, although I very much doubt they would go back there."

"Yes, I doubt this too," I admitted. "I will wait here. Please tell me if you find something."

"We will, of course," Officer Spencer said. She asked me for my contact information and told me to call them if Alison came back, or if I heard from her or the kidnappers.

Before they left, another woman arrived. She wore plain clothes and said her name was Detective Whitaker. She asked me all the same questions the others had asked and told me the same things the others had told me. Finally, they all left after I once again promised to let them know immediately if I had any news.

Ah, Dieu, I must tell Alison's father, I thought miserably once I was alone. *After promising him that I would take care of her, she has been taken. He will never forgive me, even if she comes home safe. And she will— she will come home safe. I will make sure of this.*

With this on my mind, I could not sit still. I paced the house for a half hour before finally searching for Dr. Mitchell's number in Alison's cell phone and making a call to him at his clinic. I left a message with the receptionist that there was a family emergency and Dr. Mitchell must come home as soon as possible.

I sat at the kitchen table with a glass of orange juice growing warm between my hands, the knots in my stomach becoming larger and harder by the minute. I nearly jumped out of my skin when my cell phone rang a quarter hour later.

"Joseph? What's going on?" Dr. Mitchell demanded.

"I cannot explain this to you over the phone," I replied.

"What? Why not? Where's Alison?"

"She's not here. Please Dr. Mitchell, you must come home."

"I—what? Yes, all right, I'm on my way. But Joseph, so help me, if anything has happened to her..." His voice faded and he ended the call.

Yes. I know.

Explaining everything to Alison's father when he arrived shortly afterward went as badly as I had anticipated. If he had not in fact been bound by the Hippocratic oath, I suspected that he might have ripped my head off with his bare hands.

Dr. Mitchell spent the afternoon calling every contact in Alison's cell phone. I called Michael, who had of course not heard from her, but promised to keep in touch with Roxie, who might. I was afraid to use my phone further in case the kidnappers should try to call.

With nothing else to do, I retired to my room, sat on the bed, and prayed. I prayed for Alison's safety. I prayed for wisdom and guidance for myself. I did not pray for forgiveness from Alison's father as I did not believe I deserved it.

When the telephone rang downstairs just after five o'clock, I rushed to the kitchen, where Dr. Mitchell clutched the phone receiver in both hands, his face as white as a sheet. "It's for you," he said in a strangled voice. His hand shook as he held the receiver out to me.

I grabbed the phone and shouted into it, "Alison? It's you?"

"So sorry to disappoint you, Joseph," said a man with a gruff voice, "although Alison is here with me."

"I wish to speak to her."

"Hold your horses there, bucko, you're not the one

calling the shots here. You—"

"I will speak to her! Now!" I demanded, my voice so full of authority that it surprised me. "I will not listen to you until I know she's all right."

There was a moment of silence during which I thought I would die of nerves. Then Alison came on the line, her words running one into the next. "Joseph? Oh my God I'm so sorry I never should've opened the door! He said he was looking for his dog—for Fleur—except of course, it wasn't true. He just wanted me to open the door so they could grab me. They took me to—to get to you. They—"

"Are you hurt? If they touched you, I—"

There was a muffled sound, and the man came back on the line. "Sorry, Joseph, that's all you get. Proof of life. Now, let's get down to business…"

"I will do whatever you wish to have her back safe."

"I'm counting on it."

I could almost hear the sneer in the man's voice. I thought I had probably never hated someone in all my life as much as I hated this man at this moment. "What do you want?"

"Well… as you've probably guessed, we don't actually want the girl. We want you. But as a little token of appreciation for getting her back, we want you to bring us, say… one million dollars in twenties and fifties… when you come. Unmarked bills, of course. I'll call you back Wednesday night at six o'clock. That'll give you forty-eight hours to get the money."

"I do not have one million dollars in my bank account," I admitted as my mind raced ahead to how I would do this, "but I will have it Wednesday."

"That's a good boy," the man said with a chuckle. "I

must say you're being far more cooperative than I expected. You must really care about your girlfriend. Now, one last thing: no police. I assume you've already called them and that's okay. They won't find her even if they're bothering to look. But don't call them back. If I so much as suspect you've involved them further, the deal is off. And no media. If I see Alison's pretty little face on the news, the deal is off. In either case, things won't turn out well as far as you and Alison are concerned. Do you understand?"

"Yes," I said slowly, trying to think of something defiant to say but coming up with nothing. "I understand."

"Good. Until Wednesday at six, then." The line went dead.

I did not have to tell Dr. Mitchell of the conversation. He had listened over my shoulder the entire time. Instead, I said, "I'm so sorry. I will make this right."

"You'd better believe you will, or you'll be much, much sorrier," he said, sounding not so much like a doctor as perhaps a medieval Catholic Church inquisitor.

With nothing I could say to this, I retired to my bedroom to call the only person who could help me now. Élisabeth answered, her voice slurred with sleep. "Joseph?" she said in French when I asked for our mother. "Do you know what time it is here?"

"No, uh... yes, I suppose it's close to midnight."

"What's going on? Something's wrong, I can tell by your voice."

"Yes, everything's wrong. Please Élisabeth, get *Maman*. I must speak with her immediately."

A couple minutes later, my mother came on the line.

Rather than sounding sleepy, her voice was sharp with concern. "What's happened now?"

"I have a problem, *Maman*. It's Alison…"

"Joseph," said my mother, her voice a mixture of relief and disappointment. "Don't tell me you called at this hour to talk about problems with your girlfriend."

"I wish it were only that," I admitted with a sigh. And because she had to understand how important Alison was—not only to me personally, but to the future of our bloodline and to the whole world—I told her everything.

I described the out-of-body experience I'd had when my heart stopped at the hospital. The visions I'd had while unconscious. The possibility that if I married Isobel or some other woman out of obligation to the bloodline, our son would grow up to be the one people would call the Antichrist. That if I married for love, our son would declare his heritage and somehow bring peace to the world. I told her how I felt about Alison and how I sincerely believed that she was the one I would marry. Finally, I told her about Alison being kidnapped and what the men wanted—money and me, and then probably more money—and I assured her that no matter what happened, I would protect our secret.

"So, we must transfer funds from one of the Swiss bank accounts to my bank here in New Haven," I finished in desperation. "They want one million US dollars, but I think we should transfer two million—just in case."

"Of course," my mother said after a long pause during which I could hear her breathe. "I'll call the *Crédit Suisse* Bank first thing in the morning. And I'll also call… Joseph, I've held off until now as you've wished. But I have to call the *Prieuré de Sion*. I have to call Benjamin. They need to know of this and I'm sure you know… They can help."

I hated to admit this, but I knew she was right. "Yes, of course. But they must be discreet," I warned her. "If the kidnappers suspect something they may panic. I don't believe these men are killers, but one never knows. Look what happened with Philippe and Gregory."

We spoke for a few more minutes, making arrangements for what had to be done. When I ended the call, I rose and turned to find Alison's father standing in the doorway, his jaw hanging slack in a clear state of shock.

"Dr. Mitchell! I did not see you—uh—do you speak French?"

"Took five years in high school," he said in a low, shattered voice.

"And you heard? You understood?" I asked as I reached him.

"Enough." His face was more gray than white, with splotches of red in his cheeks. "What kind of world do you live in, Joseph? That you have millions of dollars in a Swiss bank account and speak of your son becoming the Antichrist like that's something you actually believe?"

"*Bon Dieu*… I live in the same world as you, Dr. Mitchell, except that I know of truths that you do not. *Bien*… you now know a wee bit more. To be—"

"But Alison knows?" he interrupted.

It was a few seconds before I answered, "Yes, she knows."

"Oh, dear Lord," the poor man said with a shake of his head. He rubbed one hand across his eyes and gazed at me as if seeing me for the first time. "I knew you were hiding something, but I stupidly chose to ignore my intuition. I… how could anyone. I don't understand how this could be possible or what your sacred bloodline is all about, but it… it sounds like it would be some kind of earth-shaking revelation if it were made public."

"*Oui,* it would be," I admitted. "I'm sorry that you heard what you heard, Dr. Mitchell, but I must ask you now to forget every word of it."

Dr. Mitchell did not reply but turned and walked away, leaving me alone with one more thing weighing on my heart.

****

I managed to sleep for a few hours before rising to dress. I made and drank some coffee. I had no appetite for food and was surprised that the coffee stayed down.

I spent much of Tuesday on my phone, speaking with people at the *Crédit Suisse*, people in the *Prieuré de Sion*, people at my bank here in New Haven. I called Aunt Marguerite to tell her what was happening, and my mother to tell her that things were being arranged.

Roxie called three times in increasing panic to ask if I had any news from Alison. I lied through my teeth, telling her no, but I would let her know as soon as I did. I told the same thing to Officer Spencer when she called that afternoon.

Dr. Mitchell had called in sick to the clinic to hover at my side all day, but whether to offer support or to make sure that I did not run away—although I would never think of doing this—I was not sure.

I did not go to school on Wednesday, but I kept my physical therapy appointment if for no other reason than to pass the time. I forced myself to eat simply to keep up my strength and prayed repeatedly for Alison's safety.

At five minutes past four, the manager of my local bank called to tell me that he had my money and that I should come immediately to collect it.

"I'll come with you," Dr. Mitchell said, and not only because he did not look like he would accept "no" for an answer, but because I was quite sure my left arm was not up to carrying heavy bags of money, I accepted.

We gathered my backpack and Alison's, my gym bag and his, and took his SUV with him driving to my bank. The manager was waiting for us at the front door. He ushered us in silence into his private office and locked the door behind us even though the bank was closed.

"We had to get your money from the Federal Reserve," he said. "You'll have some fees to pay."

"Yes, of course, take them from my account," I replied, impatiently waving this off as of no consequence and signing all the papers he put in front of me without bothering to read them.

The manager gave me a long look as I passed the documents back to him. "Whatever emergency you need this money for, I hope you get it sorted out safely. If there's anything else I can do… please let me know."

"Yes. Thank you."

There was a knock on the door, and the manager opened it. A staff member came in pushing a trolley loaded with stacks of bills.

We counted the money as we filled our bags, thanked the manager once more, and hurried out to our car.

"Is that something you do a lot of?" Dr. Mitchell asked me in a dry voice halfway to his home.

"Withdrawing a million dollars in cash?"

"Not a lot," I replied with a grim attempt at humor to relieve the tension between us. "No. I've never done this before."

"What if they take you in exchange for Alison? You think they might, don't you?"

"Yes, to be honest, I think this," I admitted. "If they do, my mother will sign whatever papers she must and you will return to the bank for more money if they ask for it, yes?" I glanced at him and he gave me a dark look back.

"Yes," he said finally, although to be honest he sounded as if he would rather not. "I guess I will."

We passed a non-descript beige sedan parked on Ridge Road a block from the Mitchells' house. Dr. Mitchell did not seem to notice it, but I did.

The Prieuré de Sion. Bien, they made it in time.

In time for what, exactly, I did not dare to think.

Chapter 19

The Priory of Sion
Alison

If I had to be kidnapped and held captive, I supposed I was lucky to have been taken by these particular men. They kept me locked in the boarded-up bedroom but provided a couple middle-grade girl-and-her-horse novels to help me pass the time. I couldn't help wondering where those had come from. I was let out—always escorted by the black man—to use the bathroom three times a day. I even got to take a shower Wednesday morning. They fed me corn flakes and milk for breakfast and something from a can or a microwaved pasta dish for lunch and supper. Bottled water and cola. I hoped this meant they actually intended to release me alive and well once Joseph paid the ransom.

"I shouldn't be tellin' you this, but we're gonna meet up with your boyfriend back at his house," the black man told me at eight o'clock Wednesday night when he came to let me out for my last bathroom run.

"Okay, that's good. Joseph will pay you and—what? You'll just let me go?" I replied hopefully.

Rather than answering, he leaned against the dresser to face me. I was still sitting on the bed. "I'm real sorry things went down this way. Gregory Lorraine just hired me to watch the house, you know. I wasn't in on Joseph's kidnappin' and I didn't go for how he was bein' treated. When Joseph escaped, that bastard Lorraine refused to pay us unless we got him back. We all went after him but me and Ke—my partner here—we got the feelin' things were goin' south in a bad way. We bailed before the shit hit the fan. Good thing, too. We heard on the news that someone offed Lorraine. Don't know who—"

"It was the big guy," I told him. "Alec."

"Yeah?" His eyebrows shot up. "Well, that don't surprise me. He was pretty pissed about the not gettin' paid thing."

I stood up and walked closer to the man, aware that he was probably armed, yet feeling somehow that I wasn't in danger from him. "Why are you doing this? I mean, you don't really seem like... you know..." I shrugged.

"Like what? The criminal type?" He gave me a tight smile, but his hooded brown eyes were filled with regret. "My partner's not a nice guy. This is his farm, d'ya know that? Yup. Wife up and left with the kids a couple o' years ago after she had enough of him beatin' on them all."

As I thought, *Kids? Well, I guess that explains the books*, he went on, "He's got a gamblin' problem, owes a lot o' money to some real bad people. If he doesn't pay them back soon, he'll be up shit creek without a paddle, lose the farm and maybe his life. He's been from one questionable job to the next, tryin' to make some fast money so he can pay off his debts and disappear to that tropical island he was talkin' about." He gave a heavy sigh. "Me? I'm not like him, you got that right. I... uh..."

He looked down at his feet, around the room, finally back at me. "I'm just doing this for my baby girl. She's got a heart defect. Needs an operation. It's scheduled for December twelfth, but when I lost my job a couple months back, I lost our insurance too." He blinked. "I couldn't go home and tell my wife I'd worked a week at what was supposed to be a han'some job and not got a good goddamn cent. So when Ke—oh hell, his name's Kevin and I'm Chuck—called me about the ransom idea, I put in with him. Half a mil each? I could save my little girl and have some money left over to give my wife the life she deserves."

I never would have imagined I could feel compassion for my kidnappers, but I did. At least for this one. "If you'd just asked Joseph for the money, he probably would've given it to you with no strings attached," I said.

The man's eyes widened. "You think?"

I nodded. "He's a true humanitarian. All he wants to do is save the world."

"He'll probably feel different about things now," the man said miserably. He pushed off from the dresser and tried to resume his tough guy persona. "Go on down to the bathroom and do your stuff."

With my "stuff" taken care of, Chuck locked me back in my room. I heard the rumble of the van's motor a few minutes later and sank down on the bed to wait. Having had time to do nothing but think, I'd come to the conclusion that Fleur hadn't shown up in Joseph's yard by accident. The men—or more likely, Joseph's cousin Gregory—had abandoned her there with the idea that she might distract them from their usual vigilance. He'd planned everything—except of course, it had all gone horribly wrong.

Finally, after the longest two hours of my life, I

heard the van pull up, followed by the slam of doors and the faint mumble of loud voices downstairs. *Joseph?* I couldn't tell.

I listened with my ear pressed to the door but couldn't make out anything that was happening. Some time later, I heard the sound of footsteps at the top of the stairs—it sounded like two men at least, one of them stumbling and bumping into the wall. The door to the room across the hall from mine opened and closed. After a few minutes it opened and closed again.

The key rattled in the lock to my door, and I sprang to the far side of the room to avoid being smacked in the face when it opened.

But it didn't open, and I heard one set of footsteps fade as whoever it was walked away toward the stairs. I counted off ten minutes in case one of the men came back, then I tried the door and almost fell on my backside when it immediately opened inward. Unbelievably, I found the door to the room across the hallway also unlocked. I cracked it open but could see nothing in the darkness.

"Joseph?" I whispered as I stepped inside, carefully closing the door behind me. "Are you in here? It's me. Turn on the light."

"I cannot," he said from somewhere to my right.

"What? Why not?" I asked, suddenly afraid he was injured. I fumbled along the wall for a light switch, found it, and turned on the ceiling lamp.

Joseph was sitting on the edge of the bare-mattressed bed, blindfolded, his hands bound together behind his back.

"Oh my—Joseph! Hang on just a sec!" Kneeling on the bed, I yanked off his blindfold and unwrapped the duct tape from around his wrists. I looked hard at him. He was unshaved, his hair stood up in greasy little spikes, and the dark rings below his eyes told me he hadn't slept well in far too long. Since I was taken, I guessed. "Are you okay?"

"Yes," he said, absently massaging his left shoulder with his right hand and blinking repeatedly in the light. "How did you—?"

I cut him off by throwing my arms around his neck, heedless of his tender shoulder, and inhaled the good, salty smell of him. Between sobs, I exclaimed, "I was so scared, Joseph! I thought what if you don't come up with the money? What if you do and they still don't let me go? What if they take you in my place and I never see you again?" I leaned away from him to look into his eyes. I was dimly aware of tears running down my cheeks, but I no longer cared about appearing brave.

Joseph wrapped his arms around my back, pulled me close again, and kissed me hard and passionately on the lips. "I was afraid too, Alison," he said when we parted to breathe. He blinked away his own welling tears. "I did not think these men are killers, but I could not know for sure." His eyes narrowed as he reached up to gently touch the bruise on my right cheek with the palm of his left hand. "They 'urt you?"

"The white guy hit me when he didn't like how I answered him. Don't worry, I'm fine. What about you? Why'd they tie you up?"

"I do not know. I told them I would come with them, but this same man saw the need to tie my 'ands and put an, uh… eye band—?"

"Blindfold," I said helpfully.

He rolled his eyes at me. "Yes, blindfold… They

also took my phone and my gun. They—"

"Wait—what? You brought a gun?"

"Yes," he said simply, and I wondered if he now thought that was as reckless as I did. He looked me up and down. "'Ow did you get in 'ere?"

"They've been locking me in the bedroom across the hall." I gestured vaguely over my shoulder, still unsettled by the thought of Joseph once again having a gun. "But tonight, someone unlocked the door and left yours unlocked too. I'm pretty sure it was Chuck. He—"

"Chuck?"

"The black guy. The white guy's Kevin."

"Do you know where are we?" Joseph asked. "I think we were on the road per'aps a half hour, but I could not see, so…"

I shook my head. "It's Kevin's farm, but I don't know where exactly. They knocked me out with chloroform or something. I woke up in the back of the van, but I couldn't see any—what are you doing?" I interrupted myself as Joseph rose and began stalking around the room.

"I 'eard something before 'e left me," he said. He opened and closed the closet door. "Something 'eavy." He started pulling drawers open in the dresser, obviously searching for something. "Ah—*oui*!" He reached into the bottom drawer and triumphantly withdrew a black handgun. "'E left my gun!" He checked to see if it was loaded, racked the slide, and smiled grimly.

I gasped. "What are you planning to do with that? Go downstairs and shoot them in cold blood?"

"If I must." For all his talk of peace and wanting to make the world a better place, the look on his face sent a shudder down my spine.

"You can't do that! They just want money. Kevin's a horrible person who beat his wife and kids and has a bunch of gambling debts to pay before he runs off to some tropical island somewhere. But Chuck's different. His baby daughter needs heart surgery, Joseph. He lost his insurance, and he needs the money to pay for it. He had nothing to do with Gregory's kidnapping you the first time and he's sorry they had to take me. He must've unlocked our doors and left your gun for you to find. He—"

"They do not only want money, Alison," Joseph cut me off as he slipped the gun into the right-hand pocket of the gray leather jacket he and I had chosen together only days ago. "They took you to make me come peacefully and bring some money with me. But they know from Gregory that I 'ave a secret. They—*bien alors*, the white man—Kevin? 'E wishes to know my secret and then I think 'e will ask for more money to not tell anyone of it. I do not believe 'e will let either one of us go anytime soon."

"Oh. My. God. What are you—we—going to do?" I said again. "We have to get out of here."

"Yes," Joseph agreed, nodding. "Alison, men are coming from the *Prieuré de Sion.* They will study the situation 'ere and then they will come in and get us."

I gasped. "What? H-how will they do that?"

"I do not know," he said, "but they 'ave their ways."

For some reason, this wasn't a comforting thought.

"Come," Joseph said, gesturing for me to follow him. "Stay be'ind me." He cautiously opened the door, but just as he was stepping out into the hallway, we heard low voices and heavy footfalls on the stairs.

"*Merde!*" Joseph hissed. He closed the door again

and pushed me toward the bed. "They're coming."

A moment later the door to the room was flung open and Kevin entered, followed a few steps behind by Chuck.

"Well, well, what've we got here?" Kevin inquired with a sneer. He glared over his shoulder at Chuck. "Looks like some dumb ass forgot to lock the door. *Again*." He pulled a handgun from the holster on his hip and nonchalantly waved it at Chuck before pointing it at my head. "I'll take care of that later. For now, how about you sit on the bed like a good girl, and your boyfriend can just stand there with his hands where I can see them, and we'll have a little chat?"

I looked at Joseph, who gave me an almost imperceptible nod. With my heart racing in my throat, I did as I was told, sinking onto the mattress with my hands on my knees to stop them from shaking.

"Now," said Kevin with a dark look at Joseph, although he lowered his gun slightly. "I want to know what the big secret is. Obviously, your dear cousin Gregory wanted you to come clean about something. I even searched your family name on Google, but all I got was some historical shit about the Hapsburg-Lorraine dynasty and some half-baked conspiracy theories about the Holy Grail and a friggin' Jesus bloodline. I want to know the truth, and I want to know how much you'll pay me to keep the secret."

"You wish to know my secret?" Joseph asked in a bone-chilling tone of voice I never would have imagined coming from his mouth.

"Joseph… don't." My words came out in a terrified croak.

"You wish to know my secret?" A little bit louder.

"That's what I said, isn't it?" Kevin retorted, but for the first time he seemed unsure of himself. He looked sideways at Chuck, who wisely shuffled two steps away.

And that was the opportunity Joseph needed. He whipped the gun from his pocket and pointed it one-handed at Kevin's chest. "The secret is… if I tell you my secret, I will 'ave to kill you. This is not a joke."

The two kidnappers gaped at this sudden change of affairs, although Chuck seemed less shocked than Kevin.

"You will put down the gun," Joseph said with all the authority of a future world leader. "If you point it at Alison again, I will shoot you."

Apparently thinking he would call Joseph's bluff, Kevin raised his gun.

Joseph fired.

I screamed and scuttled backward on the bed to press myself against the wall. My nostrils filled with a sort of smoky chemical smell and for a few seconds, I couldn't breathe.

Kevin dropped his gun with a clatter and fell to his knees, his face contorted in pain and his hands clutched to a dark red patch growing over the lower right side of his sweater.

Chuck leapt forward and snatched up Kevin's gun from the floor as I drew breath and yelled at Joseph not to shoot him.

But Chuck didn't point the gun at Joseph or me. He pointed it—albeit shakily—at Kevin. "You greedy bastard!" he bellowed. "You weren't going to let them leave, were you? Or maybe not any of us, once you got all the money you wanted. You'd be afraid we could identify you."

"You friggin' traitor," Kevin hissed with all the

venom he could muster through his pain. "Coward! I should've known you'd cave on—" He didn't have the breath to finish his line of accusations.

Everyone seemed to freeze for a moment, then as my eardrums recovered from the shock of the gunshot, I heard a thud downstairs like the sound of a door being kicked in. Running footsteps and men's voices calling urgently in French.

"Put down the gun!" Joseph yelled at Chuck. "If you wish to live, do it now!"

Chuck placed the gun on the floor.

"Kick it away from you. Over 'ere." Joseph gestured with his head to the floor at his feet. "Put your 'ands in the air."

Chuck did as commanded and clasped his hands behind his head. "Look man, I didn't want nothin' to do with anyone gettin' hurt. I don't care about your big family secret. I just needed the money for my—"

"For your wee girl. Yes, I know," Joseph said, his gun still trained on Kevin. Without looking away, he shouted something in French.

About five seconds later, the door flew open. Three men dressed in military-style black pants, bomber jackets, and caps burst into the room, firearms drawn and pointing at Chuck and Kevin, who had managed to regain his feet but didn't look like he would remain standing for long. One of them picked up Kevin's gun and shoved it into his belt.

There was an urgent exchange of French between Joseph and the first man into the room. Joseph put his gun away and continued speaking to the men from the Priory of Sion while they kept their eyes on the kidnappers.

I managed to sit up on the edge of the bed but didn't dare to move more.

Joseph turned to Chuck. "Go away from 'ere. Take the money, as much as you need. Go 'ome and take care of your wee girl. Forget you ever saw us."

Chuck's jaw dropped and he blinked a couple times. "You gotta be kiddin' me."

"One of these men will go with you." He said something in French to the men. "Go now."

Poor Chuck didn't need to be told twice. He turned and marched out of the room with the youngest looking of the Priory of Sion men behind him.

"What about him?" I asked, pointing at Kevin who was sinking slowly to his knees with a low groan of pain.

"We'll take care of him, Miss Alison," the older man who seemed to be the leader of the Priory of Sion men replied with only the slightest French accent. "You needn't worry about him anymore." He continued speaking to Joseph in French in a familiar tone that made me think the two of them knew each other. If I wasn't mistaken, Joseph called him Ben.

Joseph took me by the arm and helped me to my feet. I was trembling so hard, I could barely stand. "Come," he said. "We must leave this place now."

My strength came back as we walked down the hallway, and I was able to handle the stairs on my own. In the kitchen, we paused at the table where Joseph's cell phone lay beside his backpack and my dad's old gym bag, both of which were filled to bulging.

"'E took only two bags of the four," Joseph remarked in surprise. He picked up his cell and shoved it into a front pocket of his jeans.

"All he wanted was to pay for his daughter's

operation," I told him, reaching for one bag as he grabbed the other with his good hand.

We hurried outside and around to the front of the house under a light but cold rain. The van was gone, and the young Priory of Sion man was waiting for us beside a beige four-door halfway down the driveway.

We'd almost reached the car when we heard three gunshots ring out from inside the house.

I let out an involuntary screech and spun around, but the man from the car rushed forward and grabbed me by the elbow. "Come *mademoiselle*, now," he said in a thick accent.

Then, somehow, I was in the back seat of the car with Joseph beside me, his arm around my shoulders, as the other man put the bags of money in the trunk. I realized my feet were soaking wet and I'd lost one of my slippers. I was shivering. Weeping. "Don't tell me—Joseph, your men—they didn't—"

Joseph pulled me close against him and whispered in my ear. "These men protect the sacred bloodline at all costs, Alison. I could not stop them if I wished to."

"B-but they let Chuck go?"

"Yes. Chuck was innocent. A good man caught in a bad situation. If he truly cares about 'is family, I think 'e will not look to bother us in the future."

The Frenchman got behind the wheel and off we went. No one spoke. I stared numbly out the window, disjointed snippets of things Joseph had told me about his family and the Priory of Sion mixed up with fragments of images from tonight spinning through my mind, until about forty minutes later we pulled into the driveway at Joseph's house. I'd stopped crying and was now feeling somewhat like I'd awakened from a dream.

A very bad dream.

The driver escorted us from the sedan to Joseph's car with the two bags of money, which we put into the trunk, then he turned without a word and left again in the beige sedan.

Joseph stashed his gun away beneath his seat and drove us to my home in heavy silence, both of us too exhausted to speak. Or maybe, like me, he was just too lost in his own thoughts to string three words together.

We'd barely reached the top of the stairs when my dad flung the front door open wide. "Oh, Alison!" he exclaimed, and for the first time since Mom's funeral, he burst into tears.

Chapter 20

The Whole Story
Joseph

On the way back to town I relived over and over the heart-stopping and regrettable moment when I shot another human being. The recoil of the pistol. The expression of pain and surprise on the man called Kevin's face. My own surprise at having actually hit him. It did not help to know that had I not shot him, he very well might have shot Alison and me. It did not help to know that I had not killed him.

Once arrived at the Mitchells' house, I took a long, steaming shower in hopes of washing away the dirty memory running through my mind. Unfortunately, the water did not help either. I dried off, pulled on some boxers, and trudged to my bedroom wondering if Alison would ever speak to me again. I dropped my dirty clothes on the closet floor and only had time to fall exhausted into bed before hearing three tentative knocks on my bedroom door.

"Joseph?" Alison's voice was barely audible through the door. "Can I come in?"

"Uh… yes. Come!" I threw back my covers and swung my legs over the side of the bed.

Alison entered my room as I turned on the lamp on my bedside table. She wore a white *camisole* and light blue leggings I assumed were her pajamas. Her damp hair hung loose around her shoulders.

"I'm sorry," she said, her voice trembling. "I didn't want to be alone tonight."

"Come," I said again, immensely relieved that she wanted to see me at all. I patted the mattress beside me.

Alison sat, hands clasping her knees and her head bowed, appearing not to notice or care about my bare legs and chest, although her gaze did fall for a couple seconds on the thin red scar along my collarbone.

I realized at this moment that I did not wish to be alone either, but I remained silent, waiting for her to speak.

Finally, without looking at me, she did. "We can't keep lying to my dad, Joseph. I don't think he believed the half of it, anyway."

After his tearful reunion with his daughter, Dr. Mitchell had demanded to know everything that had happened to us. I had lied through my teeth, telling him that the kidnappers had let us go after deciding to take only half of the money. That they had blindfolded us and driven us back to my house. We could not identify them because they had worn ski masks the entire time we were with them. Alison had backed up everything I said without hesitation. Dr. Mitchell had called the police to tell them that we were safe and arranged for them to come in the afternoon to take our statements.

"I know." I sighed heavily. "Tomorrow morning—*bien*, later this morning—we will think of something better to tell him, yes? Right now, I need to sleep."

"Don't make me go," she pleaded, surprising me. "Please. Can't we just… just sleep here together? You don't even have to put your arm around me or anything, if you don't want to." Tears stood in her eyes, making them bright. "I just don't want to be alone," she said again, her voice barely more than a whisper.

I turned off the lamp and lay down on my back, inviting her to join me under the covers in the narrow twin bed. She cuddled by my right side and after a moment I turned toward her to rest my left arm over her. She smelled lovely, of freshly washed hair and lavender. My heart skipped a beat before resuming again at a normal rhythm. My life's priority having always been the protection of my bloodline, I had never before been in bed with a girl, but I was too exhausted—physically and emotionally—to feel uncomfortable, embarrassed, or even excited by her presence tonight.

Alison turned toward me and nuzzled closer, her cheek against my chest, and while I tried to think of something intelligent and perhaps sweet to say, her deep and even breathing told me that she had already fallen asleep.

A few minutes later I had done the same.

****

"Oh, my good Lord!"

My eyes popped open and Alison, who had been sleeping wrapped in my arms, literally leapt from the bed at the sound of her father's voice.

"Dad! What the—what are you doing in here?" she shrieked. "How dare you—"

"Go to your room, Alison," Dr. Mitchell said in a voice full of venom from the middle of the room. "I'll deal with you later. You—" he added, pointing at me with an index finger that shook with rage as Alison ran past him into the hallway. "Get up and get packed! I want you out of my house by the end of the day. If I ever see your face around here again, if I hear that you've been seeing Alison, I'll call the police on you so fast you won't know what hit you."

My pulse pounding in my head from the sudden awakening, I sat up on the side of the bed. "You make a mistake," I said as calmly as I could when what I really wished to do was scream in frustration back at him.

"I made a mistake, all right," Alison's father agreed, "a big one, the moment I let you come into my house."

"Dad!" Alison was back, a fleecy white housecoat hastily wrapped around her, the belt trailing on the floor. "I know what you're thinking but you're totally wrong! Nothing happened! And even if it did, I'm an adult, you know!"

Dr. Mitchell continued to glare murderously at me. Clearly, he had noticed that I was half naked. I stood and said, "Alison did not wish to be alone last night, nor did I. We slept together. This is all we did, and I'm not sorry for it."

Even as the words left my mouth, I realized that this was perhaps not the best thing to say to Alison's irate father. His face was crimson, and his voice trembled when he spoke. "I knew you were trouble from the start, with your money and your secrets and your dubious interest in my dau—"

"Stop it, Dad!" Alison shouted, grabbing her father's arm. "You don't understand!"

"He cannot understand," I said to her. "There are too many things he does not know." Looking directly into the man's bloodshot blue eyes, I continued, "Dr. Mitchell... please go downstairs and wait for me. I will wash and dress and when I'm ready, I will come down and explain things to you as best I can."

"I want you out of our lives," Dr. Mitchell repeated,

but something in my voice or my face had settled him, and these words lacked conviction. He turned toward his daughter. "You know the rules, Alison. As long as you live under my roof… Just get dressed," he blurted before turning and stomping from the room.

"Oh my God, Joseph, I never thought he'd find us like that." Alison rubbed her hands over her face and ran her fingers through her disheveled hair. "I didn't think at all! I'm so sorry—"

"It's all right, Alison. I will take care of everything."

"What? How?" Her hands dropped to her sides. Her eyes widened with horror, and I realized that she must be thinking of the way Benjamin's men had taken care of Kevin the kidnapper.

"No! Not this way. *Bon Dieu!* I will tell him the truth."

Half an hour later, I sat at the kitchen table with Alison and her father, preparing to give what would perhaps prove to be the most important discourse of my life. Cups of coffee sat untouched in front of us.

Dr. Mitchell glared at me from across the table. "You'd better come up with a damn good reason for me not to have you hauled off the premises when the police come."

"Yes, no worries. I 'ave a very good reason." I might have laughed had the situation not been so dire. "Alison knows some of this but not all, so I will tell both of you the whole story as I understand it. I'm afraid even I don't know everything." Greeted only by two pairs of inquiring blue eyes, I cleared my throat and began at the very beginning.

"Over two thousand years ago, the man you know as Jesus Christ was born in Judea. Was he a *rabbin*? A divine man? The one and only Son of God? To be honest, I do not know. He was certainly a spiritual man who tried to teach his people of God. He was prepared to die on the cross, to show the world that he was not afraid. That there was—is—life after death.

"But he did not die on the cross. His followers took him down and placed him in the tomb of Joseph of Arimathea, where he was cared for by Mary of Magdala—yes, his wife—and his close friends and family. After three days, he was strong enough to rise and he was taken to a safe place. When he was enough recovered, he traveled to the south of France with Mary and some others. They did not remain always in France but traveled, perhaps as far as India. Over time, they had three children. The first—"

"This is utter nonsense!" Dr. Mitchell exclaimed bluntly at this point. He slammed a hand down on the table. "A made-up story to sell books and movies!"

"You may look it up for yourself," I replied calmly.

"Where? On the internet? I wouldn't believe anything I see—"

"In the Holy Bible. The Book of Acts…"

Dr. Mitchell pushed back his chair, shot to his feet without a word, and left the kitchen. He returned a moment later with a Bible in his hand and resumed his seat.

"The Book of Acts," I repeated, "Chapter Six, Verse Seven."

Dr. Mitchell thumbed through the thick black book, stopping at the appropriate page to read, his lips moving with the words. What little color he had in his face drained, and he became white as a sheet.

"What?" Alison asked, leaning toward him. "Dad?

What does it say?"

"It says…" He coughed, appearing to have trouble finding his voice, and finally read, " 'And the word of God increased.' "

"There is also Acts Chapter Twelve, Verse Twenty-four," I added, reciting in French as he followed on the page with his finger, " '*Cependant, la parole de Dieu se repandait et progressait.*' "

" 'The word of God grew and multiplied,' " repeated Dr. Mitchell in English.

"*Oui.* You may think that these passages speak of preaching, but since Jesus was often referred to as the *Logos*—the Word—this actually means—"

"That he reproduced," whispered Alison, pressing her hands to her cheeks. "It's right there in the Bible. Oh. My…"

"They had three children," I continued patiently, seeing how disturbing it was for them to hear this. "The first was a daughter, Tamar, born in the year thirty-three. The second was a son, Jesus, who is called the Justus, born in the year thirty-seven, and finally Josephes, born in the year forty-four. The line of Tamar died out. The line of Josephes descended through what history calls the Fisher kings, the Merovingian kings of the Franks, and the house of Hapsburg-Lorraine. It was believed that the line of Jesus the Justus ended with the death of his great-grandson Josue, but it did not.

"It went underground in France and remained secret to avoid persecution by the Catholic Church. There was much marrying between members of the *Desposyni*—the descendants of the family of Jesus Christ, you know?—eventually giving my family the name *de Lorraine* for the region in France where we lived, but the line of Jesus the Justus was not broken. I am the many times grandson of this man, the eldest son of Jesus Christ." I stopped, sipping my long cold coffee to ease my dry throat, and waited for some kind of response.

"Go on," Dr. Mitchell said with a grimace after taking his own large gulp of coffee. The cup shook in his hand.

I glanced at Alison, who nodded. I was encouraged by the fact that neither of them had yet run to call the police or the psychiatric hospital.

"Jesus Christ and Mary both died at an old age. I do not know where but at some point, their *ossuaires* were placed in a tomb in Jerusalem. During the *Croisades*—uh, the Crusades—the Knights Templar found these along with other treasures and brought them to France. They buried the bones in coffins in a tomb in a sacred place. When the Templars were arrested in 1307, the secret of this place was lost but for some signs... uh, clues... in some parchments that they managed to hide.

"Late in the nineteenth century, a country priest called François Bérenger Saunière found some of these parchments when he renovated his St. Mary Magdalene Church in the village of Rennes-le-Chateau, in the south of France. The church paid Saunière generously to destroy them, but he did not do this. Instead, he gave them to his maid and *confidante*, Marie Denarnaud. She could not read them as they were written in Latin, but she shared them with her friend, Antoine St. Clair, who could. Antoine fought in the First World War with my great-grandfather, Joseph Marc de Lorraine. Joseph saved Antoine's life at the *Bataille de la Somme* and after the end of the war, they remained close friends. Since both St. Clair and de Lorraine are named in the parchments, they decided together to explore the secret of Rennes-le-Chateau.

"One of the parchments tells stories of Jesus that do not appear in the Holy Bible. Stories of his life and death. It's almost certainly a copy of an earlier text taken from the great library at Alexandria, in Egypt. This is perhaps the reason why Pope Theophilus ordered the library destroyed in the fourth century, you know? He did not wish certain information—certain truths—to become known. Two other parchments tell the *généalogies* of the main bloodline families to the eighteenth century. These include the line of Jesus the Justus. My line. A fourth text gives clues through a sort of riddle for the location of the tomb where Jesus and Mary were buried in the south of France. My great-grandfathers solved the riddle and found the tomb. They opened the tomb and the coffins— yes, I know, they desecrated a sacred place—and they retrieved wee bits of bone to prove that they had found the tomb. But they never told exactly where it is; I know only that it's in the region of *Pech Cardou*.

"Seven years ago, we had tests made on the bones. The *laboratoire* of Oxford University dated them to the first century. More important... DNA testing made at the University of Copenhagen showed a lineage with my family. My parents, my sisters, and I are descendants of the two persons in the tomb. If they are Mary and Jesus as we believe, this is proof, yes?"

Dr. Mitchell let out a sort of pained groan. Alison gaped at me, her eyes wide and her hands clamped to her cheeks.

I pushed on, anxious now to finish this tale. "The parchments also have been examined and dated between the twelfth century for the oldest parts and the eighteenth century for the most recent parts. Along with several other rare texts, the bones, and the results of the tests, these are now in a safe deposit box in a secure Swiss bank. Only my family and some people very close to the secret know these things."

Suddenly out of words and needing some fresh air to clear my mind, I rose and went outside to the back yard with Fleur at my heels. I wished a vision would come to me, would tell me what to do or say, but *hélas*, this did not happen.

When I returned to the kitchen fifteen minutes later not feeling much better but determined to finish my tale, Dr. Mitchell asked me, "So the Catholic Church is paying your family to keep quiet about your presumed legacy? That's where you get your money?"

I was surprised at his question, although perhaps I should not have been. "Alison told you this?"

He nodded grimly.

"Yes," I admitted, "since over three hundred years."

"It's an incredible story," he conceded after a few seconds. "Absolutely incredible. But what the hell does it have to do with my daughter or the Antichrist?"

"Ah, *Dieu*, yes, I must explain this to you." I thought for a moment how to do this. "*Bien alors*… Antoine and Joseph Marc dreamed of uniting their families to make the bloodline stronger, you know? This happened finally when my mother, Marie-Chantal St. Clair, married my father, René Robert Joseph de Lorraine."

I went on to tell him the reason why Gregory had had me kidnapped the first time. I told him about the visions I'd had while in the hospital. About my role in preparing the world for the coming of my son, whom I would make sure would not become the Antichrist.

About my very real and growing feelings for Alison. My wish to marry her when the time came. All the while I was aware of Alison's eyes on me and eventually, aware of the tears running down her cheeks.

"The kidnappers didn't let you go, did they?" the poor man asked when I paused. "Tell me how you got away." He looked as shaken as someone who had just survived a bombing or some such traumatic event. I supposed that in his mind, he had.

"To be honest, I do not believe they would have let us go," I admitted. "There's a very old society called the *Prieuré de Sion,* which guards the true teachings of Jesus Christ and the secret of the sacred bloodline. It keeps members of the bloodline families safe at all costs. Particularly the eldest child of each generation, as I am. Men from this society came last night to help us escape." I looked briefly at Alison, then back to her father. "Please do not ask me how or what they did. I cannot tell you because I do not exactly know. This is their way of protecting me."

"Oh, good heavens," Dr. Mitchell moaned, pressing his hands to his face. "Good Lord! Somebody pinch me, please. I'm having one hell of a bad dream."

I was still searching for a reply to this when the two dogs began barking. Seconds later, the doorbell rang.

"That would be the police," said Dr. Mitchell, pushing to his feet, and I remembered that they were to come for our statements.

"We will tell them what we told you last night," I said quickly before the man left to answer the door. "We do not know where we were because the men put blindfolds on us in the van. They wore black ski masks. They changed their minds, took only half of the money, and let us go. We will not… how do you say this… press charges? The whole thing was an unfortunate misunderstanding that we now wish only to forget and get on with our lives, yes?"

"All right, fine," he said in a resigned voice. "Whatever you say."

Alison went to the sink, splashed some water on her face, and dried it with the dish towel. "Just pray my dad goes along with it."

I looked hard at her. "Do you think he will not?"

She shrugged. "I don't know, Joseph. I really don't."

Unfortunately, there was no time for prayer. We spent a tense hour telling the police our fabricated story, collaborating with each other on details we made up as we went. *Dieu merci,* Dr. Mitchell went along with everything we said, even though he looked at moments as if his head might explode. Finally, the good officers Spencer and Estevez appeared satisfied with our story. There was little hope of ever catching the kidnappers, they said, but the case would remain open should new evidence turn up that might point to their identities.

About five minutes after the police left, the doorbell rang again. This time, I followed Dr. Mitchell to the door to discover a young African-American woman standing on the porch with a tablet in hand. She introduced herself as Rachel Washington and informed us that she was a reporter with the local television station. She asked me for our story.

I looked past her to the blue and white television van parked across the road.

Merde! Did she follow the police here? Deciding it was better to give her our version of the story rather than have her investigate on her own, I agreed—on condition that neither Alison, nor I, nor Dr. Mitchell appeared on camera.

Rachel Washington reluctantly agreed. Dr. Mitchell invited her in, and we sat with Alison at the kitchen table, drinking fresh coffee made by Alison's father and giving her the exact same story we had given the police.

Eventually satisfied, she thanked us, wished us good luck, and left to give a ten-minute-long report on camera in the road beside the van while we watched discreetly from behind the living room window curtains.

Chapter 21

Decisions
Alison

After that snoopy and overly ambitious reporter left, apparently satisfied with our pack of blatant lies, I put on my jacket and boots and went out to get some fresh air. Last night's rain had stopped, and the sun had decided to come out, warming the afternoon air.

Bax and Fleur appeared from wherever they'd been lurking and trotted outside with me. I threw them a tennis ball, noting absently that Fleur was catching onto the concept of retrieving and seemed to enjoy it.

Some thirty minutes later, I heard the back door open and close. I threw the ball for the dogs one more time and turned to find Joseph sitting in one of the patio chairs.

"Hey," I said, strolling over to join him. He sat slouched against the back of the chair, his legs stretched out and his eyes closed against the sunshine. He hadn't shaved before coming downstairs. Despite the shorter hair, the several days old stubble on his face made him look as mysterious and disreputable as the evening we met. Six weeks ago, by my quick calculations; it seemed like years already. I sank into the chair opposite him and asked tentatively, "Any idea how my dad's doing?"

It was a minute or two before he even looked at me.

Finally, he sat up a bit and replied, "To be honest, I think e's per'aps in shock. 'E went into 'is office and closed the door."

"Oh," I said, my heart sinking.

Joseph sat up straighter, resting his bad arm on the table between us. "I know I 'ave upset 'is world—and yours—and I'm sorry for this, but I will not apologize for who I am."

"No, of course not," I said, searching for the right thing to say. "You have nothing to apologize for, anyway. You're kind and brave. You're an amazing person already and you're going to be a great man in the future. A great leader. I really believe that."

That earned me one of his crooked little smiles. "Come 'ere," he said, gesturing with his head for me to come around to his side of the table.

I got up and went around to sit sideways on his lap. He withdrew his left arm from the table to rest his hand on my thigh. He wrapped his good arm around my waist and pulled me close to his chest. "I think—*non,* I'm afraid—that I cannot be this great man without you, Alison. Please tell me… are you still with me? Or do you wish to never see me again?"

"What? How can you even ask me that?" I exclaimed. The sudden flicker of disappointment at the corners of his eyes made my stomach fall further, to somewhere in the vicinity of my knees. "Joseph! I know we haven't known each other for very long, but I already can't imagine my life without you in it. I'm totally with you, no matter what's ahead for us."

The disappointment melted away and a wide grin broke out on Joseph's face. His chocolate eyes fairly glowed as he looked at me. Into me.

"Ah, *Dieu*, Alison, 'ow is it that I love you so much already?" He hugged me tight with both arms and kissed my hair, his lips moving over to my mouth as I turned toward him.

We sat there for quite some time, nothing else—no one else—on Earth but the two of us. We were brought back to reality when Bax planted himself at the back door and started to bark.

"What is it, boy? Did Fleur make off with your tennis ball?" I asked uneasily. Then I heard the doorbell ring.

Joseph heard it too. He rose so abruptly he nearly dumped me onto the patio, barely catching me by the arm to prevent me landing on my backside.

For a second, I wondered if he had his gun on him but no, he'd left it in his car. As traumatic as events had been last night, I remembered that much. *Did he have time to retrieve it this afternoon?* I had no idea.

"Do you expect someone?" Joseph asked me in a wary voice. "Roxie, per'aps?"

"No, but… it could be her. I mean, I meant to call her. She's got to be worried silly about me."

But it wasn't Roxie who came out the back door a minute later. It was Father Thomas, wearing his somewhat intimidating on-duty clothes complete with stiff white collar beneath his open coat.

"Thomas!" Joseph exclaimed in surprise and something less than delight. "What are you doing 'ere?"

"I just saw the local news," the priest said. He looked straight at me. "You were kidnapped and then released?" When I responded with a vague nod, he added, "I thought maybe you or Joseph"—he glanced at Joseph to my left— "might need to talk about it."

I resisted the urge to giggle as I settled into the chair that Joseph had vacated. "I'm not Catholic," I said, thinking, *And neither is Joseph, if you come right down to it. He's totally faking it.*

"'Ow did you find us?" pressed Joseph, sounding only slightly more welcoming.

Thomas gave him an easy smile. "I'm a priest, Joseph, not a monk. I have internet. I remembered Alison mentioning that her dad's a doctor. I looked him up and dropped by the clinic. The receptionist asked me if I was there about the family emergency. I took a chance and said yes, and when I asked for your address, she was quite happy to give it to me. Guess she couldn't say no to a man of the cloth." The smile faded and he looked back to me. "You don't have to be Catholic to talk to me, Alison. You've been through a traumatic experience, and I'm concerned about you. Both of you."

Once the guys took chairs at the table, Joseph across from me and Thomas between us, to my right, Thomas continued, "I saw on the news there was a fire overnight at a farm north of town, a house burned to the ground. It belonged to a man by the name of Handfield. Karl—no, Kevin, that's it—Kevin Handfield. Apparently, no human remains were found, but police are searching for Handfield. Arson is suspected. I recalled what you told me, Joseph, about your kidnappers setting fire to your home after taking you, and I couldn't help wondering if there was any connection to—"

"No connection," Joseph said promptly. He went on to tell Thomas the same bogus story we'd given the police and the reporter whom I assumed was behind the news report Thomas had seen. We didn't know the identities of the men, nor did we know where they'd

245

taken us. We'd had enough fright and excitement to last a lifetime and we didn't want to pursue the matter.

I sat in silence, my arms crossed over my chest, wondering what had happened to Kevin's body if it wasn't found in the house and realizing I didn't really want to know.

Thomas listened attentively until Joseph was done. Then he leveled a hard look at Joseph. "I have to take you at your word, of course, but I have the definite feeling there's something you're not telling me. It's obviously serious enough that it got both of you abducted in turn so I would suggest, whatever it is, Joseph, that you get out of it while you can. If not for yourself, for your family. For Alison."

Joseph shook his head—rather defiantly, I thought. "Everything I do, I do it for my family, Thomas. Please do not ask me about this again. It's something I cannot get out of, as you say. I cannot tell you more. Thank you for caring enough to come. I will see you Sunday at the homeless shelter, yes?" He rose abruptly, indicating with this gesture that the conversation was over.

Thomas's eyes narrowed doubtfully, then he composed himself, repeated his offer to listen should we decide we wanted to talk, and took his leave through the backyard gate.

"Oh my God, Joseph!" I exclaimed once Thomas was out of earshot. "Do you think he knows... I mean, anything he shouldn't know?"

"No, I do not see 'ow 'e can," he replied, although he didn't look or sound quite as confident as I would have liked. After a few seconds he admitted, "I'm afraid Thomas may be a problem in the future, but I think for now we must forget about 'im. We 'ave already enough to worry about with your father."

We called the dogs and went inside to find my dad sitting in his armchair in the living room, staring blankly at the black television screen and nursing a can of beer.

"The way I see it," Dad said in a low voice once he became aware of our presence, "there are three possibilities…" He paused, waiting for Joseph and me to put away our coats in the hall closet and sit down on the sofa.

Joseph reached over and took my hand in his. Gave it an encouraging squeeze.

My dad raised his eyes to meet Joseph's straight on. "One: you're a pathological liar with an incredible imagination who doesn't give a damn about the difference between truth and lies. You've taken Alison and me for a ride, and you should be writing the next blockbuster bestseller. Two: you are entirely out of your cotton-picking mind and should be committed to a secure psychiatric facility for the rest of your life."

I fidgeted, pressing closer to the comforting form of Joseph's muscled thigh, and waited for number three.

Dad took a long swallow of beer and gripped the can in his fist like a lifeline. "And three: dear Lord, I can hardly believe I'm even saying this, but… three… everything you've told us is exact and true."

"I do not know if it's exact," Joseph admitted reluctantly, "but yes, it's true as far as I know. This is my life."

"And you're in love with my daughter?"

Joseph turned to look at me, his expression as gentle as I'd ever seen it. "*Oui*. I love 'er. I wish to marry 'er when the time is good."

Dad blinked and drew in a deep breath. "Well

then… What are you going to do now?"

"I will go on with my life as I must. Alison is now part of it, make no mistake about this. The real question is, what will you do, Dr. Mitchell?"

For the first time in my life, I experienced what they called "deafening silence" as seconds and then minutes ticked by. I didn't dare look at Joseph or my dad, choosing instead to focus my gaze on the clock that sat on the mantelpiece above the brick fireplace.

The silence was broken by the sound of the doorbell, nearly jolting me out of my seat. The dogs rushed to the door, Bax barking the alarm once again.

"Now who could it be?" Dad asked more to himself than us. "After the police, a reporter, and a priest?" He got up to answer the door and stepped back to let a distinguished-looking, middle-aged man with short, salt-and-pepper hair, wearing a navy overcoat above black trousers into the house.

"Ben," Joseph said, the name whooshing out with his breath. He left me on the sofa and covered the distance to the man in three long strides. Joseph and the visitor embraced the way French men did, with a polite peck on each cheek. Then the older man threw his arms around Joseph and hugged him the way a father would hug his son.

But Joseph's dad is dead, I reminded myself as I got to my feet, only to hover where I stood. I had time to recognize the man as the leader of the Priory of Sion men who had come to our rescue last night. The men who had done something unthinkable to Kevin the kidnapper and covered up the evidence with a fire that burned his house to the ground.

"Alison, Dr. Mitchell," Joseph said as he and the

other man stepped away from each other. "I must introduce to you Benjamin Barreau. He is—was—my father's *aide-de-camp* and my friend Philippe's father."

Mr. Barreau shook my dad's hand. "I'm sorry I didn't come sooner," he said to Joseph in English, "but we had some things to take care of."

Oh my God, I'll bet you did, I thought. I crossed my arms over my chest as if that could protect me from whatever was coming next.

"I did not know if I would see you again so soon," Joseph said, "or if you returned right away to France."

"The others are on their way to the airport as we speak," Mr. Barreau said as we drifted toward the living room. He removed his overcoat and laid it over the arm of the sofa before taking a seat beside Joseph. Dad and I more or less collapsed in the two armchairs. "I stayed… to try to talk some sense into you, Joseph." He continued in French, but whether it was because he preferred speaking in his mother tongue or because he didn't want us to understand, I didn't know, although I suspected the latter. Of course, he didn't know that my dad spoke some French.

Joseph replied to Mr. Barreau in French, and the conversation quickly grew heated. Joseph shot to his feet to pace the room in palpable agitation.

My dad looked pretty much as lost as I was, despite his high school French. When I mouthed, "What's going on?" he only shrugged and shook his head.

Mr. Barreau stood to confront Joseph. Their voices rose and fell until suddenly, Joseph glanced at my dad and his eyes widened. I suspected he'd remembered Dad understood French. He grasped the other man's elbow with his good hand to physically steer him from the room. Their footsteps went upstairs, down the hallway, and into Joseph's room, and were followed by the slamming of the door.

"What was that all about?" I asked Dad again. "Did you get anything?"

"Not all of it," he told me. "Mr. Barreau said that Joseph's mother told him—Barreau—everything. That he—Joseph—should go back to France and let him—Barreau—take care of things here. They were arguing about that, I think, and then they lost me."

"I heard my name," I said as that sinking feeling came back, "and yours."

"Yes, so did I, but I don't know exactly what they were saying, Alison. I don't want to venture a guess for fear of being way off in left field. I'm sorry."

"I'll ask Joseph when they come down. They can't talk about us like that and not tell us what they're saying."

It turned out we had to wait quite a while. We hadn't eaten all day, and I was beginning to feel light-headed from stress and lack of food. After I heated up some chicken soup and threw a freezer-to-oven loaf of bread in the oven, Dad and I ate in relative silence, expecting at any moment that Joseph and Mr. Barreau would join us.

"So, what do you think, Allie-cat?" Dad finally asked in his most cynical tone when we'd finished our meal and found ourselves still alone. "Is that invitation to spend Christmas at the Lorraines' house in France still going to be open?"

I couldn't hold back a half-hysterical giggle. "I have no idea, Dad. I don't know what's going to ha—" I stopped at the sound of footsteps on the stairs.

A moment later, Joseph appeared with Mr. Barreau behind him. Both men looked completely burned out—Joseph was pale and heavy-lidded, and the older man's eyes, while dry, were rimmed with red.

Whatever else they talked about, they must've talked about Philippe. About the end of his life. Of course they did. I should've realized that.

"We must speak with the two of you," Joseph said, and I knew that they'd discussed other things too. Serious things. The two men took their seats in the empty kitchen chairs, Mr. Barreau on the side opposite me and Joseph at the end of the table, facing my dad.

"I asked you earlier, Dr. Mitchell, what will you do now that you know… what you know?" Joseph began, leveling a look at Dad. "You must understand that you are now part of the family, yes? That you must keep the secret of our bloodline without fail, until the time comes when this is no longer necessary."

"Dad?" I prompted when he didn't answer. My heart was throbbing in my temples. "Please. You have to…"

Dad's forehead creased in a frown. He pulled at the neck of his sweater with one hand as though for air as he thought this over. "I get the feeling this is one of those 'you're either with us or against us' type of situations," he said at length.

Joseph coughed to clear his throat and replied, "Unfortunately yes, it is."

"Dad?" My voice came out in a croak. I clasped my hands together to stop them shaking.

"What if I don't agree?" Dad asked, pressing the matter. "What if I want to call that reporter—what was her name? Washington?— and give her the biggest story of the century? What will your secret society do?" He directed a suspicious look at Mr. Barreau. "Will you protect Joseph, as he says, at all costs?"

"We will," Mr. Barreau replied in a tone of voice that sent shivers through me from head to toe.

Oh. My. God. I felt sick to my stomach; the chicken soup threatened to come up in a hurry. "Dad, come on," I said with a gulp. "Think about it. You can't fight them on this. They've been protecting the bloodline for like two thousand years."

I could practically see the wheels spinning in my dad's head. I expected to see steam rising from his ears at any second. After another heart-stopping moment of silence, Dad nodded almost imperceptibly and looked hard at Joseph. "I do." He sounded like he was taking a marriage vow. "I understand. You have nothing to worry about."

"*Bien alors…*" Joseph settled back in his chair in obvious relief. There was no mistaking the fact that despite Mr. Barreau's greater age and intimidating presence, Joseph was in charge of the situation. "In this case, I 'ave an offer to make to you. You once told me that you wish to sell your 'ouse, that every day you wake up 'ere brings painful memories. That you would like to go away."

He did? I thought with something of a shock.

"I did," Dad said, nodding.

"Then this is what you will do: you will put your 'ouse for sale, yes? It will be sold quickly, believe me, and any remaining debts you might 'ave will be paid. Come—with Alison, of course—for Christmas vacation at my 'ome in Carcassonne. Afterward, do what you wish. Visit Paris"—he still pronounced it "*Paree*"— "travel or join *la Croix Rouge* as you told me you would like to do."

He did?

"Let's say I do that," Dad replied cautiously. "What happens to my daughter?"

"I'm sure she can take care of 'erself," Joseph said. "But I would like the chance to do this." He looked at me. "When we return to New 'Aven in January, after our vacation, Ben will stay in America as my *aide-de-camp* and bodyguard. If you wish it, Alison, you may move into my 'ouse. It's large enough for you to 'ave your own bedroom, bathroom, and sitting room. I do not wish to pressure you but to protect you. And yes, selfishly, I wish to be with you as much as I can be. Of course, if you do not wish this, you may live where you choose."

My eyes filled with sudden tears at the thought of leaving the house where I'd lived my entire life. "What about my pets?" I croaked. "Can I bring them?"

"But of course," Joseph said easily, with the tiny crack of a smile. "I would not leave the wee creatures be'ind." He got up and came to stand behind me, his hands on my shoulders.

The power of his conviction seemed to seep into me, and I said, "We have to do this, Dad. I want to do it. I want to be with Joseph. I love him."

"I—I just don't know, Allie," Dad replied. He looked and sounded totally drained. "I have to think about it." He got up and left the kitchen. I heard the hall closet door open and close, and then the front door.

Mr. Barreau moved to go after him, but Joseph intervened. "No! Alison and I will follow 'im."

As I rose from my chair Mr. Barreau said, "You want to make sure he doesn't go to the police or the media. He must not tell—"

"Yes, I know this!" Joseph snapped.

"He won't tell anyone," I said. "I'm pretty sure I know where he's going."

We grabbed our coats and headed outside after Joseph told Mr. Barreau to wait in the house. From the tone of his voice, it wasn't a suggestion.

The beige sedan was parked in the street, blocking our driveway. I could see my dad's form walking along the grass verge; we followed discreetly, keeping our distance.

Joseph took my hand—just a regular young couple out for a stroll—and we walked along Ridge Road for a while, eventually turning left on a side road and then following a well-worn path through the narrow strip of woods to the park.

"Wait," I told Joseph. "Give him some time. Please."

"But of course."

We sat on a bench and talked, basically re-hashing everything that had happened over the past weeks and conjecturing about what might come to pass in the near future. The thought that everything hinged on what my dad was going to do nearly paralyzed me. An hour went by before Joseph insisted we move. We crossed the baseball diamond and entered the Centerville Cemetery.

Dad was standing beside my mom's grave. He must have heard us approaching because he turned suddenly, then seemed to sag when we saw it was us. "You know I always discussed it with your mother whenever I had a dilemma or a decision to make," he told me in a choked voice.

"I know. That's why I knew you were here." I noticed Joseph taking a couple steps away from us, giving us our privacy. "So… um, did it help?" I stopped at asking him if she'd actually answered.

It was a few minutes before he spoke. "It did. I think I see things more clearly now." He looked past me to Joseph and went on, "Your very compelling story notwithstanding, Joseph, I can't… You can't expect me to just abandon my faith or my belief in the resurrection of Jesus Christ and trade them for the belief that he survived the crucifixion, had a family, and… well, all the rest of it… just because you say so. But I can see that you and yours believe it."

I gave him an encouraging smile when he glanced at me. "That's exactly how I felt when Joseph first told me who he is, Dad. I needed some time for it to sink in."

He returned a smile that was more like a grimace and looked back to Joseph, who had stepped up beside me. "I understand that we're talking about the future here. Not only Alison's future, or yours, or even mine, but if what you say is true—not that I believe it's anything more than a long-standing collective delusion, mind you—the future of the entire world. When I became a doctor, I naturally took the Hippocratic oath. Part of that states that I will tread with care in matters of life and death. I think that aptly applies here."

The tears that had suddenly sprung up in my eyes began to drip down my cheeks. I wiped them impatiently away with the palms of my hands and waited for Dad to say something more.

"So yes," he went on, his voice steadier now. "I'll join your family and keep the secret of your bloodline—whether it turns out to be what you say it is or not. I'll do everything in my power to protect Alison and the child you say will come from her union with you, if that should eventually come to pass."

I couldn't hold back a squeal of joy and practically leapt on my dad, throwing my arms around his neck in the most heartfelt and relieved hug I'd probably ever given him.

A tiny nagging voice in the back of my mind warned me that I still didn't truly know what I was getting into, but I promptly shut it down. Whatever was to come, I would face it with my dad at my back, the man I loved at my side, and my son—next in line in the sacred bloodline of Jesus Christ—in my future.

A word about the author…

Donna Marie West is an educator, translator, author, and freelance editor. She has published some 500 drabbles, short stories, and non-fiction articles in a wide variety of Canadian and American magazines, web sites, and anthologies. She loves unusual and unexplained phenomena, dystopian futures, and alternative history, and often finds ways to weave these themes into her stories.

In 2019, she co-authored a collection of horror-themed short stories and poems titled Haunted Horror, which is sadly now out of print as the publisher closed its doors. A novel, The Mud Man, was published in April 2022 by an independent American publisher.

Having recently retired from teaching, Donna now spends most of her time working as an editor, helping other authors with their stories. Her precious free time is devoted to reading, writing, and doing research for her current projects. She lives in Québec, Canada, with her long-time partner and two beloved kitties.

You can follow her on her Amazon author page or her public Facebook page, both under her name.